Broken Dreams

Glenda Thompson

ISBN: 978-1-963680-01-0

This is a work of fiction. Names, characters, places, and incidents are either the product of the author's imagination or are used fictitiously, and any resemblance to actual persons living or dead, business establishments, events or locales, is entirely coincidental.

Broken Dreams

Chapter One

A suffocating stillness permeated the walls of the conference room. Only the occasional scuff of a boot, clearing of a throat, or a quickly whispered conversation broke the silence. The air hung heavy, tainted by the acrid stench of burnt coffee, reminiscent of a skunk's musk. Texas Ranger Rhyden Trammell felt the weight of eyes upon him whenever he turned away from the somber group. While grateful for their concern over his abducted daughter, he bristled at their pity. It stepped on his last nerve.

We're going to save you, Bree. I promise.

Perched on the edge of the conference table, his right leg bounced uncontrollably as they waited for Sheriff Prescott to enter the operations order meeting. Acid roiled in his stomach. His jaw clenched and his cheek twitched as he ground his molars against one another as he attempted to keep his stomach contents where they belonged.

His fingers joined the rhythm of his leg, tapping on the table next to the empty white pastry box. Only crumbs remained. *Stereotypes become stereotypes for a reason.* Slamming his hand against his knee, he stilled both. His gaze darted around the room.

Next to him, his best friend Texas Ranger Noah Morgan leaned against the fake wood paneling lining the meeting room, tapping his fingers against his thigh. A growing sense of urgency swamped the crowd of law enforcement. Time grew short. If they missed this window of opportunity, the kidnapped children would be sold across the globe and Rhyden would never see his teenage daughter, Bree, again.

Why are we wasting so much time? He edged toward the door. *We need to go...now.*

"Okay. We clear?" Chief Deputy Dannar scanned the room, making eye contact with each deputy, ranger, tactical officer, pilot, and medic there. "We will assemble at the abandoned convenience store on Old Kyote road. That leaves us about a quarter mile to cover on foot, most of it through some pretty rough brush. The ambulances will remain in the store parking lot until the scene is contained, and we call them in. Understood? No one approaches the building until Deputy Hendrickson completes the drone fly-over. Once we get the all clear from the deputy, we will approach on foot. People, we don't know what we're going to be dealing with out there. We know two of the kidnappers, Patrick and Seamus Gorman, are Travelers. Patrick is especially dangerous, a sociopath with sadistic tendencies. We don't know who the purchasers are but suspect they could be cartel. Keep your head on a swivel and watch your six."

Photographs of Bree, Patrick, and

Seamus were passed around the room. Chief Deputy Dannar continued, "This young lady is the daughter of Ranger Trammell. She's a good guy." A strained chuckle circled the room. "The other two are the bad guys. I want to thank all of you for being here and a special thank you to the Atascosa County Sheriff's Office Critical Response team for helping us out as well. Make sure you activate your IR markers. We don't want to mistake any good guys for bad guys. Radio silence. Got it?"

To the chorus of ayes, yesses, and sirs, the chief deputy gave a sharp nod.

Sheriff Prescott entered the room. After acknowledging Dannar, he turned to Rhyden and Noah. "Gentlemen, am I correct in believing asking you to sit this one out would be a waste of my breath?"

Rhyden flinched as if struck. He swallowed visibly. "Sir, my daughter…"

The sheriff cut Rhyden off with a sharp, chopping hand motion. "Like I said, a waste of my breath."

With a casual circular motion of his finger, he beckoned the group to come closer, his gaze sweeping across the room. The anticipation in the room was palpable, as everyone leaned in, their undivided attention fixed on his every word. "You've had your briefing. You know what's at stake here. Do your job. Do it well. Those kids are depending on us." He scanned the room one more time as if assessing the capability of his team. Apparently satisfied with what he saw, he said, "Okay, team, load 'em up and head 'em out."

Rhyden held the door open and glanced back to where Noah stood arguing with his paramedic girlfriend. "We're burning daylight. Noah, you coming?"

Noah shook himself and said, "Let's go."

***

Rhyden, Chief Dannar, and members of the SWAT team huddled around a laptop. Video footage from the drone streamed across the monitor. Rhyden leaned in closer, searching for any glimpse of his daughter. *Hold tight, baby girl, we're coming to get you.*

"Seems like we've got fifteen or sixteen heat signatures." Deputy Hendrickson pointed at the screen. "One here. One here. Two over here. And eleven smaller ones huddled together here." He surveyed the officers clustered around him. "I'm betting those are our hostages." They watched the video feed for a few more minutes. "These two appear to be stationary guards while these two patrol. Although they've been standing here together for the past few minutes. Earlier, however, they were circling the building in opposite directions."

Once the breach teams were established and geared up, the chief asked, "Ready to do this?"

Affirmative replies echoed all around. Chief keyed his microphone. "620-Bennett County. Close the channel please."

"10-4, 620," the dispatcher responded. "Attention all officers, all units not involved in the special assignment. This channel is now closed. Switch to analog. Repeating, channel is now closed. My time out 20:04."

Chief signaled for the teams to move forward. Rhyden's heart raced. *I'm coming, Bree.* Following his partner forward, moving easily through the brush, he crept silently toward the decrepit shack housing the children, slipping beneath the branches of the mesquite trees. For once in his life, his short stature was an asset.

A thick mist rolled in as the temperature dropped. Dusk deepened. Rhyden and Noah communicated using hand signals. As they approached the structure, a dark shadow rose up in front of them. Throat tight, weapon clenched in sweating palms, Rhyden inched closer. The shadow gradually gave form to the twisted spine of a mesquite tree. Relief whispered through him. He loosened his grip on his rifle.

A shuddering crunch of gravel signaled danger. Rhyden watched as Noah melted into the shadows. Skills learned growing up with his grandfather floated to the surface of Rhyden's mind. He slipped backwards, eased into a crouch, blending with his surroundings. The patrolling guard walked past within touching distance.

Noah's radio crackled. "1480-Bennett County. Traffic stop in front of HEB on 35. John-Robert-Mary six-four eight."

What the hell? As Noah struggled with the radio's volume knob, the guard whipped around, rifle at the ready as he searched for the source of the noise.

Dispatch responded to the officer on the radio. "Bennett County-1480. Switch to analog. The channel is closed. Repeat, the channel is closed."

Before Rhyden could move forward to help Noah, a guard materialized in front of him holding a bowie-style knife and grinning maniacally. Waving the blade in a series of figure-eights, he advanced, confidence shining in each step.

Twenty-one feet, Rhyden thought, *a man with a knife within twenty-one feet of you can kill you before you can draw your gun and shoot.*

Dropping his rifle, the Ranger drew his own blade from a sheath in his boot and circled the aggressor. He wove from left to right, tossing his knife from hand to hand. As quick as a rattlesnake strike, he lunged forward. Flicking the blade of the knife, he drew first blood from his opponent. He pulled back, still circling.

The guard charged him, slamming his back to the ground. The impact knocked the breath from his chest and the knife from his hand. Grinning evilly, the guard clamped his hands around Rhyden's throat.

Clasping his hands together, fingers interwoven, Rhyden raised his arms and slammed down on the arms of the man strangling him. Nothing. He clawed at the hands cutting off his air. He fought for breath as the larger man dug his thumbs into his windpipe.

Confident of victory, the guard squeezed tighter and leaned closer to whisper taunts.

Rhyden's head shot up, smashing into the other man's face like a hammer. Blood spurted as the attacker's nose shattered. The man fell to the side clutching his nose. The Ranger, gasping for air, rose to his knees. Hands scrabbling across the ground, he found a rock and smashed it against the cartel soldier's skull. Flipping the unconscious man over, he dragged him to the base of a nearby mesquite tree. Rhyden bound his arms behind his back and around the trunk of the tree with flex cuffs and shoved a dirty bandana in the guard's mouth.

He scooped his rifle from the dirt and worked his way over to Noah in time to see his best friend annihilate his opponent. He watched him deliver a right to the face, a left to the kidneys, another right to the face. A satisfying crunch accompanied a spurt of hot blood as another nose shattered. Noah rolled off the man, collapsed in the dirt, and struggled to catch his breath.

"Hey," Rhyden asked, "you okay?"

Still too winded to speak, Noah rubbed his throat. "Fucking PD," he croaked in a whisper. "Damn near got me killed. What part of channel closed did that motherfucker not understand?"

Rhyden reached a hand down to help

Noah to his feet. "Come on, pansy, quit your bellyaching. Bree's waiting for us to save her."

A hoarse chuckle escaped Noah's lips. "Pansy, my ass. I whooped two of them. You only fought one." He pointed to a second body on the ground. "Grab that one, will you?"

The Rangers dragged the unconscious guards to the base of the mesquite tree next to their buddy."I hope you get prickly pear stickers in your ass," Noah muttered as he cuffed the man's hands around its trunk with nylon flex cuffs before gagging him. "I may never sing again."

Thinking of last month's karaoke night, Rhyden asked, "Should I leave him a thank you note?"

"Hardy, har, har."

Rapid rifle fire split the air to the east. Rhyden's pulse spiked. A frantic voice broke radio silence. "We're pinned down. Taking fire."

More gunfire erupted.

"It's hitting the brush around us. Can't see anything."

Fear for the children flooding his system, Rhyden grabbed his radio microphone. "Where are you?" he asked.

"About four hundred yards southeast corner of the building. We're pinned in the brush."

"Are the kids in the line of fire?"

"Not that we can tell. Shooters are between us and the building."

A veteran of many firefights, the chief's calm tones issued from the radio. "Stay put. Keep your heads down. Back up's on the way. Perimeter is set."

"We can't tell where the shooter is. We're hunkered down in a tiny hollow, surrounded by brush."

Rhyden and Noah rushed in the direction of the gunfire. "We're gonna try to flank them," Rhyden radioed.

"Bennett County to all officers. DPS chopper is on the way."

Noah slipped his pistol from the holster. He motioned for Rhyden to follow as he edged forward toward the shack. He pointed toward the back of the structure. A bright yellow spark of light momentarily cut the thickening gloom of dust. "Muzzle flash," he whispered as he corrected course. "We're almost there."

"This is DPS 107, airborne, we're about seven mikes out. I'll circle when we get there. We should be able to spot the shooter for you."

"10-4, we just took three more shots. Not sure we can hold out for seven minutes. Shots seem to be coming from the northeast. Uncertain if we have one or more shooters."

"Roger that. Heading northeast from

your location. Picking up the pace. Five mikes out. Make sure all the good guys have their IR markers activated, please."

Rhyden and Noah met up with a line of officers moving toward the structure they hoped held the children. A rustling in the brush caused the officers to pause. As one, they all pointed flashlights and guns at the brush. The brush wriggled again. A member of the San Antonio Police Department's critical response team stumbled out. He threw his hand in the air. "Whoa! Hold fire. Hold fire. I'm with you."

A nervous chuckle swept through the group.

The SAPD officer quipped, "Man, give me the concrete jungle over this shit any day."

Noah pointed to the northwest. "We're gonna circle around this way."

"This is DPS 107. I see your bad guys. Looks like two armed with ARs. I've got a line of seven good guys in a semicircle, then two others moving west, northwest. Two more goodies hunkered down about 500 yards to the east. Okay, your baddies are on the move. Heading back to the structure. Repeat, bad guys are on the move. I've got them pinned in the spotlight."

News that armed men were headed to the place where his daughter was held captive struck Rhyden like a fist to the gut. His breath whooshed from his body. Cold sweat broke out all over him.

A volley of rifle fire mixed with small-arms fire split the night. The chopper pilot called out. "We're taking fire. We're taking fire." The helicopter returned fire. "They're down. I repeat, bad guys are down."

Rhyden and Noah gave up all pretense of stealth and raced toward the house. Rhyden left Noah in the dust.

Rhyden's heart racing, he fought his instinct to storm the building and rescue Bree. Rash action could cause more harm than good at this point. He and Noah eased up to the fence surrounding the dilapidated house. Even with night vision, he couldn't see much. Just another ramshackle structure. "Hendrickson, we're getting close but can't see anything. Can you be our eyes?"

The drone buzzed overhead. It dropped low, waggling its wings at the Rangers, before zooming off to circle the structure and surrounding area. "I've got nothing in the area outside the shack. Thermal imaging shows eleven, no twelve, no eleven... I'm not sure. They keep moving, huddling up, but I've got eleven or twelve heat signatures inside." A pause. "Good guys are joining you."

Rhyden and Noah dropped back to the brush line and waited for the rest of the team. Rhyden let Noah take the lead as he fought to control his fear for Bree.

"Okay, who has the rakes?" Noah asked when the group gathered.

Three men held up metal poles with pointed ends and teeth on them. Noah nodded in acknowledgment. "I need one of you on each team. Bravo team, take the back. Charlie, the left. Delta, the right." Noah pointed to where he wanted each group to go as he spoke. "Ranger Trammell and I are marching right through the front door."

"Damn straight," Rhyden muttered, fidgeting in place.

Noah glanced at the illuminated dial on his watch. "Fifteen seconds. Rake the windows. Toss in the flashbangs. We'll make entry right after that. Everyone ready?" Affirmative nods circled the group. "One more thing. We have a minimum of eleven children inside—children— possibly including Ranger Trammell's daughter.

No mistakes, people, and no unnecessary gunfire. Got it? Good. Go."

The men split into three groups and approached their designated areas.

Hold on, Bree. Daddy's here.

"Chief? Ranger Morgan here. Have EMS ready to roll. We go in five… four… three… two…"

Breaking glass and children's screams echoed through the brush. Bright lights and loud explosions lit up the night sky. Rhyden rushed through the door, sweeping low. His eyes scanning, searching.

"Clear." Rhyden stepped to the left.

Noah stepped past Rhyden, swinging his rifle from left to right. "Clear," he said, pointing the rifle at the ceiling.

Anxiety ate at Rhyden as they continued

through the house, the pier and beam foundation creaking and groaning at every step. He cringed with each sound. *Just what we need. To crash through a rotten floor and never find the kids.*

They entered the last room.

"Daddy!" Bree launched herself at Rhyden, burying her face in his shirt. She sniffed. "You smell like gunpowder and sunshine."

Tears streamed down her face. Rhyden wrapped his arms around her, clinging to her. Tears clogged his throat.

Noah slid deeper into the room. "All clear." He keyed his microphone. "Send in EMS now. We've got them." Emotion colored his voice. "We've got the children."

The police cars and ambulances formed a circle of red and blue flashing lights around the makeshift yard of the falling-down structure where the children had been held. Cop cars surrounded ambulances, forming a safety fence around the children. Relief filled the air.

Officers roughly moved suspects—the ones not stupid enough to pull guns on law enforcement—into the back of the marked police units. Forensic techs and investigators swarmed the scene. Camera flashes filled the air. Teams from the funeral home, with the okay from the scene investigators, loaded the others into body bags and placed them in the back of hearses.

Paramedics tended to the children. Bree clutched Rhyden's hand, squeezing hard. He loved every moment of feeling her hand in his. A tiny blonde child clung to Bree. Noah walked up to the group and Bree wrapped an arm around his waist, but she never released her father's hand. "Uncle Noah. I knew you and Daddy would find us. I knew it."

Rhyden worried a bit about Bree's

regression to calling him Daddy. He'd been Dad for the past five years, but he figured he would worry about it later. Right now, he had his daughter back, and that was all that mattered to him.

Noah hugged Bree fiercely, then released her. "Hey, jump off any cliffs recently?" he asked, referring to a prank she'd pulled a month ago that almost kept her from graduating high school with her senior class.

Noah kneeled and spoke to a few of the former captives. Standing, he gestured to the children and asked Rhyden, "How are they?"

Rhyden gathered Bree close again. "Physically? None the worse for wear. A little dehydrated, a few bruises." He smiled down at Bree. "Hungry."

She smiled back at him. "Starving...and I never want fast-food burgers again, ever." She shuddered.

He pulled her tighter to him. "We'll have steaks tonight. Cooked exactly the way you like them." He pretended to gag. "Burned on the outside, raw on the inside." He winked at his daughter, pulled her tighter to his side for a moment before releasing her. Returning his attention to Noah, he continued, "Overall, not too bad." He shrugged. "Emotionally? That's a whole other ball of wax."

Noah grasped Rhyden's upper arm. He squeezed and released. "I'm glad she's home, man." His voice cracked. "I am so glad she's home. I'm going to go try to talk to Cat."

"Hang on a minute, man." He turned to Bree. "You okay while I go talk to Uncle Noah? Just for a sec?"

Bree hesitated before releasing his hand and drawing herself up to full height. "I'm good, Dad. I'll be right here."

Taking a deep breath, letting go of the

ball of anger buried in his chest, Rhyden squared up face-to-face with Noah. "I want you to know I forgive you, man. I don't understand what you did or why you felt you couldn't trust me, but I forgive you. Now, go talk to your lady."

Noah swallowed visibly. His eyes filled with tears. "Thank you," he whispered and raced over to where he'd last seen Cat.

Before Rhyden could return to Bree, a sharp scream split the air. "Daddy!"

Rhyden whirled around. The color washed from his face. A spike of fear shattered his heart. One of the kidnappers hid behind Bree, his arm wrapped around her throat, a pistol pressed to her temple. A grubby bandage on his cheek peeked out from behind her head.

Rhyden took a faltering step forward and raised his hands in a non-threatening gesture. "Easy now, Patrick," he said, "let's talk this through for a minute. You know that you're surrounded, right?"

Blood drained from the kidnapper's face. He blinked rapidly. "You know who I am?" He tightened his grip and scanned his surroundings agitatedly. "Yeah, okay. I know who you are, too. That's okay." He nodded to himself. "I got your girl." He tightened his grip around Bree's throat and gestured to his wounded face with the barrel of the pistol. "I owe this bitch one for carving me up. I'm walking out of here with her."

"Like hell you are." Bree slammed her foot down on his instep as she shot an elbow straight back into his solar plexus, followed by a headbutt to his nose. "I have had about enough of this bullshit." She punctuated each word with another strike.

Dazed and bleeding, Patrick faltered momentarily, loosening his grip on Bree. She wrenched free and darted away from him. He raised his pistol and fired wildly as Rhyden charged forward.

A concussive force slammed into Rhyden—*bam, bam, bam*—hitting him square in the chest. His ballistic vest stopped those bullets from penetrating his flesh. Another slammed into his shoulder while yet another hit him in the thigh. Rhyden's legs crumpled beneath him; his bones dissolved. He collapsed in a heap. A searing agony lanced through his thigh, radiating outward like a spider web of fire. The white hot inferno of pain stole his breath and blurred his vision. Blackness descended, accompanied by the crunch of breaking bone as the side of his face collided with the concrete parking lot.

Chapter Two

Rhyden's world went from dark to hazy. Time had no meaning, but he registered the whomp-whomp-whomp noise created by the helicopter rotor blades. Felt the shaky lift-off as the chopper left the ground.

Disjointed phrases drifted over his head. "Calling in report... forty-seven-year-old male... multiple gunshot wounds... compound fracture right femur... shattered right shoulder... possible internal bleeding... probable fractures of the zygomatic bone and orbital floor... A and O times one... ETA five mikes."

Pain surrounded him, eating him alive. Gratefully, he succumbed to unconsciousness.

***

The world exploded in pain. Rhyden's body convulsed. Pressure around his neck and plastic wrapped around his face made him feel as if he were suffocating. He tried to swipe the oxygen mask away but couldn't move. Tried to turn his head but couldn't. The ceiling tiles clicked past his half-opened eyes during the brief trip from the landing spot to the emergency operating room. In an instant, the light intensified. He squeezed his eyes shut, but the glare seared his retinas through his closed eyelids. It seemed a hoard of people swooped down on him, pulling, tugging, and cutting off his clothing. One mask was ripped away and another slapped over his face. He felt a sharp prick as they started a second IV. Then an icy wave—freezing cold—hit his chest and leg right before the anesthesia carried him away.

***

Floating in a dark cocoon, Rhyden heard the rhythmic click of multiple footsteps echo against the industrial tile of the hallway. Papers rustled. Muffled voices grew louder as a doctor with a group of residents entered his room. He tried to open his eyes and failed. The harsh chemical smell of antiseptic cleaners burned his nose. A voice pierced the darkness.

"Morning, nurse. We're making rounds. How's our patient doing today?"

A murmured reply came too quiet for Rhyden to make out. He barely heard the sounds of the nurse leaving the room.

The doctor continued speaking to his residents. "We have a forty-seven-year-old male recovering from multiple gunshot wounds. Shattered his right femur. We removed multiple bone shards and replaced the fractured bone with a titanium rod. It's too early to determine how much nerve damage he sustained, but it will probably cause him pain for the rest of his life. We have him sedated to allow the swelling in the brain to continue to decrease. It was touch and go for a while. I'm most concerned about the injury to his right orbital socket. He may never see from that eye again."

Before Rhyden could process this newest information, a flash of warmth flooded his bloodstream. As he slipped back into the chemically induced darkness, he heard the doctor ask if anyone had questions.

"What are these other scars from?" a baritone voice asked.

The doctor replied, "Not that it applies to his current condition, but according to his medical history, this man used to be a bull rider. Any other questions?"

A female voice piped up. "Just one, sir. What could possibly entice a sane person to climb onto the back of a 2,000 pound pissed-off bull for fun?"

As he descended into darkness, a thought crossed his mind - who had ever claimed he was sane?

***

Guttural, rhythmic chanting in a deep, raspy smoker's voice pierced the void surrounding Rhyden. The familiar cadence pulsed through his very core, summoning him. Strident beeping filled his head. He cracked open his eyes. The view through his left eye blurred. His right eye, his shooting eye, wouldn't open. Something held it closed. Panic flared through his chest. *I can't see.* Alarms sounded as his heart rate elevated. He heard the rumble of rhythmic chanting increase and became aware of others in the room. The scent of burning sage filled the room.

"Sir! Sir! You can't burn that in here."

Rhyden couldn't understand the response, but he recognized the voice. *Grandfather.* His pulse lowered, steadied. A soothing calm swept over his mind.

The nurse's voice reached an outraged

note. "I assure you, sir, there are no evil spirits here."

A slight smile tugged at the corners of Rhyden's mouth. Feeling protected, Rhy let the darkness pull him back under.

***

The sweet, high-pitched voice of his youngest daughter, Maddie, broke through the darkness. "But Grandfather, if the Great Spirit created the people, who created the Great Spirit?"

A constant hum punctuated with sharp beeps rumbled just below the surface of his awareness, providing a background for the voice.

She's got you there, Grandfather. Scratchy cotton sheets surrounded him. The harsh, metallic tang of bleach invaded his senses, leaving the scent of an over-chlorinated swimming pool clinging to his taste buds.

Before Granddad could answer, Maddie followed up with, "And why did Coyote have to trick Humpback to get the buffalo released? Didn't Humpback know it's better to share? Then his son wouldn't need to bring in stray animals. He would have real friends."

"Well…" Grandfather said.

Maddie interrupted. "When is Daddy going to wake up?" The words tumbled from her lips laced with fear and worry. Her voice hitched with tears. "I want my daddy!"

At the pain in her voice, Rhyden struggled to lift his eyelids or move his fingers, anything to let Maddie know he heard her. He tried to find his voice in the gloom, but the sedative held him too tightly. He drifted back beneath its grip. Deep beneath its grip.

As Rhyden's heart rate slowed to below

forty beats per minute, the alarms blaring and lights flashing teased his awareness but soon didn't even register as he drifted deeper into the comforting, pain-free darkness.

Chapter Three

Rhyden stretched his shoulder, swinging his arm in a full circle as he stood next to his crew-cab pickup truck in the parking lot of the Bennett County Law Enforcement Center. The doctor was amazed at his recovery. Doc didn't think he would ever regain a full range of motion with his shoulder, but he did. *Thank God for physical therapy.*

The tiniest hint of fall lingered in the air. It was that time of year when temperatures raged between freezing in the morning and sweltering by midday. Dark clouds hung above him, threatening to unleash a downpour. Static electricity crackled in the air as the wind picked up. An empty soda can skittered across the sidewalk.

He slid his hand up and down the outer seam of his jeans, feeling the scar tissue underneath. Biting at his lips, he stared at the double glass doors set in the limestone façade of the building that housed the Bennett County Sheriff's Department, the county jail, dispatch center, and the Department of Public Safety offices. Years ago, someone way above the Ranger's pay grade convinced the county legislators to go in on the joint effort to save the taxpayers a bit of money. The way the oilfields worked these days, the county never knew if incoming taxes would provide a feast—or dry up like a years-long famine.

Anxiety bubbled in his chest, spread through his limbs. Sharp pain shot through his shoulder and down his arm. A sheen of cold sweat covered his skin. He dragged a callused hand across his forehead. Sure, Doc said the gunshot wounds to his shoulder and leg had healed, but was he truly ready to return to duty? What about the injury to his mind?

Suck it up, buttercup. There's nothing wrong with you. You can handle the pain. Mind over matter and all that other shit the therapist keeps throwing at you. Rhyden pulled in a deep cleansing breath through his nose and blew it out his mouth.

He shoved his trembling hands deep into the pockets of his freshly starched jeans. It felt weird wearing real clothes again after so long in shorts and t-shirts. His fingertips brushed against the hard, oblong object in the pocket's corner. His heart rate slowed. Pulling the white pill out, he slipped in his mouth and cracked it between his molars. The bitter taste flooded his mouth further calming him. He grabbed an ice cold coke from the cup holder in the pickup's console and washed the fragments down with a long sip.

Stiffening his spine and raising his chin, Rhyden scooped his brand new silver belly beaver felt hat from the dash of his truck. The hat, a welcome-back-to-work or more likely a please-get-out-of-the-house gift from his daughters, brought a smile to his face. *Those girls.* He snugged the hat down on his head and headed toward the building.

Inside the LEC, none of the usual chaos greeted him. The lobby stood silent and deserted. No families waited to welcome a newly-released inmate, no individuals demanded to make a complaint to the sheriff, no kids created a ruckus as their parents sought to free a prisoner. The receptionist's desk sat abandoned. Not a single, solitary soul stirred in the building. The hair on the back of his neck stood up. The place was never this empty. He flinched, startled by a deafening crack of thunder that sent tremors through the glass doors he'd just slipped through.

As he approached the secured area of the center, he heard the distinctive but subtle click of the bullet-proof reception door unlocking. Scalp prickling, he pushed open the door. *Something's wrong.* Silence surrounded him, too much silence.

His hand dropped to his service weapon.

He pressed the release on his holster and lifted his gun partially from where it nested. The gun felt good in his hand, reassuring. Stepping carefully, he entered the hallway leading to the bullpen and beyond it to his office. Crazy thoughts pinged around the inside of his head like a pinball lighting up his fear receptors. He bit the inside of his lip, pausing as he listened. The place felt abandoned. A shiver of fear slid down his spine.

Movement ahead caught his attention. He drew his weapon fully from the holster as Sylvia, the law enforcement center receptionist, raced around the corner toward him. She grabbed his empty hand and squeezed. Tugging him further down the hallway, she said, "Ranger Trammell, it's so good to see you. Come quick. You're needed in the conference room."

Relief at seeing Sylvia mingled with the confusion at the state of the building and both flooded through Rhyden as he replaced and secured his weapon. Picking up his pace, he allowed himself to be pulled toward the conference room.

Rustling noises came from behind the drawn shades concealing the interior of the room from Rhyden's sight. He tensed again, part of himself wishing he was still safe at home with the girls.

"Surprise!" Exclamations of 'welcome back' and 'good to see you' mixed with laughter flooded the air.

Heat rushed from his chest to his hairline as Rhyden felt himself blush. *What an idiot!* He berated himself silently for making a mountain out of a molehill. Of course everyone hid in the conference room—with cake, he was certain. It's what they did anytime anyone came back from a leave of absence. Any excuse for a celebration—and baked goods—was welcome in the law enforcement center.

The soothing, chatty effect of the pill kicked in. Rhyden's shoulders relaxed. His lips lifted in a smile.

Noah Morgan, stood with his now-fiancée, Cat Ramos, closest to the door. Cat's swollen, undulating abdomen announced that John Wyatt Morgan would be making his appearance in the world sooner rather than later.

Rhyden shook hands with Noah and hugged Cat. "How much longer do you have?" he asked.

Cat rubbed her belly ruefully. "Too long. I'm past ready."

Noah's face paled.

She grinned. "The doctors tell me about another six weeks." She elbowed her fiancé in the gut. "I may be ready, but someone else isn't."

Rhyden laughed aloud. "I've missed you

guys."

"Hey, Morgan, quit hogging the celebrity. Trammell, get your butt in here and cut the cake. We're hungry already," called out Lieutenant Dylan Gregorio.

Rhyden smiled and walked deeper into the room. He shook hands with Dylan. "Not used to seeing you on the ground, buddy."

"Yeah, well, I couldn't miss this welcome back party, now could I? How did your PT test go?"

Rhyden winced and rubbed his shoulder. "It's a lot harder at my age now than when I first joined the department. Seriously though, what are you doing here? I thought they had you stationed on the border."

"They do, but with them housing the illegals we capture in the hotels along the border, there is no place for us to stay."

Rhyden raised his eyebrows. "So you mean to tell me you work twelve-hour shifts and then drive three hours back here to have a place to stay? Every day?"

Dylan nodded. "That about sums it up. So when do you re-qualify at the range?"

Worry flitted through his mind at the thought of shooting qualifications. His vision still not one-hundred percent, the world swam at the edges. He felt a pang of anxiety, knowing he should tell someone, but held his tongue. He feared the doctors or his commanding officer would prevent him from returning to duty if they knew. He shrugged. "I'm not sure. I guess as soon as the commander schedules it."

"Well, let me know when you're ready to go up again. I bought the sweetest little Mooney Ovation the other day. Well, I went in with some partners and we purchased her together. I'd love to take you flying."

Chapter Four

Vintage dark brown cowboy boots, spit-shined to a mirror-like finish, stood sentry near the foot of the bed. From where he stood at the bathroom sink, he saw the cracked leather around the creases that ran across the base of the toes. Severely rolled and worn soles told him he'd need new boots before too terribly long. Or maybe not. The wear and tear was a testament to their many years of service and a reminder of the father he'd inherited them from. He only wore them on days like today. Days which seemed to come more and more often.

Bent over the sink, he scoured his hands with a pumice-filled soap. The orange scent filled the room as he scrubbed his fingers until his knuckles bled. Rinsing the blood away, he scrubbed his hands again and again. Finally satisfied, he dried them and coated them lightly with baby powder. He donned a pair of latex gloves making sure the cuff covered his wrists. Over those, he tugged on a snug pair of black leather, steel-weighted SAP gloves.

He shrugged into a baby-soft cotton t-shirt, which caressed his torso and protected his sensitive skin from the coarse fabric of the tan uniform shirt. He tucked the shirt into his heavily starched, sharply creased, chocolate pants. The sleeves of both shirts dug uncomfortably into his oversized biceps. He pulled the long sleeves down and buttoned the cuffs at his wrists hiding the latex gloves.

Pulling an extra pair of socks from his dresser, he shoved a balled-up sock into the toe of each cowboy boot before shoving his feet in. He slipped a knife into a sheath at the top of his right boot. Grabbing a nine-millimeter pistol, he slipped in a full magazine and chambered a round. He tucked the pistol securely into the holster on his belt, right next to the handcuffs, mag light, and pepper spray. He placed the straw cowboy hat on top of his head and scooped a paper-tagged set of keys from his pine bureau top. Admiring himself in the full-length mirror gracing the back of his bedroom door, he straightened the badge pinned to his chest and rubbed his sleeve across its face to give it more shine. He brushed the brim of his hat between his forefinger and thumb in a mock salute.

Moving outside, he slid into the front seat of the marked patrol vehicle and dropped his "special" tool kit on the front passenger seat beside him. He reached under the dash and disabled the county's GPS unit. Opening his kit, he reviewed its contents: zip ties, duct tape, a spare knife, blindfolds, and condoms.. Satisfied, he started the engine, turned on the unit radio, and placed the car in gear.

Twenty minutes later, he reached an undeveloped brush-lined stretch of Highway 97 between Gato Montes and Wild Rock. He pulled the sheriff's department unit to the shoulder of the road. Lowering the driver's side window, he leaned back in his seat as far as he could, pulled his hat down over his eyes, and waited for the sunset. In case he fell too deeply asleep, he set the alarm on his phone for 8:00 p.m.

Gradually, the headed-home-from-work rush hour traffic slowed. The constant roar of tires on pavement faded to the occasional whisper. Darkness filled the car. His hand hovered over the siren switch as he waited. He inventoried every vehicle that passed. *Too many passengers. Too old. Too male.* He squirmed in the driver's seat, trying to increase the blood flow to his legs. Patience had never been one of his strong suits, but he knew she would drive down this road. He just wasn't sure how long he would have to wait.

A cramp in his calf increased his squirming. *Why are these cars designed for short people?* As he reached for the door handle to get out and walk the charley horse away, the perfect vehicle zipped past. Cramp forgotten, a wave of euphoria swept over him.

He flipped the switch for the red and blue lights on top of the car and hit the sirens. The piercing high-low wail of the siren alternated with the urgent yelp of sound. The car that had passed him slowed. A smile spread across his face before he smothered it with an expression of professional neutrality. His hands tightened on the wheel as he whipped the patrol unit off the shoulder of the highway and slid in behind the Grabber Blue Ford Mustang. The car pulled off the highway, kicking up a cloud of dust.

The officer sauntered up to the vehicle, gravel crunching beneath his boots. Careful not to touch the car, he tapped on the driver's side window with his mag light.

The window purred down. A delicious wave of vanilla-based perfume floated out. He closed his eyes and breathed it in. His lips turned up in a slight smile. *Yummy.*

Opening his eyes, he shone his light into the backseat and passenger side seat before shining it into the driver's face.

Tear-filled blue eyes dominated a pixie face surrounded by a mass of golden curls. She blinked rapidly as she squinted up at him past the bright light. Fear radiated from the young woman behind the wheel. She anxiously toyed with the top button of a white button-down shirt.

His eyes laser-focused on her blouse. In his mind, he saw himself ripping it open, buttons flying everywhere.

"Yes, Officer?" The teenager's voice trembled. "I didn't think I was speeding. Was I?"

Her fear ratcheted his heart rate. Adrenaline rushed through his veins, sucking the moisture from his mouth. He lowered the flashlight and made eye contact with the girl.

His imagination ran wild. Scenes of violence and control swamped him. He swallowed hard. "License and insurance, please."

Her hand shook as she passed the documents to him. "Oh, man. My dad's going to kill me. He bought me this car last week and warned me what would happen if I got a ticket." She cast a pleading look at him. "Can you let me off with a warning? Please? I promise I'll slow down."

He examined her driver's license— eighteen years old. *Perfect.* Blood raced from his brain to the lower regions of his body. He handed back her insurance card without looking at it and tucked her driver's license into his uniform shirt pocket. "Kind of late to be out. Where are you headed this time of night, ma'am?" Mentally, he slapped his forehead. *Late? It's what 8:15?*

She didn't seem to notice the time discrepancy. "Home."

"Home from where?"

"W-work, sir."

"When are you due home? Who's waiting for you?"

"Um—soon? And no one? My parents are on a Caribbean cruise this week. For their anniversary?"

The deputy clicked his tongue as he admired himself in the dark tint of the back driver's side window. Turning his attention back to the girl, he asked, "Are you asking me or telling me?" He reached for her door handle. Locked.

Irrational anger swamped him. His nostrils flared, and he planted his feet wide apart. The muscle in his cheek pulsed as he ground his teeth. Heat flushed through his body. He took a deep, calming breath. *Not yet. Keep the monster under control. Soon, okay? Soon.* He exhaled and consciously relaxed his facial muscles. His shoulders slumped. "I'm going to need you to step out of the vehicle, ma'am."

"Do I have to?"

"Now, please."

Sniffling to hold back her tears, she unlocked the door and slid out of the vehicle.

He took her by the elbow and led her to the passenger side of the car. Her arm trembled in his grasp as she attempted to resist his guidance. He tightened his grip and tugged. "Let's step to this side of the car for safety."

As they reached the far side of the car, close to the deeply shadowed, thick brush on the side of the road, she stumbled over a rock, turning her ankle. With a whimper of pain in her voice, she said, "You never told me why you stopped me. What did I do wrong, sir?"

He slammed her face-first against the side of the car and quickly tie wrapped her hands behind her back. Grabbing her by the hair, he dragged her toward the shadows.

She struggled to escape his hold, kicking and screaming.

He laughed out loud and quivered with the effort to control himself. Avoiding her flailing legs, he leaned forward and whispered in her ear. "You want to know what you did wrong? You were born beautiful."

Chapter Five

Rhyden picked up his ringing phone. The screen read Principal Harkness. *Sam, what have you done now?* "Hello, Mrs. Harkness."

"Mr. Trammell, we need to talk. Immediately and in person. I'll expect to see you at the school in twenty minutes."

"Mrs. Harkness, I —" He was talking to empty air.

Arriving at the school, he glanced at his watch. Eighteen minutes had passed. He breathed a sigh of relief. He wouldn't be late. *Not that that woman frightens me.* He shook his head. *Who am I kidding? That woman terrifies me.* He climbed out of the pickup and headed into the school.

Principal Harkness stood with her back ramrod straight and arms crossed over her chest in front of the double glass doors leading into the school. She checked her watch as he climbed the concrete steps leading to the school's entrance. She opened the door and motioned for him to follow her. The click-clack of her ridiculously high-heeled stilettos broke her sullen silence.

From behind a closed door, he heard the murmur of excited voices and the high pitched screeching of chairs being shoved across the floor.

Her nostrils flared. The air grew thick with her disapproval. She glared at the closed door before turning her attention back to Rhyden. Clipped words fell from her lips. "This way."

She turned left down another hallway lined with closed doors. Finally they reached their destination. Entering her office, Principal Harkness stabbed her finger toward the chair in front of her desk.

Once seated in the hardback, plastic chair in front of her desk, Rhyden asked, "Mrs. Harkness, what did Sam do?"

"It's Principal Harkness. I'm not married, Mr. Trammell, which you would know if you spent a bit more time here at the school." She sniffed disapprovingly.

"Principal Harkness, I apologize. You do know what I do for a living, don't you? I'm lucky to see the girls at home. I don't have the luxury of being able to spend time at the school. To be honest, I don't have time to be here now. You are aware of all the pursuits going through the area, aren't you? I'll ask again. What did Sam do that required me to come to the school?"

Folding her hands primly on top of the desk, Principal Harkness said, "It's not what she did so much as what she hasn't done. She's not applying herself in her classes. At the rate she's going, she may not graduate. If Samantha spent as much time on her studies as she does," the principal pursed her lips and paused as if searching for words, "tinkering with automobiles with that group of boys perhaps we wouldn't be having this conversation. Girls should not be up to their elbows in dirty engine oil nor should they be called by a boy's name. Now, Mr. Trammell, I realize not having a woman in the home is detrimental to a young lady's growth, but I assumed after the issues we had with your eldest daughter that you would have found a way to rectify this issue."

Heat rushed through Rhyden's core. He clenched his fists and shot to his feet, knocking the chair over. *No wonder they call her Hardass Harkness.* He inhaled for a count of five and exhaled for a count of eight before speaking. It didn't help. Sarcasm coated his words. "I apologize if my wife's murder inconvenienced you. I assure you we neither planned nor desired it. I will speak to *Sam* about her grades."

Principal Harkness removed her glasses and polished them on a soft cloth before speaking again. "If I remember correctly, Mr. Trammell, that… woman… ran away many years before someone murdered her."

Pain shot through Rhyden's injured leg. A craving for a pain pill caused him to tense his jaw. "That, Principal Harkness, is none of your damn business." He stepped to the office door and flung it open. "And it's Ranger Trammell."

Principal Harkness drew herself up to her maximum height of five feet eleven inches. She towered over Rhyden by four inches. She stretched her neck and dipped her chin to glower down her nose at the Ranger. "Why I never…"

Fatigue swamped Rhyden, pushing away his anger. Sadness swept through his soul. He turned back in the doorway and met her eyes. "Neither have I, ma'am, neither have I."

A microscopic twitch of her lips told him his words had hit their target.

Chapter Six

What the hell is that? Rhyden slammed his truck door causing Samantha to jump, banging her head against the open hood of the pickup truck she huddled under.

"Son of a …" She stepped back rubbing the back of her head and glanced behind her. Brushing dark curls off her sweaty forehead with the back of her other hand leaving behind a dark splotch, Sam waved her socket wrench. "Dad! What are you doing home?"

"Samantha Elaine, what is this beast doing in my driveway?" Rhyden walked over to the F100 leaking oil on the concrete. Looking under the hood, he spotted Maddie perched on the fender well inside the engine compartment. "Pumpkin, what are you doing in there?"

Maddie grinned, flashing the gap where her front tooth should be. "I'm helping Sam,

Daddy." Her seven-year-old eyes sparkled. A streak of grease decorated each of her pink cheeks.

Rhyden turned back to Sam. "Where did this monstrosity come from?"

"I bought it. Isn't she cool? 1974 F100 with a 240 cubic inch, 150 horsepower inline six. I wish it was a 302 but she'll do. Man, you can't kill a straight six. Grandfather said so. The guy who sold it to me thought he was ripping me off. I got it for $500. Dummy thought the tranny was out. Said it jerked on hills."

"Why would you buy a truck with a bad transmission? And where did you get the money?"

Sam rolled her eyes. "I *said* he was a dummy, Dad. There's nothing wrong with the tranny. The truck needs plugs and wires. I'm changing the fuel filter, too. Then I'm going to sell it and make ten times what I paid for it—

minimum." She thrust her fist into the air. "Yes!" She tossed a 'I'm so smart' smile at him.

Rhyden fought to hide a grin. *How did I end up with such a smart kid?* Samantha, otherwise known as Sam, was his middle daughter. Tall, slender, with dark curly hair and upturned, almond shaped, hazel eyes laced with flecks of gold and brown, she could have been a model, but girly things didn't appeal to her. She didn't even realize all the boys were chasing her. In her mind, they were all buddies. The girl could rebuild an engine with her eyes closed. A swell of pride expanded his chest. "You never told me where you got the money."

"I've been working part-time at the mechanic shop that fixes the sheriff's office vehicles after school."

"How did I not know this? I thought you were taking care of Maddie after school?"

Sam's jaw jutted out as she shot a

glance at her father from the corner of narrowed eyes. "If you were ever home, perhaps you would know what goes on around here. Grandfather has been watching Maddie. She likes him better than me anyway."

"I do, Daddy. He tells me stories. Sam just yells at me."

Sam spun around and glared at her little sister. "Hey! I'm letting you help me on Bessie, aren't I?" She caressed the fender of the pale green pickup truck.

Maddie nodded. "That's true. I got to change the fuel filter."

Rhyden raised a single eyebrow.

His youngest daughter shrugged, "Well, I got to hand Sam the tools and the parts."

Rhyden smiled for the first time all day. He loved seeing his girls working together. Some days he worried about the ten year age gap between them.

Thunder rolled across the sky vibrating inside Rhyden's chest. The first giant raindrops fell from heavy clouds above them. "Come on, ladies, let's get inside."

Rhyden's phone rang again. "Ranger Trammell speaking."

Chief John Dannar's voice came over the phone's speaker. "Ranger Trammell, something's come up. I need to talk to you now."

***

After receiving Chief Dannar's call, Rhyden sat in his truck. He fished in the console until he found his bottle of hydrocodone. His hands trembled as he twisted it open. *Been too long.* He'd been trying to cut back, but it wasn't working. Tapping the bottle against the palm of his hand, two of the precious white pills tumbled out. He looked into the bottle and shook his head. He dumped the pills into his hand and counted them. *There should be more pills in the bottle. Note to self: call Doc for a refill.* He poured all the pills except for two back into the orange plastic bottle. He quickly dry swallowed the two remaining pills. Leaning his head back, he waited for them to kick in. Still angry at Principal Harkness's last comments, his mind wandered back to the last time he saw his wife, Cara, alive. The two older girls had been rolling across the yard, fighting over a boy, while the neighbors stood around recording it on their cell phones. Thank goodness Noah had been there to help.

Rhyden tried to pull the girls apart and caught an uppercut to the chin. "Son of a bitch. Break it up. Now." He kept trying to tug the girls apart. Maddie stood on the porch, watching.

Noah leaned against the hood of the unmarked sedan and waved the two Bennett

County sheriff's deputies back. "He's a Ranger. Those are his daughters. Let him handle it."

After watching for a few more minutes, Noah let out a sharp, high-pitched whistle to get the girls' attention. They raised their heads and saw him. Sheepishly they broke apart, glared at each other, and ran into the house. Rhyden rubbed the bruise forming on his chin.

Maddie flew across the yard and latched on to Noah's long legs. "Uncle Noah. Uncle Noah. Bree said that Mark was her boyfriend, but I saw Sam kissing him. Isn't that gross? Everyone knows boys have cooties. And then when I told Bree, she started crying and yelling and hitting Sam and then Sam hit her back and I didn't know what to do. I tried to call Daddy, but he didn't answer his phone. Boys are stupid. Don't you think so, Uncle Noah? Well, except for you and Daddy. Y'all are boys, but you aren't stupid." She paused for a moment, as if considering that last remark. "You aren't stupid, are you? Why would anyone want to kiss a boy? Yuck." Maddie paused to take a breath. She threw her arms up in the air. "Pick me up, Uncle Noah. Are you staying for dinner? Bree was cooking jambalaya. I got to pour in the rice, but I bet it's burned now cause Bree started beating up on Sam but Sam hit her back, so I think Bree got beat up too. Boys are disgusting. They stink. I don't like boys. Do you, Uncle Noah?"

Noah stared at her, lost in bewilderment. A panicked expression skittered across his face.

Rhyden walked over and rescued Noah. He picked up Maddie. "Hey, Pumpkin, how are you?"

"I called you, Daddy, but you didn't answer your phone. Why didn't you answer your phone? I called you. Three times. Aren't my sisters silly? Boys are gross. I'm never gonna like boys. Yuck."

Rhyden ruffled Maddie's hair. "If only that were true, Pumpkin. Here," he handed Maddie to Noah, "go to Uncle Noah while Daddy talks to the nice policemen." He turned to the crowd of bystanders. Disgust dripped from his words. "Show's over, folks. Really appreciate all your help. You can go on home now. Got to get your videos posted, right?" He walked over to the officers. "Sorry about this, gentlemen." He shrugged. "Teenagers. What can I say?"

The officers laughed, shook his hand and got back into their patrol car to leave.

As the crowd disbursed, Rhyden heard a sarcastic, throaty female voice behind him. "Well, I see you are doing a great job raising our daughters, now aren't you?"

Rhyden saw his estranged wife dressed to the nines in a tight black pencil skirt, red silk blouse open to show too much cleavage and stiletto heels standing on the sidewalk blocking his path to the house. First time he'd seen her in five years. She'd walked out a week after Maddie's first birthday. Just packed up and took off. He pushed past her. "What do you want?"

"Is that my mommy?" Maddie slid out of Noah's arms and ran to the woman. "Mommy! Mommy!" She threw her arms up for the woman to pick her up.

Cara tensed and stepped away from Maddie, aghast at the thought of getting dirty. She brushed off her skirt, then reached out a hand and patted Maddie on top of the head as one would pet a dog. "Madison," she said.

"Mommy?" Confusion crossed the little girl's face. Tears pooled in her eyes and slowly slipped down her cheeks. Rhyden reached down and picked her up.

"You always were too good for us, weren't you?" Anger vibrated in his voice. "I asked you what you wanted."

"*Well, I tell you what,* honey, *why don't you put our little darlings to bed and we'll discuss it.*"

"*Let's not and pretend we did,*" Rhyden said.

Noah walked up and took Maddie from Rhyden. To Rhyden, he said, "I'll take care of the girls. You take care of this." He nodded at Cara. "Hello, Cara. Long time no see."

"*Not long enough,*" she muttered under her breath.

"*Back at you,*" he said before turning *toward the house with Maddie in his arms. "Come on, sweetie." Noah tickled her tummy. "Let's go check on those silly sisters of yours and see if they have made up yet. What do you say?*"

Maddie giggled. "Okay, Uncle Noah. Want to see if Bree burned the dinner?"

"What do you want, Cara?" Rhyden asked for the third time. "I thought you and Michael were in Cancun or Cozumel or some such place. What are you doing back here?"

Cara glanced around the yard at the remaining nosy neighbors still lingering outside. "Let's take this inside, shall we?" She squeezed past Rhyden into the house. Once inside, she stalked through the living room, past the kids without a word, and into the kitchen. She turned up her nose at the dishes in the sink, the scorched rice on the stove and the cookbook propped up in a corner of the counter. Turning to Rhyden, she said, "I want $150,000.00."

Rhyden choked on a bitter laugh. "People in hell want ice water too."

"Yes, that's true," Cara examined her freshly manicured nails, "and you want to keep those precious little brats in the next room, too. If you don't give me what I am asking for, I will take you to court and take them away from you.

After all, that scene in the front yard shows what an exemplary job you have done of raising them…not."

"Like any judge in his right mind would give them to you? You haven't contacted them in over three years. I'm their father and the only one who has been taking care of them for the past five years. You pop in and out of their lives on a whim between highs. The rest of the time, you can't even be bothered to drop a birthday card in the mail. What makes you think a judge would give these girls to a crack whore like you?"

"That's ex-crack whore, thank you very much. I've been clean for eight months now. Besides, you know how the courts love a success story. And don't all little girls need their Mommy to teach them all the things Daddies don't know about? It's not my fault their mean old daddy kept me away from them because he was angry that I found someone who made me

happier than he ever could. Why, Michael will testify that I've cried myself to sleep every night for the past three years because you threatened to hurt me if I tried to contact my precious angels."

"You may be off the crack, but you're still a whore. How much did Michael pay for those new boobs of yours?"

A sharp crack echoed through the kitchen as Cara slapped Rhyden across the cheek. "How dare you? I am not and never have been a whore. Just because I needed more than you to keep me satisfied does not make me a whore. I never sold it. Maybe if you had paid more attention to me or were better in bed, I wouldn't have had to go looking for it somewhere else."

"Do you even know what grade Bree is in? Or what classes Sam has trouble in? Or how many nights a week Maddie creeps into my room after waking up terrified from a nightmare?"

"Why would the courts let you keep Madison?" Cara tossed a folder of papers onto the kitchen table. "She's not yours."

Stunned, Rhyden grabbed the back of a kitchen chair to steady himself. "What the hell are you talking about? What kind of lies have you cooked up this time?"

She slid the folder closer to him. "Go ahead. It's all in there."

Rhyden opened the folder and read the paper inside—a paternity test proving Michael, not Rhyden, was Maddie's biological father.

Cara laughed. "You wouldn't want to break up the girls, now would you? Give me what I want and I will go away."

Rhyden's hands shook. Red tinged the edges of his vision. "Get out. Get out of my house right now. Before I rip your heart out of your ass and shove it back down your throat."

He took two steps toward Cara, who backed up to the kitchen counter.

Reaching behind her, she grabbed a butcher knife off the granite counter and waved it at Rhyden. "Stay away from me. Give me the money and I'm gone."

"Yeah, is that a fact? For how long? Til you burn through this installment and come back for more? I'm not made of money, you know."

"No, I won't come back. I promise. Give me what I want and I'm gone. Don't and the girls are gone. That's also a promise."

"You will never take the girls from me. Not one of them."

The next time he'd seen Cara she'd been on a stainless steel table in the morgue, and ice-cold, metal handcuffs had been digging into his wrists. It still hurt—Texas Ranger Rhyden

Trammell, arrested for the murder of his ex-wife.

***

A hand slammed onto the hood of Rhyden's truck. Jarred from his memories, he looked up to see Sam motioning for him to roll down his window. The relief from his favorite little white pill flowed through his bloodstream. The memories might've been painful, but his body no longer ached.

Creases formed on her forehead between squinched eyebrows. "Dad? What are you still doing here? I thought Chief Dannar needed you."

"Shit." He reached for the keys dangling from the ignition. "Yes, you're right. I gotta go. Want me to pick up a pizza on the way home?"

"You don't have to. I can cook."

A grimace crossed Rhyden's face. "Like

last time? We still haven't gotten the smoke smell out of the curtains."

"Hey! That's not fair…" She saw the smile he tried to hide and laughed. "Pepperoni?"

"You got it. See you in a bit."

Chapter Seven

Rhyden bounced his truck over the speed bumps in the Bennett County Law Enforcement Center parking lot. As he stepped out of the truck, Rhyden watched Chief Dannar exit the building through the double glass doors set in the limestone facade. *Like stepping back in time.* Rhyden thought the same thing each time he saw the chief deputy.

John Dannar strode across the parking lot like an old-timey Western lawman. Long and lean, his gun belt rode low on his hips. His bow-legged gait, along with the straw hat perched on big ears and shiny badge pinned to his pearl-snap shirt, added to the illusion. After shaking hands with Rhyden, Chief Dannar fished a crushed box of Marlboro Red cigarettes from his pocket. He tapped one loose and offered it to Rhyden.

"No, thanks, Chief. What's up?"

The chief lit his cigarette and drew in a lungful of smoke. He exhaled audibly. Looking at the cancer-stick in his hand, he shook his head. "Nasty habit. I know, but right now I need the calming effect." He met Rhyden's eyes.

The Ranger imagined he could see the distressing burdens of command crushing the other man's soul. "You okay, Chief?"

"Walk with me." He turned and headed toward the helipad where the life flight chopper sat. He sighed before crushing out his cigarette beneath the toe of his boot on the pavement. He bent down, retrieved the butt, and tucked it into his shirt pocket. "Wife'll know I'm smoking again. Gonna be hell to pay when I get home." He shrugged. "And I'm stalling."

He nodded toward the little log cabin representing the original Bennett County courthouse. "We can talk over there in the shade."

Rhyden maintained his silence. Whatever bothered the chief would come out in due time.

Once they reached the cabin, Chief collapsed into one of three straight-backed, wooden rocking chairs sitting on the porch. He gestured for Rhyden to sit as well. Elbows on his knees, he leaned forward, twisting his hands together, lost in thought. He ran a hand across his chin before taking a deep breath. He nodded once sharply as if coming to a difficult decision. "Rhyden, how long have we known each other?"

"You mentored me through the academy. Before that you were on the street with Dad. Before the ambush. I've known you my whole life. John, you know this. You're scaring me. What's wrong?"

"I need your help. I can't believe I'm even considering this." Chief's voice drifted off. He stared off into space.

"Considering what?"

Chief shook himself. "Did you know we have a serial rapist terrorizing the Wild Rock corridor?"

"I've heard a rumor. Between working the border and rescuing Bree, I'm not up on what's been going on here in Bennett County. Do you think it's true?"

"It's definitely true."

Anxiety sent a tingling through Rhyden's limbs. A flash of heat raced up the back of his neck. He began planning the talk he would be having with Sam when he got home. *No more running the roads for you, young lady.*

Anguish carved deep creases into the chief's face. He closed his eyes momentarily before opening them and meeting Rhyden's. "I'm terrified it's one of my guys."

Fuck, really? Before Rhyden could

answer the chief, Sylvia, the sheriff's department receptionist, flew across the parking lot. "Chief," she gasped trying to catch her breath, "we need you. Now. It's bad."

Sylvia shoved through the double glass doors ahead of Rhyden and Chief Dannar. She slid her ID badge through the lock on the bulletproof door separating the public area from the secured employee-only section. The lock snicked open. She held the door for the officers.

"You're needed in dispatch, Sir. A 10-80 has turned into an active shooter situation. Someone has a hot mic. We can hear everything, but we can't communicate back. The situation is bad. Sounds like big guns. And lots of them."

"Where was the pursuit?" Chief asked as he walked into the communications office.

One of the dispatchers held up a finger as he pressed his headset closer to his ear. Squinting his eyes, he listened—hard. In a rush, he typed urgently into the computer-aided dispatch screen.

He faced the chief. "Sorry, Sir, we're trying to get information out to uninvolved officers using the system, and I couldn't hear. The 10-80 started in Atascosa County. Their sheriff's office lit up a stolen Dodge truck based on a license plate reader camera. The chase headed south into our county near Redus Crossing.

"Atascosa County broke off when our deputies and border patrol took over. The truck crashed out. Most of the illegals bailed, but the coyote and a few of his compadres dug in and opened fire on our guys. Right now, they're engaged on County Road 2817 five miles north of the Frio River."

"Of course, they did. Put the system on speaker. I need to hear what's going on." Instantly, a barrage of semi-automatic gunfire and frantic shouts echoed off the office walls. A shrill scream filled the room before gunfire cut the scream short.

Beads of sweat popped up on Rhyden's upper lip. He wrapped his arms around his torso, jamming his hands into his armpits. For a split-second, he found himself back in the parking lot with Bree's screams ricocheting inside his brain pan. *Pull it together, damn it.* He rocked back on his heels. A craving for a pain pill swamped him. His heart crashed against the inside of his rib cage. His teeth itched.

A young deputy's pain-soaked voice came from the speakers. "I'm hit. Oh God, oh God, oh God, oh God. I'm hit. Help me. Please, I don't want to die. Please help me." His voice trailed off, buried bemeath the bark of submachine guns.

Chief Dannar's legs gave way beneath him. Color drained from his face.

"John," Rhyden stepped forward and

caught the Chief before he collapsed. "What is it?"

Chief stared at the radio. He swallowed noisily. "Is that… ?"

The dispatcher grimaced and slid his palms up and down the thighs of his uniform pants. In a strained voice, he replied, "Yes, Sir." He cast a beseeching look at Rhyden. "That's John, Jr."

"Who else is in the area?" snapped Dannar.

"Timmons and Ellis, sir. We've tried reaching their cell phones but no one's answering. Ambulances and air life are on stand-by but can't enter the scene until it's secured."

Chief's knees buckled as another rapid exchange of gunfire split the air. Straightening up, he spun on his heels and headed toward the door.

Craving forgotten, the Ranger dashed after him. "Hold up, John. I'm coming with you. I'll drive." He waved his phone at the dispatcher as he raced after the chief. "I'll be on my cell. Keep me updated."

***

Tires spitting gravel, Rhyden careened to a stop outside the range of the long guns being fired at the deputies and border patrol agents. A sudden silence fell over the scene. The opening bars of Proud Mary rang out from his cellphone.

"Trammell speaking."

The passenger side truck door ripped open, and Chief Dannar scrambled out.

"John, wait." Rhyden unbuckled his seatbelt.

"Ranger Trammell," Sheriff Preston's voice echoed tinnily from the truck speakers, "let him go but keep an eye on him. The shooters are deceased and ambulances are en route for our wounded. Just wanted to let you know."

"Thanks, Sheriff."

"Take care of my friend."

Rhyden found Chief Dannar crouched over a pale carbon copy of himself, blood-covered hands pressed firmly to a weeping wound.

"Hang in there, JJ."

"Ambulances are on the way, John." A lump formed in his throat. Rhyden knelt beside the chief but bit his tongue before promising John that everything would be fine. Color bleached from John, Jr.'s skin. His chest shook with tattered breath.

A light hand fell on his shoulder. The absolute last voice he expected to hear said,

"Ambulances are here."

Cat, extremely pregnant, stood above him. His eyes darted past her searching for Noah. His friend was nowhere to be seen. A momentary flash of panic overwhelmed him. *In through the nose, two, three. Out through the mouth, two, three, four, five.* He released the trepidation with his breath exactly as the department psychologist taught him. *Oh, shit!*

"Step aside, Ranger. I've got this."

Rhyden stepped back. "What are you doing here?"

Catalina Ramos crossed her arms over her burgeoning belly. "What do you think I'm doing here? I work here."

Rhyden stammered. "Does Noah know you're here? What does the doctor say?"

Her jaw jutted out. Temper flashed in her eyes. "The doctor…" She placed strong emphasis on the word 'doctor', "said I'm pregnant, not sick. As long as I don't lift more than forty pounds, he said I can work right up to my due date. Which, for your information, is still two weeks away."

"But Noah…"

Cat growled at him. Literally growled like a feral mountain lion.

Her partner, Jim, dropped the jump bag beside John, Jr. "Argue later. Save lives now," he said as he nudged Chief Dannar out of the way and expertly slipped an IV needle into the deputy's rapidly collapsing vein. He exchanged a look with Cat. "We've got to move—now."

With Rhyden's help, they rolled JJ onto a backboard.

Chief nodded as he clung to his son's hand. "Hang in there, son." He tried to reassure his son by cracking a joke. He took a deep breath, trying to control his emotions, but the bob of his Adam's apple betrayed him. "Your mama will skin me alive if anything happens to her boy. And I kinda like my skin."

A ghost of a smile crept across JJ's face right before his color continued to fade. His eyelids fluttered closed, the weight of his injuries crushing them against his eyes like a vise. A gasping breath rattled around inside his chest.

Stark terror clouded his father's face.

"Chopper," Cat snapped. "Double time it."

Jim and Rhyden grabbed the board and raced for the chopper.

As the chopper took off, the two men bent at the waist, hands on their knees, and tried to catch their breath. Rhyden closed his eyes and sent up a quick prayer.

"Oh, fuck," Cat whispered.

Rhyden opened one tired eye and peeked in her direction. She stood in a puddle. He raised one eyebrow questioningly.

Alarm tinged her voice. "My water broke."

She frantically canvassed the scene. Her bottom lip trembled. "Where's Noah?"

"I'll go grab the ambo," said Jim.

Cat inhaled through her nose, filling her lungs to capacity and holding it for a slow count of ten before blowing the air out through her pursed lips. She wrapped her arms around her belly. Inhaled again.

Rhyden scooped his phone out of his pocket and tried calling Noah. No answer.

The ambulance whipped into the parking lot next to Cat. Jim jumped down from the box and raced around to the back, tugging the doors open as he went. "Your chariot awaits, madame," he said with a sweeping bow. Supporting Cat's lower back, he helped her into the back.

Cat chuckled. Rhyden breathed a sigh of relief. *Good job, Jim. Thought we were going to have a hysterical pregnant woman on our hands for a minute.*

Rhyden's cell rang. "Chief, how's JJ? Good. Good. Glad to hear it."

He listened. "About that. We're on our way, but we have to take a tiny detour. Cat just went into labor. Can you have someone find Noah for us, please? Send him to Bennett Memorial."

Cat swatted at Jim. "How many times do I have to tell you no one calls an ambulance an ambo? I don't care how many television shows you watch. There are only three options: the ambulance, the box, or the bus—period." She rubbed her lower back and sat on the gurney. "Give Rhy the keys. He'll have to drive."

Color blanched from Jim's face. "But… it's my turn to drive. You drove last time."

"Jim, you're the paramedic. To quote Gone With the Wind, I don't know nothing 'bout birthing no babies. And she sure can't do it by herself." Rhyden winked at Cat. "Well, I don't know. This is Cat. She probably could."

***

Screeching into the hospital emergency parking lot, Rhy slammed the box into park. He jumped out and raced around to help Jim pull the stretcher out.

On the landing pad, the air life helicopter crew hosed blood from the interior of their bird. The lead paramedic recognized Rhyden and jogged over to the ambulance. "Just wanted to give you a quick update. The deputy looks like he's going to make it. He lost a lot of blood and it was touch and go for a bit, but he's young and strong. Of course, we won't know anything for sure until he gets out of surgery, but the hospital staff seemed optimistic."

Rhyden shook hands with the paramedic. "Thank you." A sharp scream of pain drew their attention back to the ambulance. "Whoops, gotta go. Pregnant women wait for no one."

The life flight paramedic laughed. "Better you than me. Good luck."

As they entered the emergency department, Cat latched on to Rhyden's hand. "Please, don't leave me. Not until Noah gets here."

As the adrenaline of the firefight faded from his body, the craving for a pain pill crept in. A throbbing pain pounded the base of his skull. The titanium rod in his leg vibrated, sending tremors of pain through his entire body.

The skipping heartbeats threatened to send Rhyden into a full-fledged panic attack. *Come on, heart. Pump blood, not air.* His brain itched. He clenched and unclenched his fists. *Breathe, two, three. You can do this. Cat needs you.*

Screams and moans of pain reverberated up and down the hallway. Cat tightened her grip on his hand and opened her mouth.

A six-foot tall, 280-pound labor and delivery nurse whipped around and shook a meaty finger in Cat's face. Lines of exhaustion accentuated the pallor of her complexion. "Do not even start that. Every single baby in Bennett County decided to make its appearance here tonight, and each and every one of their mothers was a screamer. Don't you dare. Holy mother of God, I can not handle another scream." The nurse pushed the stretcher into the hospital room and kicked the door shut behind her. "So suck it up, Buttercup, and let's get this baby out of you. No one ever claimed it would be as much fun as putting it in there. Come on. Move it. In the bed.

Now.”

Wide-eyed and cowed, Cat slammed her mouth closed and transferred to the bed.

The nurse pinned Rhyden with an expectant look and raised a single eyebrow. “Well, Dad? Don't think you are going to make her do all the work. You put it in there. Help her get it out.”

“Whoa!” Rhyden sputtered, “I'm not…”

At the same moment, Cat said, “He's not… “

“Hey, I don't care if you're married or not. Got nothing to do with having a baby. We've got work to do and I don't have time to waste. Come on, now. Let's go.”

The door swung open behind her. Noah scrambled through it. His garish neon-orange and lime green tie lit up the room and seared Rhyden's eyeballs.

"Sir! We are busy here. Get out."

"But… " Rhyden, Cat, and Noah started speaking at the same time.

"But nothing. Out now." Muttering beneath her breath, the nurse advanced on Noah. "Not even a full moon. Lord help me, I don't have time for this kind of monkey business." She placed a massive hand on his shoulder and shoved him toward the door.

Noah ducked under her arm and dashed across the room to Cat, with the nurse chasing him.

Rhyden took advantage of the distraction and slipped out of the room.

Sighing heavily, Rhyden slid down the wall to sit in the hallway. The sensation of cotton filled his mouth, absorbing what little moisture he had left. He dug in his jeans pocket to find a pill, when a shadow fell across him. He jerked before looking up, scattering the contents of his pocket across the floor. *What the ever-loving, holy hell does someone want with me now? Can't I have five freakin' minutes to myself?*

Thick, unruly auburn hair shot through with streaks of a lighter, strawberry color piled on top of an oval face with apple-round cheeks filled his vision. Long red eyelashes tipped with black mascara surrounded ocean blue eyes with streaks of caramel radiating out from the pupil. Damn! Sparks of electricity shot through his chest, sucking his breath away. *I think I'm in love. Or I would be if I believed in love.*

"Ranger Trammell?" She tilted her head to the side. An inquisitive expression crossed her face.

All thoughts of a pain pill vanished from his thoughts. Rhyden scooped up his belongings and scrambled to his feet. "Ma'am?"

"I'm Michelle Ross, the sexual assault

nurse examiner. Can we talk?"

Chapter Eight

Sam bounced into the mechanic shop and plopped her backpack onto Lawrence's metal desk with a heavy thud. She reached to the ceiling, stretching out her shoulders before rolling her head from side to side. *I hate school.*

She took in the long legs encased in denim protruding from beneath a dismantled Chevy truck. *But I sure like coming here after it.* Butterflies nothing; a flock of birds took flight in her stomach. She ran her hands through her hair, fluffing it out. She straightened her top and slid her hands down her skinny jeans. After running her tongue across her lips, she approached the side of the truck and kicked the bottom of the boots sticking out. "Hey."

Lawrence slid out from beneath the pickup. The wheels of his red creeper scraped against the concrete floor. Scrubbing a hand across the dark stubble covering his sweaty head, he chuckled. "Hey, kid, what you keeping in that thing? Rocks?"

"Ha-hardy-ha-ha." Sarcasm dripped from Sam's voice. "I wish. Rocks would make more sense than the stupid books they make us carry around." *And I'm not a kid. Would he ever see me as a grown woman and not just her father's daughter. It didn't help that Lawrence was her father's co-worker and in the process of teaching her auto mechanics.*

Hoping he watched her, she sauntered across the shop, one exaggerated hip swing at a time to where a Bennett County Sheriff's Department Tahoe sat on a lift in the shop's corner. She wrinkled her nose. "This one's going to cost the county a pretty penny."

"Why would you say that?" Lawrence wiped his hands on a red rag. "I haven't had a chance to check it out yet. Are you psychic now?"

Sam smiled. She loved knowing something he didn't. "Let's see, why don't we?" She closed her eyes and held her hands out toward the SUV. Peeking beneath her eyelashes, she made sure Lawrence watched her. Squeezing her eyes shut again, she wiggled her fingers at the vehicle and muttered, "Abracadabra."

Opening her eyes, she tilted her face to the ceiling and held the back of her hand to her forehead. "I'm getting a vision."

Lawrence shook his head. "Okay, smart alec, I'll bite. What's your *vision* showing you?"

She giggled. "I hear howling noises." She strolled around the vehicle. "Hmmm, a little grinding and metallic clunking." She rested her chin on her palm and tapped her pointer finger against the tip of her nose. Cutting her eyes to the corner, she verified she still had Lawrence's full attention. "I see the vehicle being difficult to steer. I feel vibrations on acceleration."

"All that from a 'vision', huh?" He stuffed the oil-stained rag in his back pocket, walked over and picked up the work order from where it hung on the board behind his desk beneath the key box. He flipped to the page that listed the driver's complaints. His eyes widened as he looked over his shoulder at Sam. He tilted his head to the side and narrowed his eyes. "You know the deputy that drives this unit?"

"No. I didn't check out the unit number." She joined him and tried to peek over his shoulder to read the work order.

Lawrence scratched his head. "Then how did you know what was wrong with the Tahoe?"

"Was I right?"

"You know you were."

Sam dropped into Lawrence's desk chair and spun around. She leaned back in the chair, propped her feet onto the desk, and folded her hands behind her head with a secretive smile.

"Come on, Miss Fancy Pants, I'm dying of curiosity over here because I know you aren't psychic." He reached into his pocket and withdrew a worn, silver Zippo lighter. *Click, clack, click, clack.* He flipped it open and closed as he waited for her response.

Their eyes met. A flash of electricity shot through Sam. *Focus, Sam.* She sat up straight, letting her feet drop to the ground. "Seriously?" She furrowed her brows. "You really can't smell it? Are you still smoking? You know that's not good for you."

"Smell what?" He tucked the lighter back into his pants' pocket.

"The burned differential fluid. It hit me in the face when I walked in." Sam idly opened and closed the flat top drawer of the desk. "Are you sure you're not humoring me?"

"Nope. Didn't notice it."

Sam reached over and fiddled with the top drawer on the left side of the desk. Peeked in. "You got any snacks in here?" She shut it and pulled open the one beneath it. An old guy with a cane and a Hitler-type mustache peeked up at her from the orange lid of an antique pencil case. She reached for it.

"Stop!" Lawrence slammed the drawer shut, almost smashing her fingers.

Sam froze. Her eyes darted around the room. Her mind whirled. "I... "

"Don't mess with my stuff," he growled before he stepped back. Inhaled deeply. Arms crossed over his chest, he blew out a noisy breath. "Just don't, okay?"

Sam stood and gathered her backpack. Hot tears filled her eyes. "I'll..."

"Hey, Nubbin," a voice called from the

shop door, "is Trammell's daughter in there with you? She's needed at the hospital. ASAP."

The color drained from Sam's face. Her breath locked up in her chest. She couldn't speak. Shoulders tight, she pressed her elbows into her side, trying to make herself as small as possible. Memories of the last time she raced to the hospital overwhelmed her. She couldn't move. An image of her dad, unmoving, wrapped in bandages with tubes running in and out of his body surged through her mind. Eyes wide, she turned to Lawrence.

He grabbed a set of keys off the board behind his desk. He pointed to the cruiser parked closest to the open bay door. "Get in. I'll drive."

Chapter Nine

Rhyden paced the emergency department waiting room. His boots clicked against the gray industrial floor tiles. He felt a tickle in his throat from the smell of antiseptic and bandages. The fluorescent light over the outside doors flickered, the ballast buzzed.

The conversation he had shared with that annoying SANE nurse careened off the inside of his skull like a pinball at the hands of a wizard. *No way in hell is that rapist a sheriff's deputy. Or any type of law enforcement.* He unclenched his fists and shook out his hands. *Call me Mikki, she said. What is she? A mouse? Not likely. Nothing timid or cheerful about that, that,* Rhyden ground his teeth, *that woman at all.*

Where in the hell is Sam? I need to get out of these clothes. She should be here to pick me up already. He picked at the dried blood on his pants and continued pacing. *I need to check on JJ and Chief Dannar.* His mind bounced from thought to thought. He tapped his hands against his thighs as he paced. Returning to the elevator, he punched the up button and waited for it to open and carry him to the surgical floor.

His legs ached. His head throbbed. *Maybe I should go to the truck and take a pill. Just one.* He stepped toward the exit. *Damn it.* He'd left his truck at the crime scene. *Damn it, damn it, damn it.*

"Rhyden! There you are. Thank you," said Noah. The grin on his face and bounce in his step made him appear to be floating. He clutched a four-foot tall fuzzy brown teddy bear wearing a blue bow.

Rhyden forced a smile. "Baby's here already? That was quick."

Noah puffed his chest out. "All nine pounds and fourteen inches of him. Come see him. If Cat will let you anywhere near him." He raised his eyebrows. "She won't even let me near him... and I'm the father."

"I need to get out of these clothes first. Sam's supposed to be coming to get me. And I need to pick up my truck." He glanced at his watch. "Any other time, she'd be burning rubber to get wherever she's headed. I called the office forty-five minutes ago."

Brakes screeched outside the emergency room doors. Car doors slammed. "Dad!" Sam rushed through the doors and threw herself into Rhyden's arms. She held him tight before pulling back to examine his bloody clothing. "What are you doing out here? Why aren't you being taken care of?"

Rhyden squeezed her tight. "It's not my blood. I rode in the ambulance with Cat..."

Sam pressed a hand to her heart. Jerking back from Rhyden, she spun to face Noah. "Is—

?"

"Sam." Her dad gently turned her back to face him. He slid his hand beneath her chin and lifted her face, bringing her eyes to his. "Focus. It's not Cat's blood either. She was working the scene and her water broke. A deputy got shot, but he's doing well. I'm headed up to check on him, since it took you forever to get here."

"Forever? Lawrence broke every speed limit in town. He even borrowed a cruiser and drove with the lights and sirens on."

"Lawrence? Who is Lawrence, and how did he get a cruiser?"

Noah waved the bear at Rhyden and his daughter. "On that note... Sam, good to see you. Come meet John Wyatt when you get a chance. Rhy, don't be too hard on her. I can only imagine the message you left at the Sheriff's department."

Sam hugged Noah. "I will, Uncle Noah. Congratulations. Give Aunt Cat and the baby a hug for me."

"Now, young lady…"

A tall young man built like an NFL linebacker with hazel eyes and wearing a camouflage cap walked up behind Samantha. He rested a banged-up hand with dirty fingernails on her shoulder. "You okay, Sam?"

Rhyden advanced on the man crowding into his personal bubble. "Who are you? What are you doing with my daughter?"

He pulled off his cap revealing close cropped dark brown hair. He tucked the bill in his back pocket, and held out a hand to Rhyden. "Ranger Trammell, we've met before. I'm Lawrence Walker from the Sheriff's Office. I think you knew my dad."

Rhyden scanned him up and down, taking his measure. "Walker?" He shook the man's callused hand. Taking in the small, round growths poking through the stubble on the man's head, he asked, "You're the one they call Nubbin? Damn good mechanic, right?"

"Yes, sir."

Rhyden glared at him. "What are you doing with my underage daughter? You are familiar with the term jailbait, aren't you?"

"Dad!" A bright red flush crept up Sam's chest and neck onto her cheeks. She buried her face in her hands. "I'm seventeen," she mumbled. She dropped her hands and stuck her chin out. "I am not a child."

Rhyden whipped around to his daughter and shoved a finger in Lawrence's direction. "And he's twenty-nine if he's a day over eighteen."

Lawrence cleared his throat. "Um, actually I'm thirty-two."

"I repeat, what the hell are you doing with my teenage daughter?"

Sam stomped her foot. "Dad," she whined. "He's my boss. Remember? I'm working at the shop to earn money to fix up Bessie? Lawrence..." She winced at the hard glare her father sent the man. "I mean, Mr. Walker is teaching me."

She tugged on Rhyden's arm, pulling his attention back to her. "Why did you say you needed me at the hospital ASAP? I was terrified you had been shot again and no one even hurt you?"

"Is that the message you got? I told dispatch to ask you to come pick me up at the hospital because I didn't have a vehicle to get home." He opened his mouth to say something and then thought better of it. Shaking his head, he said, "They never listen. I'm sorry if—"

The red-haired, green-eyed SANE nurse

swept around the corner. "You. Ranger." Eyes narrowed, she pointed at Rhyden and crooked her finger. "Come with me. Now. I need to prove something to you."

Chapter Ten

"Damn it. I wish someone would tell the new dispatcher that cleaning my office and bringing me fresh coffee is not part of her job."

Rhyden hastily grabbed the styrofoam coffee cup that he had knocked over by tossing his cellphone onto the desk. "Damn it." Hot coffee flowed like a muddy river. The skunk-like scent of burned coffee filled the room. The cup had not been sitting there before he darted around the corner to the men's room. He turned up his nose. "I don't even like coffee."

Noah jerked his boots off the corner of the desk where he had them propped and swept up a handful of paper napkins. He thrust them at his partner. Taking a bite of the tart cherry pastry that had been resting on the napkins, he swallowed and grinned. "You don't mind the pastries, though, do you?" He brushed crumbs from today's outrageous tie. This one had a glaring yellow background covered with pink and blue storks carrying chubby, diaper-wrapped babies.

"Fuck. My. Life." Rhyden scrambled to rescue his phone and wipe up the spilled coffee. "If this day was a fish, I'd throw it back."

"What has your tail twisted in a knot? Don't tell me it's a clean desk or positive attention from the cute dispatcher, either, because I won't buy it. Tell her she can clean my office if she wants. No one ever cleans my office."

Rhyden tossed the sopping wet napkins into the empty wastebasket beside his desk. "That damn, crazy…" he threw his hands up in a gesture of frustrated defeat, a gesture that said he couldn't find strong enough words, "…SANE nurse in the emergency department at Bennett Memorial. She cornered me again when I stopped to check on JJ this morning."

"Must be her bubbly personality."

Rhyden's eyebrows arched nearly to his hairline as he snorted. "Bubbly personality? Are we talking about the same nurse? The sexual assault nurse examiner? Nurse Michelle-call-me-Mikki-but-not-the-mouse Ross?"

"Five foot nothing ball of energy? Blunt? Perpetually pissed off? Curvy? Sparkling green eyes that light up a room? Not that I noticed." Noah held his hands up in surrender. "Cat would kill me. Bright auburn hair usually shoved into a messy ball on top of her pointed little head? That Nurse Ross?"

"You have met her. Have you ever actually spoken to the woman? How can you call that abrasive personality bubbly?"

"Hey," Noah grinned, "acid bubbles."

Stunned silence filled the room for a split-second before both men broke out in laughter.

"Acid bubbles," Rhyden repeated, shaking his head. "True that."

"So, what did Nurse Bubbles do to set you off today?"

"Only threatened to feed me to the wolves, that's all. Hang on." Rhyden strode to his office door and scanned the busy hallway. "I definitely don't need anyone to overhear this." He shut the door, blocking out the noises of phones ringing, handcuffs rattling, and the background buzz of officers talking in quiet tones.

"We're overrun with stolen vehicles, armed coyotes, and pursuits, and she's cornering me in the emergency department with some half-baked theory about a serial rapist." Rhyden paced across his office, back and forth, from wall to wall, his temper mounting with each step.

"I get it. She sees a lot of victims, way

more than she should, but that doesn't mean it's the same perpetrator each time." He slammed his fist against the wall. "I don't know what's worse—the thought of a serial rapist or multiple rapists on the loose. We shouldn't have any rapists. Period."

Turning back to his desk, he plopped into his chair. The leather squeaked in protest. His arms felt too heavy to lift. Defeat permeated his entire being. "The victims won't talk to us. Won't answer questions, much less give us a description. They're terrified. How can we help them if they don't give us anything to work with?" He shuffled a stack of papers in front of his keyboard.

"Oh, and get this." Rhyden stood up and began pacing again. He tugged at his tie. A flash of heat rushed across the back of his neck. "To top things off, not only do we have a serial rapist rampaging the Wild Rock corridor, she believes he's not just any standard joe blow psycho. No, nothing so simple. She's convinced—and somehow convinced Chief Dannar—that this rapist is a cop. One of the Bennett County sheriff's deputies." He made eye contact with Noah. "Can you believe it? Which, of course, dumps this whole sticky, smelly ball of wax in our lap."

"Oh, shit."

"Yeah. And that's not even the half of it."

Noah scowled. "What could be worse than a serial rapist cop?"

Scrubbing a hand across his face, Rhyden let out a breath he didn't even realize he held. "If I don't do something about it, muy pronto, like right this minute, she's going to the press with her theory." He scratched the back of his neck before turning to face Noah. "She's giving me until the end of the week."

Chapter Eleven

The pot lid on the stove clanked and rattled. Boiling sauce splashed over the top of the pan, extinguishing the gas flame and making an enormous mess. Gas hissed. The scent of rotten eggs filled the room. His already taut nerves drew tighter. *Breathe, two, three.* He forced his fisted hands to relax. He snapped the knob on the stove to off. Dinner could wait.

A metallic grinding noise came from the living room. *Now what?*

Smoke rolled from the vents on the front of the window air conditioning unit. Condensation flooded the windowsill and dripped down the wall, flooding the already moldy carpet. *Great. Triple digits and the a/c's out.*

He grabbed his phone and dialed his landlord. "Mr. Sauer, this is unit 3C. My air conditioner is on the fritz." His jaw tightened. "What do you mean, you can't fix it? You do realize by law you are required to fix it. Do you know who you are speaking to?"

A beep-beep-beep indicating a waiting call rang in his ear. He pulled the phone from his ear and scanned the caller ID. Sheriff Preston. *He can wait.* With a quick movement, he sent the call to voicemail. "I expect someone to be here within the hour to fix or replace the air conditioner." He disconnected the call without waiting for a response.

The monster in his head woke up demanding to be fed. Violence… and preferably dished out on a slender brunette. Things were spinning out of control. He needed control.

The man squeezed his eyes closed, rubbed his temples. His pulse pounded in his temples. The muscle in his cheek jumped as he ground his molars together. The voice in his head kept egging him on. He reached under the bed and pulled out his tool kit. Unzipping the case, he spread the implements out on the bed.

Bam-bam-bam! A fist slammed against the wooden front door.

Startled, he jumped. Dropped the roll of duct tape which rolled beneath the bed. *Fuck!*

He crept to the door and snuck a peek through the fisheye lens of the peephole.

A dust-coated black Tahoe emblazoned with Constable sat in his gravel driveway. An impatient, uniformed constable holding a packet of papers stood on the doorstep. Face red from the heat, sweat soaked the collar of his polo shirt, the officer beat against the door.

He slid down the wall and sat on the floor next to the door. *Don't these people ever give up?* He didn't know what they wanted, but he knew it couldn't be good. He'd been ducking them for days. *Go away already.*

The fist pounded against the front door again. "I know you're in there. Open up." More pounding. "Hiding won't do you any good."

His hands curled into fists. Muscles tightened. He needed to hurt someone, needed to see blood. Now more than ever.

The sounds of ripping tape and rustling plastic came from the front stoop. Footsteps moved away. An engine started. Tires crunched on the gravel.

He waited a few more minutes before he rose to his feet and opened the front door. With hands trembling from rage, he ripped the plastic packet from the front door where the constable had taped it. He read "You have been sued." Wadding up the papers in his hand, he slammed his fist through the sheetrock. "Motherfucker!" he yelled. *No wonder the bastard won't fix the air conditioner. Eviction? How? Why? When* was *the last time he paid rent?*

His cell phone rang again. Sheriff Preston again. He sent the call to voicemail and threw the phone across the room.

Pressure built inside his head. It felt like someone had wrapped an oil filter wrench around the top of his skull and cranked it down good and tight. Simultaneously, they jammed an ice-pick through his right eye. Nausea roiled in his stomach. *I don't have time for a migraine on top of everything else.*

He loosened the collar on his uniform shirt. *Damn thing choked him.* He stomped across the room, bent, and scooped the phone from the floor. Putting it on speaker, he played the voicemail from the sheriff.

"This is Sheriff Preston. We have a problem. Meet me in my office tomorrow morning. Eight a.m. sharp. Do not be late."

He can't know. I've been careful.

He hit play again. And again. The

sheriff's voice morphed into his father's. "Problem… problem… useless… weak… waste of human flesh… dead to me…" His nostrils flared. Face tightened. "Oh, yeah," he muttered aloud, "who's dead now, huh, Daddy dearest? How did that work out for you?"

He shoved his phone into his pocket, repacked his tool kit, and headed out to hunt.

His emotions bubbled beneath the surface. He suppressed the rage and struggled to keep his shoulders relaxed, his gait normal. *Can't alert the nosy neighbors.* He strode past his mother's flower bed, amazed the roses survived beneath the wild vines smothering them. No one had touched the bed since she disappeared all those years ago. He paused for a moment. His mom's big green eyes and rich brown curls flashed through his mind. He reached to pull a vine from the bed. A thorn pierced his palm. *Fuck it! You didn't care. Why should I?*

His vision tunneled on the unmarked

F150 in the driveway. *Escape.* Climbing in, he started the engine and checked to see if the computer was still logged in. Deputies were supposed to logout of their software at the end of each shift but rarely did. It took too long to log back in. He wiggled the mouse. The computer aided dispatch screen popped up.

He clicked on the map showing the location of each unit. *There.* He spotted the little vehicle icon representing the truck he sat in. Reaching beneath the dash, he unplugged the GPS and watched the icon disappear from the screen. He turned on the two-way radio to listen to the chatter. Between the map and the radio, he knew he could avoid the on-duty deputies

The monster in his head rubbed its hands together. *Time to hunt. Time to feed.* A tight smile curved his lips but never reached his eyes.

Restless, he decided not to sit in his regular spot. Instead, he patrolled the Wild Rock corridor. He fought against his father's voice in his head and the memories that haunted him. He lost the battle. Pulling to the side of a deserted county road, the memories swamped him.

He walked into the house after school and tossed his backpack on the entryway table. He drew up short. His dad and a strange blonde were wrapped around one another on the sofa.

"Where's mom?"

"Get out of here. You're bothering me." His father continued groping the woman in front of him.

Slowly entering the living room, he repeated, "Where is my mother?"

Father ignored him.

"Sweetie," the woman asked, "why don't you tell him?"

The muscle in his father's jaw jumped, and his face turned red. The boy froze, his feet rooted to the orange shag carpeting. When he noticed the warning signs, he held his breath and hoped his father wouldn't direct his outburst towards him.

Father slammed his fist into the woman's face. "Did I ask you to speak?" He drew his fist back again.

The boy turned and ran, holding his hands over his ears to block out the woman's screams of pain.

The sound of oncoming traffic pulled him from the past. He inhaled a deep, shaky breath and let it out in an extended exhale. A silver Dodge pickup raced past him. Glancing at the radar, he saw it traveled well above the speed limit. He pulled onto the road as red brake lights flashed in front of him. He pulled up behind the truck. *Damn it.* A young man in his early twenties drove the pickup.

He pulled a U-turn and drove back to

where he had been sitting. *This is a bust.*
Studying the map, he noticed no one patrolling
the Chili Pequin area near Gato Montes. A little
out of his usual comfort area, but the pressure
continued building and this area was not
providing an outlet. Traffic was dead. He needed
release—soon.

Turning on his red and blue lights, he
accelerated southwest away from Wild Rock. He
cranked up the satellite radio and tuned it into an
alternative metal station. Puddle of Mudd's 'She
Hates Me' blared from the speakers. He tapped
the steering wheel in rhythm with the song and
roared out the chorus. "She fucking hates me."
Well, I don't like her much either.

He pulled into the rest area near the
Chili Pequin creek, shutting off his overheads.
Two vehicles sat in the picnic area. As he pulled
in, one left. He glimpsed the driver of the second
vehicle. Positively female. Curly shoulder-
length brown hair. He licked his lips. *Exactly my
type.* A tingling sensation shot through his body,

straight to his groin. Thoughts of what he planned to do raced through his mind. His lips curled upward. *This was going to be fun.*

He tugged on a pair of latex gloves and covered them with leather driving gloves. *Never be too careful.* Checking his appearance in his rearview mirror, he snugged his father's old Stetson on top of his head. Brushed off the badge pinned to his shirt. He eased the truck up behind her car and flipped the red and blues back on.

Her shoulders hunched. Leaning to the right, she reached for the glove compartment. Something about the way she moved looked familiar. A warning itch crept up the back of his neck. Tapping the mouse, he woke up the computer and typed in her license plate. A notification dinged. He read the screen. *Fuck, fuck, fuck.* He threw his pickup into reverse and took off.

The registration information of the vehicle

flashed on the screen. It belonged to Ranger Rhyden Trammell.

Chapter Twelve

Rhyden gathered up the case file of the first sexual assault reported. He had read it cover to cover multiple times. *Useless.* The victim refused to answer questions. He flung the folder and its contents across his office. He massaged his temples. He could feel a migraine building. With regret, he thought of the white, oblong-shaped pills hidden in his truck. He pinched the bridge of his nose. *I can do this. I don't need the pills. I don't.*

He tossed the file to Ranger Noah Morgan. "Help me out here. What am I missing?"

Noah plopped into the leather visitor's chair in front of Rhyden's desk. He propped his feet up on the corner of the desk.

With a quick swipe of his hand, Rhyden knocked Noah's boots to the floor. "Come on, man. Keep your feet off my desk. Feet are nasty.

Think about all the places you walk. I don't want your germs contaminating my desk." He grabbed an alcohol wipe and scrubbed the corner of his desk.

"OCD much?" Noah asked. He straightened up in the chair and tugged on his tie. Today's tie sported a Confederate battle scene from the Civil War, complete with cannons, smoke, blood and guts. He flipped through the thin file. "Not much in here, is there?"

"The victim has apparently been quite uncooperative. Won't talk to the sheriff's investigators. I need to go talk to her. I can't shake the feeling that she's not the first victim. Just the first one brave enough to speak up, even if she's not giving us much. Do you want to come with me?"

Noah ran his hand over his chin. "Why not? I need to talk to you, anyway. We can talk on the road."

Once they settled in the F150, Rhyden started the engine and grabbed the gearshift to put her in drive. He quickly let go and shook his hand. "Son of a bitch. I burned the crap out of my hand."

He cranked up the air conditioner to max cold and rolled down the windows to blow the heat out. "I don't know about you, but I'm so ready for fall. These triple digit days are killing me."

Noah fastened his seatbelt. "I hear you. At least they aren't physically killing us, yet. Unlike that boy and his dad in Big Bend. Kid died of heat stroke. Father died in a car accident trying to get help. They think he crashed over one of the big embankments. I mean, temps here are 110°F to 113°F but at the national park, they're hitting 119°F and above." Noah fidgeted in his seat. "So..." He stopped speaking and pulled on the seatbelt.

Rhyden rolled up the windows and

pulled out of the Law Enforcement Center parking lot. "So what? You said you wanted to talk. What's up?"

"Umm, well," Noah stammered. "I need to ask you something. I know not that long ago that you were furious with me for hiding my identity, so I'll understand if you say no. But I really... well, I... umm..." He let the sentence fade away. Swallowed audibly. Rubbed the back of his neck.

"Hey, I thought we were past this. You helped rescue Bree." Rhyden paused as images of his teenage daughter held captive flashed through his mind. He remembered his anger when he thought Noah was involved. His muscles tightened as his hands fisted. Consciously, he relaxed his shoulders and shook out his fists. "You explained your deception, and I said I forgave you. I meant it. You're Uncle Noah." Rhyden smiled reassuringly at Noah. "What do you need?"

Noah took a deep breath. He tugged on his seatbelt again. In one rapid sentence, without taking a breath, words spewed from his mouth. "You know Cat said yes, and the wedding is coming up soon. Will the girls be bridesmaids and Maddie flower girl? And you're the best friend I've ever had. Hell, you're the only family I've ever had that wasn't trying to kill me. I mean I know we're not actually family, but you know what I mean. What I'm trying to say is I love you, man. Will you be my best man? There, I said it." He collapsed back against the seat, closed his eyes, and squeezed his hands together while he waited for a response.

After an extended silence, Noah opened his eyes and looked at Rhyden with an expression of hope mixed with apprehension.

"I would be honored to be your best man," Rhyden said with a smile. "We'll have to check with the older girls, but I know Maddie will be over the moon to be asked to be your flower girl."

Noah slumped in his seat. Shaky laughter came from him. "I was terrified to ask you that after our big blow up. You and the girls truly are the only family I have. You mean the world to me."

"It's all good."

They pulled onto a circular cement driveway in front of a two-story log cabin. The turquoise front door boasted an oval, cut-glass center. Rose beds filled with roses of all colors lined the front of the cabin. Rhyden double checked the address on the case file. With a nod, he parked behind a blue Mustang. "That's her car. She should be home. Keep your fingers crossed she will talk to us."

Noah's brows drew together. He bit his lip and wrinkled his brow. "Do you really think the perpetrator is a sheriff's deputy?"

Rhyden paused, opening his door. His

mouth dried. A sharp pain shot through Rhyden's leg. His heart rate increased. "God, I hope not." He rubbed his leg and blew out a heavy breath. He gestured toward the cabin. "You go on ahead. I'll be right there."

Noah gave Rhyden a curious look. "You okay? Anything I can do?"

Rhyden squeezed his jaw tight. Shook his head. "I'm fine. Just need a minute."

"Okay." Noah started toward the front door.

As soon as the passenger door of the truck shut, Rhyden reached for the pill bottle he stashed under the seat. With trembling hands, he opened the bottle and removed a hydrocodone. He paused a second, thinking. He shook out a second pill. Popping them both in his mouth, he crunched them between his molars before swallowing. He grimaced. Grabbing his soda, he took a large swig to flush the bitter taste from his mouth. *Hurry, hurry, hurry.* He couldn't wait for the pills to kick in and settle both his pain and his anxiety. *What if sitting in the heat of the locked truck decreased their efficacy? Fuck it.* He fished the pills back out from their hiding spot and dry swallowed one more. He squeezed his eyes closed and tossed out a prayer. *Lord, help me. I have to stop.*

***

Straightening up, Rhyden secured his hat on his head. The feel of the hot, heavy air weighing down on him fit his mood. He braced himself for a nightmare of an interview, if she even spoke with them at all. Sometimes, having daughters made his job more difficult. He adjusted his holster on his belt and slammed the truck door closed. He smoothed a hand down his long-sleeve white shirt hoping the starch held up and straightened his tie. Thinking of Noah's garish torture-Rhy-tie-of-the-day, he muttered, "My normal, plain black tie." Most Rangers paid close attention to their uniforms. They had a proud heritage to represent, after all.

As he and Noah approached the front door, they saw a lace curtain, the yellow of dandelions, twitch in the front window of the cabin.

"Does she know we're coming?" Noah asked.

"No, based on her previously uncooperative manner, I thought a surprise visit might be best," Rhyden answered. He rang the bell. No answer. After waiting a few minutes, he rang the bell again. Too much longer outdoors in this heat and he would be as wilted as his shirt.

Still no answer, although the curtain twitched again.

Walking through crunchy brown grass that had succumbed to the ongoing drought to the window, Rhyden tapped on the glass. "Crystal? Can you open the door? We know you're here. We need to talk to you for a few minutes." He walked back to the door and waited.

Several minutes passed before he heard the sound of the chain being removed and the door unlocked. The door swung open. A young lady, approximately eighteen years old, stood in the doorway, arms crossed over her abdomen. Swollen, red-rimmed eyes blinked rapidly. Her blonde curls lay limp and unwashed on her shoulders. Wrapped in a wrinkled, oversized man's chambray work shirt that probably belonged to her father, she resembled a faded version of her ID photo: the sparkle evident in the photograph gone.

Rhyden removed his hat, spun it between work-worn hands. "Crystal Davis? Do you have a moment to speak with us?"

She pressed trembling fingers to her lips. Her eyes dropped to the badge on his chest and widened in fear. Shaking her head, she said,

"I didn't say anything. I promised him I wouldn't. And I didn't. Why are you here?" She stared past the Rangers, surveying the front yard and the empty street beyond the yard. Shimmery waves of heat rose off the pavement. "Did he send you? I promise…" her voice broke, "I-I haven't said anything. Not a word to a single soul."

Rhyden gentled his voice. "Promised who? Crystal? No one sent us. We're here to help you. I'm Ranger Rhyden Trammell and this is Ranger Noah Morgan. We just want to talk to you. Are your parents at home?"

Still shaking her head, she said, "No. No one's home. They're at work."

Rhyden pressed lightly against the door. "May we come in? Please? I promise, all we want to do is talk. No pressure."

With quick, jerky steps, she backed away from the door. She gestured for the

Rangers to enter before pressing her elbows into her side as she tried to make herself small enough to disappear.

Rhyden reached a hand out to touch her shoulder in reassurance.

She flinched. "No," she whispered as she folded in upon herself. "Please. Please don't touch me."

He withdrew his hand immediately. "I'm so sorry, Crystal. I wasn't thinking. Is there somewhere we could sit and visit for a minute or two? Would you like to call your mom? Have her come home?"

Crystal sucked in a steadying breath and stiffened her spine. She shook her head again. "No. I'm an adult. I don't need my mom." She drew in a deep breath, released it slowly. She appeared to be gathering her strength and resolve. She gestured toward the oval kitchen table. "Please, come in. Would you care for a soda or water? I don't have anything else."

"No, thank you, Crystal. All we want to do is talk for a minute and maybe see if you could answer some questions." Careful not to spook the girl, Rhyden and Noah took a seat at the table. The scratches and scars on its wooden surface hinted at the many family meals shared around it. Rhyden pulled out a notepad while Noah brought out a small digital recorder.

"Do you mind if we record this?" Noah asked.

Crystal raised her hands in a gesture of surrender. "I guess not. But I can't tell you anything. He has my license. Knows where I live. He'll kill me and my family. He promised. Swore he would know if I talked."

Rhyden laid his pen down on the open notepad. He opened his hands wide, palms up, and rested his wrists on the tabletop. "Look, Crystal, I don't know what you are going through. I don't. I can't even pretend that I do. But what I do know is that you have information that can help us stop the same thing from happening to other young women."

He reached for his cellphone and pulled up a family photo. He turned the screen toward Crystal. "I have three daughters of my own. Bree is nineteen, Sam seventeen, and that little monkey," he pointed at the image of Maddie, "is seven. I need to stop him, whatever it takes." He laid the phone on the table where she could see his girls.

In the back of his mind, he could feel the hydrocodone beginning to kick in. His shoulders relaxed. Tension fled from his body. He leaned forward. Tossed a quick glance at Noah sitting in silence recording the conversation. *I cannot believe I am going to say this aloud.* "Crystal, I've heard a rumor that a police officer who attacked you. Is that true?"

Her panicked gaze whipped up to meet

his. Her mouth fell open as the color faded from her face. "I-I-" she stammered.

Rhyden raised a hand to stop her. "Before you speak, let me explain a few things to you. I don't work for the sheriff's office or the local police department. Texas Rangers are called in to investigate crimes when it's suspected a law enforcement officer is involved in a crime. Nothing you say to me will go any farther than myself and Ranger Morgan. No one at the sheriff's office or the police department will know you have said anything. Does that help?"

Noah gave a nod of agreement. "It's true. What you say is safe with us. It will remain between the three of us, at least until we arrest this piece of shit."

Crystal turned away and covered her mouth. Ragged fingernails bitten to the quick and covered with peeling ruby nail polish topped slender fingers. She looked back. Fear mixed with hope clouded her eyes. Tears clung to long, pale lashes. With a trembling voice, she asked, "Are you sure? Can you promise me he won't find out?" She carved her hands through her curls, scraping them back into a ponytail before releasing it, letting her hair fall forward to cover her face. She scrubbed her hands over her cheeks and eyes before studying Rhyden. Next, she turned her attention to Noah.

He met her eyes with a gentle, even look.

She rubbed her hands absently on the tabletop and asked, "Do you promise me?" She pointed at Rhyden's cell phone. "Do you promise me on the lives of your daughters that I will be safe? That he won't find out I told you anything?"

Rhyden reached forward to hold Crystal's hands but pulled back at the last moment. "Crystal, I promise you. On my honor. No one will know." The room swirled around him. The floor pitched up and down beneath his boots. He blinked slowly—once, twice. *Whoa.* He rubbed his palms up and down his denim-clad thighs. *Shouldn't have taken that third pill.* Ignoring the dizziness, he made eye contact with the girl. "Do you believe me? Will you talk to us?"

Rocking slightly in her chair, Crystal stared into the middle distance, her eyes hollowed out. She chewed on her bottom lip. Indecision painted her face. She cleared her throat, fiddled with the silver cross hanging from her neck. She tapped her pointer finger against the table and tapped her foot against the floor.

Rhyden and Noah waited patiently. They knew they were at a critical turn, and one wrong word could shatter the rapport they were building.

Minutes passed. The tick-tick-tick of a cuckoo clock hanging above the gas range in a corner of the kitchen filled the silence. A shudder shook her body. Raising her eyes, she turned to the Rangers. Strength fought the fear in her eyes. Blowing out a long breath, she said, "What do you want to know?"

Rhyden slumped in relief. He rubbed the bridge of his nose. Scrubbed his hands across his face. Straightening in his chair, he said, "Thank you, Crystal. You don't know how much this means to us."

Her forehead wrinkled as she twisted her hands together. "I'm still not certain what I can tell you. Everything happened so fast." She dropped her gaze. Mumbling slightly above her breath, she added, "And I'm trying hard to forget."

He nodded encouragingly. "It's okay. Take your time. Tell me what you remember and I'll ask questions if I need more clarification. Sound okay?" Rhyden removed the cap from his pen and prepared to take notes.

Crystal shuffled her feet. Stood up. "Are you sure you don't want a drink?" she asked as she moved toward the stainless steel refrigerator. "I'm grabbing a bottle of water."

Both Rangers declined and waited patiently while she reseated herself at the table.

Cracking the seal on the plastic bottle, she took a long drink. A distant expression crossed her face as she played with the blue bottle lid. "What do you want to know?"

"Let's start easy. Where did the… assault… take place?"

She snapped the Rangers a look, her eyes narrowing at the corners. Anger creased her face. "Assault? You mean rape?" She jumped to her feet, knocking her chair to the floor. She paced the kitchen. "Don't make it less than it was. He didn't just 'assault' me. Yes, he hit me, but he did so much more than that. That son-of-a-bitch raped me. He took what I didn't want to give him and discarded me like a piece of trash when he finished. He left me laying in that brush like an empty candy wrapper." She whirled around to face the Rangers, panting. "Don't sugar coat it by calling it an assault. He fucking raped me."

Contrite, Rhyden held out his hands, palms up in a placating manner. "I'm sorry. You're right. I don't mean to trivialize what happened to you. I'm truly sorry." He rose to his feet and righted her chair. Gesturing to it, he asked, "Can we start again?"

Crystal stood for a long moment, assessing the Rangers. As if reaching a decision, she nodded. "No, I'm sorry." She took her seat. "I know you're taught to pretty it up. To make it less offensive. The nurse at the hospital acted the same way. I wish I'd never gone." She hid her face in her hands. "I can't stand being around my parents. My mom hovers. She studies me with such pity, like she's afraid I'm going to melt down at any minute. And Dad? He can't meet my eyes. Like he's embarrassed. Pisses me off. That bastard did more than have sex with me. I could deal with that. He stole what wasn't his. He's destroyed my entire family."

She inhaled deeply. Exhaled slowly. She did it again and once more. She gave the Rangers an embarrassed half-smile. "The therapist they recommended suggested I try deep breathing exercises." She shrugged. "I guess it helps."

Rhyden smiled encouragingly. "They taught me the same thing."

Picking up the water bottle cap, she concentrated on rolling it between her fingers. The ticking of the cuckoo clock filled the room. The ice maker in the refrigerator dumped a load with a loud rumble. She expelled the words on a voice roughening whisper. "I drive home from work on 97 every night around eight p.m. I don't think I was speeding, but sometimes my foot gets heavy. Mom says I inherited my lead foot from Grandpa." She shrugged and shared a sheepish grin with the Rangers.

Rhyden chuckled. "Don't feel bad. My daughter got hers from my grandfather. He calls them 'speed suggestions' and tends to ignore them. Not that I condone that train of thought." He rolled his eyes.

Crystal giggled before sobering.

Like watching shutters slam shut, blocking out the sunlight. "Crystal, I already told you I can't begin to understand what you have and are still going through, but I know it can't be easy. Please, take your time. Try to tell us everything you remember. What did you see, hear, smell? In the file, it says you fought back. That you bit him. What did he taste like?"

A tiny grin flitted around the corner of her mouth. "I did. Almost got away, too." The grin fell from her face as she stared at her hands, remembering. "But then he tangled his hands in my hair and jerked me off my feet."

"I'm so sorry. Where did this happen?"

"At that deserted S-curve about seven miles south of Gato Montes. I was headed into Wild Rock."

Rhyden scribbled notes on his pad. "Please," he waved his hand in a go ahead motion, "continue."

"I don't know what else to tell you." She avoided making eye contact with the Rangers. "I got out of my car and walked around to the passenger side like he had told me to. Next thing I know, he slammed me against the car and wrapped my wrists with those plastic tie-wrap thingies." She absently rubbed the fading bruises ringing her wrists. "He dragged me into the thick mesquite thicket right there. Punched me a few times. I bit him. Tried to run. It didn't work. Just made him angrier." The more she spoke, the flatter her voice became. All emotion drained from her. "Flung me to the ground. Shoved my skirt up, ripped my panties off, and did his thing. Then he left after reminding me he knew where I lived and threatening to kill me and everyone I love if I said anything." She gave a half-hearted shrug. "What more do you want to know?"

"I'm so sorry to make you relive this, Crystal. I sincerely am. Is there anything else you can tell me? Any detail, no matter how small. Hair color? His skin? What about his eyes?"

"He had bristly cocoa-brown hair, military cut—lots of stubble, super thick but short—like shaved but not. Bronze colored skin." She paused, skimmed her eyes across Rhyden's face. "But not natural like yours. Less coppery. More like he spends a lot of time outdoors without sunscreen. He wore those sunglasses cops like. What are they called? Ray Ban airplanes? Pilots?" She shook her head. "Something like that."

Noah reached into his pocket. "Ray Ban Aviators? Like these?"

She nodded yes.

He tucked the sunglasses away. "Crystal, you're doing really well. Is there any other detail you can share with us?"

Crystal thought for a moment. She crinkled up her nose. "He smelled like gasoline."

"Gasoline?" Rhyden asked.

"Yeah, like when you fill your tank too full and it splashes on you."

Rhyden gathered up his notepad. A sense of relief eased the tightness in his chest. Nothing the girl had said pointed to a sheriff's deputy being the culprit. He stood and held out a hand for Crystal to shake. "Thank you for your help." He dropped his hand when she didn't reach to take it. "We'll show ourselves out. We appreciate your help. Immensely." He and Noah stood and walked toward the front door. With his hand on the glass doorknob, he glanced back over his shoulder at the girl.

She stood by the table, one arm wrapped around her middle, her other hand tucked into her mouth as she chewed on her fingernails.

He paused. "Crystal, I have one last question."

She squeezed her eyes closed. She lifted her lashes. Both arms wrapped around her stomach, she lifted one shoulder. With a heavy sigh, she asked, "What?"

"Why did you stop your car?"

She raised a single eyebrow. Her expression said Rhyden had just asked the stupidest question on earth. She dropped her arms to her sides, turned her palms up and raised her hands slightly before dropping them again in surrender. "He turned his red and blue lights on behind me."

Chapter Thirteen

"Damn, I'm not looking forward to this." The thermometer on the dash of Rhyden's truck registered 113°F as he and Ranger Noah Morgan pulled up to the location Crystal had given them. He tugged at his tie and collar. "Tell me again why our uniform comprises a long sleeve shirt, tie, and hat. In Texas? During a triple digit heat wave? Whoever designed it must have been on crack… or a Yankee."

Crystal couldn't or wouldn't tell them much about the attack or her attacker. She did reveal the location of the assault on the condition that they keep her name out of it.

Noah looked across the console at Rhyden. "Can you believe… ?"

"My heart plunged into my stomach. Until that last moment, I thought I could tell Chief and Nurse Bubbles they were crazy." He climbed out of the truck and opened the rear driver's side door to grab his kit. "Fuck me. A cop? Do you know how much that complicates things? I don't even want to think about it."

He tossed an extra roll of yellow crime scene tape to Noah before placing orange traffic cones in the lane closest to his pickup to close the lane. Not that much traffic existed on this stretch of road.

Motioning wide of the area they suspected the assault occurred, he said, "You take that side. I'll tape off this one. Let's take it from the shoulder of the road to about 100 feet back that-away. It's been over a week, so I don't expect to find much."

"At least it hasn't rained. Maybe we can find something." Noah tied the yellow tape around the trunk of a twisted mesquite tree and began walking away from the road, stretching the tape behind him.

Rhyden took the other side. He wrapped the caution tape around several other mesquite trees as he walked. Once he had gone approximately 100 feet from the road, he turned and headed toward Noah. When they met in the middle, they tied the plastic tape together, creating a rectangle enclosure around the suspected attack site. "Did you see anything?"

"Not yet. Brush is pretty thick. I'm not looking forward to working our way through it."

"Me neither," said Rhyden, "but I don't see any way around it. Ready?" He edged into the thick brush made up of prickly pear cactus and mesquite trees. Here and there he saw turkey pear growth. *I hate turkey pear.*

"Son of a bitch."

"Noah? You okay?"

"Yeah, stumbled into that damn turkey pear. I didn't see it. Damn thing took a piece of my hide and my shirt."

"Here's hoping the rapist stumbled into it, too."

Noah nodded as he pulled thorns from his arm. "Serve the bastard right, but I'm not holding my breath. He seems smarter than that. And I can almost guarantee Crystal wasn't his first victim."

"I agree with you. He's too smooth to be a virgin."

"Virgin?" Noah raised his eyebrows.

"Fine. Bad choice of words, but you know what I meant." Rhyden ducked beneath a mesquite limb and tried to dodge a stand of prickly pear. "Damn! Everything in this place either wants to stab me or cut me. Do you see anything yet?"

Noah dragged a torn, blood-stained sleeve across his forehead, wiping away the sweat dripping into his eyes. "Nothing yet."

The men worked their way closer to the road.

"Over here." Noah pointed to a spot in the brush. Crushed weeds and bent, broken mesquite limbs gave the impression that a struggle had taken place here. Watching where he stepped, he moved closer to the artificial clearing. "Look, footprints. I think."

Rhyden made his way through the brush to where Noah stood. Kneeling down, he took photos of the footprints. "Something's not right about these prints. All the weight is in the boot's heel. No weight at all in the toes." He placed a measuring tape beside the print and took another photo. Cautiously, he surveyed the ground, searching for more prints. Unfortunately, the hard packed ground yielded nothing.

"Can you dig the plaster of paris out of my kit? There should be a bottle of water in

there, too. I want to make casts of these prints."
He indicated the boot prints in front of him.
"Something about these really bothers me."

As they waded through the brush toward
the road after finishing the casts, those prints
nagged him. Something about them nagged his
memory, but he had no clue what.

After another hour of combing through
the brush and finding nothing, the Rangers
called it quits. Walking back to the truck,
Rhyden said, "If an asshat like this one came
after one of my girls, I'd have to invoke the
three Ss."

Noah cocked an eyebrow. "Three Ss?"

Rhyden stopped and turned to face
Noah. Sweat soaked the back of his shirt. He
propped scratched-up hands on his hips.
"You've never heard of the three Ss? How long
have you been in Texas?"

Noah shook his head. "Nope, afraid not."

"I'm surprised, that's all." He pulled the Stetson from his head and used it as a fan. He turned and headed to the truck.

"Well, are you going to leave me in the dark or let me in on the secret?"

Rhyden laughed. Placed a hand on the butt of his gun. "Shoot, shovel, and shut up."

"Never heard of it before today, but hand me a shovel. I'm in."

Chapter Fourteen

He flipped on the siren and overheads. The red and blue lights reflected off the silver Jeep as it slid to the side of the road and eased to a stop in front of the deserted roadside park. The park had been closed for remodeling for several months. Something about plumbing problems. A smile crossed his face. Finally, he could release this pressure building up in his head.

He grabbed the cowboy hat off his passenger seat, snugged it down tight, and opened his door. He stuck one boot covered foot to the ground; then the other. Stepping out of his vehicle, he adjusted his gun belt. Unhooked the clasp on his holster. A cool breeze loosened the stranglehold the heat had held on the day.

He sauntered up to the Jeep. Tapped on the window with the butt of his Mag light. The glow of the full moon reflected off his badge.

The window buzzed down a crack. "Is everything okay, Officer?"

"Ma'am, I need you to open the window the rest of the way."

She hesitated.

He smiled. Dimples creased his cheeks. "Please, ma'am." *Where do I know this one from?* Dark curls, olive skin. *Reminds me of someone.* His heart rate increased.

The window lowered the rest of the way down. He leaned in the window. Casually rested his crossed arms covered by the tan long sleeves of his uniform on the Jeep's window sill. He noticed her pretty green eyes dart to the leather gloves covering his hands. "Beautiful night, isn't it?" he asked.

She cocked her head to the side flirtatiously and said, "That depends on whether or not I'm getting a ticket." She smiled coyly and winked at him.

The skin around his eyes tightened, but his smile never faded. "I need to see your driver's license and insurance card, please."

She handed him the documents.

"Shannon Brown?" *Name means nothing to me. Guess I don't know her after all.* He grinned. "It says here you're twenty-one. I need you to step out of your vehicle, please. Have you been drinking?" He tucked the driver's license into his shirt pocket.

"No, sir. I don't drink. Alcohol tastes nasty." She grimaced. "Officer, why did you stop me?"

"Your license plate light is out. Come here. I'll show you."

"What? I passed the safety inspection earlier today when I went to get my new registration sticker." She jerked the door open and stomped toward the back of her Jeep. "Damn mechanic. You think he'd have told me the bulb burned out, wouldn't you?"

He slipped up behind her and slammed her head against the rear window of the SUV. BAM! He slammed her head against it again. Jerked her arms behind her back. Slid tie wrap restraints around her wrists and pulled them tight. "He might have… if your light was actually out."

He grabbed her upper arm and tugged. The ground was clear of rocks or debris. A fine layer of red sand crunched beneath their feet as he dragged her deeper into the roadside park, past the picnic tables. Into the ominous shadows by the dry, rocky creek bed.

She struggled against him. Tried to break free. She clenched and unclenched her fists. Pulled against the restraints cutting into her wrists. She stomped on his toes hard, but he didn't feel it.

He backhanded her across the face. Punched her in the stomach. Blood trickled from her split lip.

"Don't fight me." He panted. "Do what I want, and this will be over so much faster." He buried his fists in her hair and jerked her head back. He lowered his mouth to the delicate shell of her ear and whispered, "See those stars? I could make you one of those stars."

He pulled back and studied the blank expression on her face. "Stars? Heaven?" He went silent. Waited for her to catch on. He curled his lip. "You're not the brightest crayon in the box, are you? I'm saying I can kill you, you stupid cunt. But I won't if you behave. Don't fuck with me."

He pressed a kiss against her mouth. Forced his tongue between her lips. Squeezed her tight.

She whimpered but didn't struggle.

"Good girl," he murmured. He threw her to the ground. Shoved her skirt up and unfastened his duty belt and uniform pants.

She scrambled back away from him. Screamed for help.

"Uh, uh, uh." He grabbed her sandaled foot and dragged her back towards himself. "Trying to get away isn't very nice." He ripped her blouse open. "Go ahead, scream again." He smirked. "I like it."

Shannon swallowed her scream and curled into a protective ball. She kicked her foot out at him, striking a glancing blow against his thigh.

"What did I say about being nice?" He heard the echo of his father's voice in those words. Tried to shake the memory away before it could fully surface, but failed.

"Just be nice, boy. Who knows, you

might even like it." His father cackled as he thrust his son at the old hag waiting on the bed. "Make the lady happy."

He backed away, shaking his head no.

"You defying me, boy?" The old man reached for his belt buckle. Thrust his chest out.

The boy's eyes came to rest on the badge pinned there. He shuddered.

The old man gloated. Lifted a foot and kicked the boy in the butt, knocking him into the greedy grasp of the naked woman on the bed.

Wrinkled hands tugged at his clothing. Gin-soaked breath hit him in the face. Caused him to gag. His eyes returned to his father's badge.

"That's right, boy. I'm the law and there's not a damn thing you can do about it. When I say jump, you best ask how high. Now, you take care of the lady like I done told you."

His father stepped away, pocketing the money the woman left on the bureau for him. "What are you, boy? One of those faggots? Get busy."

Derisive laughter brought him back to the present. "What's the matter?" she asked. "Can't get it up?"

His nostrils flared. The vein in his temple pulsed. He balled up his fist and punched her in the ribs. Punched her in the stomach, in the face. He stepped back and kicked her. As he did, he tripped over his loose pants and fell to the ground beside her. He reached out to grab her.

The grating ch-ch-ch buzz of a rattlesnake filled the air. Anger faded to fear.

A rattlesnake slithered toward Shannon. Full body tremors engulfed her. A cold sweat covered her body.

The snake coiled up. Drew back to

strike.

She moaned and reached for the officer. Her fear of the snake outweighed her fear of him. Her eyes pleaded with him for help. Surrendering to the inevitable, she squeezed her eyes shut.

At the last moment, he thrust his arm between her and the snake. A grunt of pain escaped him as the snake struck.

"Fuck!" He flung his arm around, but the snake wouldn't release. He shook his arm. Tugged at the snake until it came loose. He threw it as far as he could.

The snake slipped away into the brush.

He grabbed his arm. Raspy breaths escaped his lips. "Help me. Please."

Stunned, she gaped at him. "Why did you do that? It was going to strike me. Why did you jump in the way?" She pulled her shirt closed and fumbled with her skirt. She gasped. "I-I don't understand. Why?" She frowned, then bit her lip. "I don't get it."

Pain surged up his arm as it swelled. His voice elevated in pitch. "Please. Help me." Adrenaline raced through his body. The world seemed to spin as spots danced in front of his eyes. He gasped for air. "Can't breathe. Please…" He reached for her, but his hand fell to his side. The world went dark.

Chapter Fifteen

Rhyden unwrapped the plaster of paris casts of the footprints made at Crystal's rape scene. He laid them on the table beside the 8 x 10 photographs of the footprints. "What do you think?" he asked Noah.

"Not sure." Noah dragged the photos of Crystal's injuries taken at the hospital closer to his side of the conference table. He cringed. "Damn, she's lucky. It could have been so much worse."

Scanning the room, Noah noted all the windows set in the faux-wood paneling. He watched deputies traveling up and down the hallway between the communications area and the bullpen. He flipped the photos facedown. "I think we need to move this discussion to a place more private. Maybe your office?"

Rhyden gathered up the case file and the evidence. "I'm an idiot. I should have thought of that." He ran a hand down his leg, pressing hard on his surgical scar. His heart skipped a beat. "Fuck," he muttered under his breath.

"Here." He shoved the evidence at Noah. "Take this stuff. I'll meet you in my office. Go ahead and pull up the sex offender registration on my computer. You remember the password?"

Noah's eyes snapped up, surprised. "Yeah, I got it. Where you going? You okay?"

"Just go, okay? I'll be back in a minute." Rhyden spun on his heel and stormed out of the conference room. An itchy sensation crawled through his chest. He clenched his molars.

Fuck, fuck, fuck. He couldn't remember if he put the pain pills back in his pickup's console or not. Last night, he remembered counting pills and crunching a few, but couldn't recall what he did with the bottle afterwards.

Picking up his pace, he quick-stepped it to the truck. He fumbled and dropped his keys as he tried to pull them from his pants' pocket. A shiver danced down his spine. He scooped the keys from the pavement, unlocked the truck and all but dove inside. His pulse raced.

Please, please, please. He popped the console open. The orange pill bottle lay nestled in the top tray. *Oh, thank God.*

Rhyden twisted the lid off and shook two white oval pills into the palm of his hand. Tossing them into his mouth, he grabbed the bottle of water sitting in the cup holder. He swallowed the pills with a swig of hot water.

He blew out his cheeks and wiped the sweat from his forehead. Shoving the bottle into his pocket, he locked up the pickup and headed back into the law enforcement center.

Walking into his office, he draped his Stetson over the antlers of the trophy buck hanging by the door. He closed the office door.

Noah glanced over at him. "You okay?"

Rhyden nodded. "Yeah, fine."

"Okay. Good." Noah crinkled up his face. He shuffled the photographs awkwardly through his hands. He puffed his cheeks with air and blew out. "Can we talk?"

Unease washed over Rhyden. "Um, yeah? What's up?"

Panic painted Noah's face. "I am so afraid of fucking John Wyatt up. I never had a father, or at least not one that I want to acknowledge. Grandda did what he could, but damn, Rhy, he was a criminal—a con artist." He tugged at his tie. "Why the hell did I think I could be a father? Cat's going to take JW and run as far away from me as she can. I'll never see him again."

"Whoa, Noah, what happened?"

"Nothing. I just know I'm going to fu—er, screw this up. I don't have a clue what I'm doing. And Cat says I have to quit cussing. Me? Quit cussing. I can't do that." He rubbed at the veins standing out on his neck.

"Settle down, partner." Rhyden knelt in front of Noah and pressed a hand against his knee to stop his leg from bouncing up and down. "You're going to be fine. You and Cat will be wonderful parents. Follow your instincts. Follow your heart and for God's sake, listen to Cat."

"But how do we know if we are doing it right? Someone posted on social media last night that we can't raise our kids the way our parents raised us. In my case, that's a good thing, but Cat had good, no she had great parents. They raised her right."

"Why would anyone say we can't raise our kids that way?" Confused, Rhyden stood and walked around his desk. He sank into his chair.

"He said the world our parents raised us in no longer exists."

Rhyden scrubbed his hands across his face. "But if everyone raised their children the way our parents or grandparents raised us, wouldn't the world revert to the way it was before the snowflakes and the politicians screwed it up? Doesn't this make it even more important to raise our children the way we were raised? Think about it."

"I don't want to think about it. I'm confused enough as it is. Can we change the subject to something easier to talk about? Let's get back to the search for the infamous Officer Rapist."

A knock on the door caused both men to jump. They exchanged nervous looks.

Noah shrugged. "Guess I shouldn't say that so loud, huh?"

The knock repeated, and the door

cracked open. Chief Dannar stuck his head into the room. "How's it going? Please tell me the nurse at the ER got it wrong."

Rhyden gestured for the chief to come in and shut the door behind him. He winced and swallowed hard before speaking. "I wish I could. Crystal Davis confirmed the only reason she stopped on that deserted stretch of road because a marked sheriff's unit pulled her over."

He handed a cast of the footprint to the chief deputy followed by a stack of photographs. "We found this print at the scene and it's bugging the crap out of me. Appears to be a size 13, but it's not right. What do you think?"

Chief Dannar studied the cast and the photographs. He tapped one of the photos against the palm of his hand and stared off into space. "You know, way back in the day, a friend of mine used to wear his daddy's boots. They were way too big for him. They made tracks like that—deeper in the heel and almost nonexistent in the toes because he stuffed them with newspaper. He didn't put any weight on the toes. We used to play tracking games in the back pasture. I could always tell which trail belonged to him."

He handed the photograph back to the Ranger. "This guy is not wearing boots that fit."

Noah wadded up the piece of paper he had been scribbling sex offender names on. He tossed it into the wastebasket. "Well, that rules out these men. They actually wear a size fifteen boot." He stood up and stretched. "Of course, if this guy truly is a sheriff's deputy, we won't find his name in the registry. Not his real name, anyway."

Rhyden grabbed his hat from the deer mount. "Damn it. I guess there's no way around it. I'm heading back to the hospital to talk to Nurse Bubbles."

Chapter Sixteen

Standing outside the privacy curtain in the emergency department, Rhyden heard a crash and a metallic clatter.

"Dag-nabbit and fudge nuggets! Can someone bring me a new stitching tray? Stat."

Rhyden peeked around the curtain as a tray and tools of some sort skittered across the floor. Nurse Bubbles, better known as SANE Michelle Ross, stood in the center of the cubicle with her hands clenched into tight fists.

The corners of his lips twitched as he tried to hold back a grin. Rhyden winked at a young boy about twelve years old sitting on the gurney, holding a blood-soaked towel to his chin.

Nurse Ross swiped at the wild strands of auburn hair that had escaped her bun and stuck to the perspiration beading on her forehead. She glared at the Ranger. "What do you want now?" she asked as she shoved him out of the cubicle. "Have you never heard of patient privacy?"

He held his hand up protectively in front of himself. "Checking on you. I heard a crash. Are you okay?"

Frustrated, she said, "I'm working a double shift in the emergency department of a trauma hospital on a Friday the thirteenth with a full moon. How do you think I am?" Before he could answer, she continued, "I'm frickin' peachy keen. Now, I repeat, what do you want? I'm in the weeds here."

"In the weeds?" He chuckled. "Did you say dag-nabbit?"

"What of it? I hear so much cursing in here from pain and disrespect, I choose not to curse." She popped her hands on her hips and stepped toward him, crowding his personal space. "Yes, my coworkers tease me unmercifully, but I refuse to bow to peer pressure. Do you want to make something of it?"

"No, ma'am, absolutely not." He stepped back. "Nurse Ross, I needed to see if you had a moment to discuss that... hypothesis you had."

"Name's Mikki." She cast a glance over her shoulder into the curtained cubicle she had vacated a moment before. She blew strands of hair out of her eyes. "Let me finish stitching up this young man, and I'll be right with you." She shook her head and sighed. "Friday the thirteenth." Her shoulders slumped. "Who knew shenanigans with a plastic baseball bat could cause a wound needing twelve stitches? Are you hungry? Meet you in the cafeteria?"

"If you don't mind, I'll wait right here. I'd hate to miss any of the excitement. Then we can cop a squat and gobble."

Mikki raised her right eyebrow. In a

voice thick with resignation, she said, "Whatever flips your tail feathers. I'll be done in a few."

Lifting the bread on the edge of his sandwich, Rhyden frowned at the wilted lettuce drowning in giant glops of mayonnaise. "You actually eat this stuff?" The chatter in the cafeteria almost drowned out Mikki's reply.

"It's not that bad if you don't think about it... and you're starving." She handed him a bottle of ketchup. "Try this. It helps."

Rhyden shuddered and pushed the plate away. The hospital smell of disinfectant and illness brought back terrible memories and killed his appetite, anyway. Folding his hands on top of the table, he leaned forward. "Back to the subject at hand. What convinced you the rapist was law enforcement?"

Mikki grabbed half of Rhy's abandoned sandwich. "You aren't going to eat this, are you?" She took a huge bite and swallowed before reaching for her soda. "Each victim reports being pulled over by an officer in a marked sheriff's unit and forced out of their own vehicle."

"But how do you explain the fact that none of the sheriff's office's vehicles were anywhere near the location of the assaults? After the Atascosa County massacre, they equipped every single vehicle in the fleet with a GPS tracker. Dispatchers always know exactly where the vehicles are, and how long they've been there. They can even tell you how fast the officers were driving. All the vehicles were accounted for and none were in the area."

Mikki rolled her eyes. "Are you genuinely that simple? It's a plug-and-play device stuck into the onboard diagnostic port. You can buy them for a buck two ninety-eight online. Heck fire, my teenage demon can disable the tracker in about two seconds flat. All you have to do is unplug it."

Before Rhyden could reply, Mikki's pager went off. "Crap. He's struck again." She ran her eyes up and down Rhyden's clothing. "Take off the gun belt and the badge and I'll show you another reason I know the sorry S.O.B. is a cop."

After placing his gun and badge in a secure locker, Rhyden followed Mikki into a curtained-off cubicle in the emergency department. He stood quietly in the corner after Mikki introduced him as a colleague in training.

The young lady on the gurney in front of him caused his heart to squeeze in pain. With her short, dark curls and tanned skin, she resembled his middle daughter, Sam. She had a swollen and split lip. Bruises were blossoming on her face. She clutched the pieces of a torn shirt closed.

Mikki gentled her voice and approached

the girl. "Shannon? Is it okay if my colleague remains in the room? I need to ask you some questions, and with your permission, perform an examination." She glanced over her shoulder at Rhyden. "If you don't want him here, I can ask him to leave."

Shannon's breath hitched. She shrugged. "It's okay. He can stay."

"If you are sure?"

The girl nodded.

"Okay, I'm going to pull this curtain around the bed and ask him to wait on the other side. I need you to slip out of your clothing, all of it, and place it in this bag. I'll set out a gown for you to put on."

Shannon tugged her shirt tighter around her chest. She shook her head no. "He didn't rape me." Her gaze darted around the emergency department. "Is he here?"

Mikki frowned. She tugged on her earlobe. Holding her hands palm up, she peered through the curtains into the triage area. "Shannon, why would he be here?"

"The rattlesnake. That's why he didn't rape me. He planned to." She shuddered, then gulped air. "He threw me to the ground and was going to... going to... but then the rattlesnake struck. It stuck in his arm. The snake was going to bite me, but he got between us. He threw his arm in front of the snake." Her gaze clouded over. She stared into space before returning her eyes to Mikki's. "Why did he do that? He was going to hurt me." She gestured to her bruises. "He did hurt me, but then he saved me." Her gaze traveled between Mikki and Rhyden. "Why?"

Before either of them could answer, a uniformed officer pushed his way into the cubicle. "Miss Brown? I'm Deputy Williams. I need a statement from you."

Mikki tried to stop the officer from entering, but the deputy rudely shoved past her.

Shannon cringed away from Deputy Williams. "I didn't say anything. Honest, I didn't tell them anything. I promise." She backed into a corner of the cubicle. "Please, don't kill me. Don't kill my family. I promise." She melted into hysteria, lashing out at the deputy.

Rhyden motioned for the deputy to leave. He approached Shannon and tried to calm her.

She kicked out at him, catching him painfully in the shins.

Mikki slipped up behind Shannon and injected her with a sedative. She held onto the girl until she relaxed into a semi-conscious state. After securing Shannon on the gurney, she pulled up the railings so the girl couldn't fall off.

She gestured for Rhyden to follow her

into the hallway outside the cubicle. "She isn't the first one."

"First one what?" Rhyden asked.

"First one to react in such a negative manner to the arrival of the investigators. She's the third one this week alone that I've had to sedate."

"I imagine the sight of any male would cause a similar reaction, wouldn't it? Considering what they've experienced."

"Generally, yes, I would agree with you, but you are not listening to me. It's not the person. It's the badge."

"What makes you think it's the badge?" he asked in a voice like raspy sandpaper.

Mikki rubbed the back of her neck. "After the second victim, I tried an experiment. Last night, another victim came in. Both investigators were female. When the first investigator walked in and the victim melted down, I asked her to step out. I asked her partner to come in without a badge or any other trappings of law enforcement. The second investigator asked the same questions the first tried to ask without identifying herself. The young lady responded calmly. She remained guarded and kept details of her attacker to herself, but she stayed calm."

She locked eyes with Rhyden. "Your rapist is a sheriff's deputy." She squinted at him, inspecting his face. Her nostrils flared. She crossed her arms across her chest and crowded into his space. Her tone deepened. "But you already knew that, didn't you?"

***

"Ranger Trammell?" A voice like fingernails on a chalkboard assaulted his ears, pulling his thoughts from the curvy, sarcastic nurse who looked oh-so-good in scrubs.

"Ranger Trammell, may I speak to you for a moment?" Principal Harkness waved at Rhyden from across the hospital cafeteria as she beelined it straight to him. "Is everyone okay? I do so hope Samantha is feeling better. You know you are required to call the office to keep us updated on her condition."

"Condition?" Rhy scratched his ear. "Um, okay." Mental note—find out what the hell Sam is up to now.

"We will be so happy to have her back at school as soon as she's capable." The principal twisted the double strand of pearls at her neck. "You've done such a good job with her as a single father. I swear, if my daughter turns out half as sweet as Sam, I will know I did my job as a parent. I don't know how you do it with three girls all on your own."

What the… Confusion flooded Rhyden's mind. His eyebrows beetled together. *Principal Hardass, er Harkness, is singing a way different tune than last I heard her.* He examined her face trying to understand what she wanted. This woman was never this pleasant, and she never, ever complimented his daughters. *Not even the one who deserved the accolades.*

"How is Bree doing?" The woman continued talking. "Does she like the university? Now, that one was a handful."

"Principal Harkness, are you sure you don't have the girls mixed up? Bree made straight-As. Sam is, shall we say, a bit too… sassy to focus in class."

"Nonsense. Bree is the one with an attitude." Principal Harkness sniffed and raised her chin. "Always a mite too big for her britches if you ask me. Knew everything. Didn't think I knew a thing. Samantha is perfectly well-behaved and polite every time I see her."

"O-kay." Images of Sam mocking the principal flooded Rhyden's mind. Sarcasm flowed from Sam's lips like honey. *Perhaps Principal Harkness wasn't the sharpest pencil in the box.* That's what the girls had always claimed. He shrugged. "Well, it's, uh, good seeing you again, but I need to get back to work. I'll tell Sam you were checking on her." *Right after I ground her for skipping school—again.*

Rhyden tossed his soda cup in the garbage can as he headed to the exit.

"Ranger Trammell, wait. Please."

Here it comes. He turned to face the principal. "Ma'am?""We have a fundraiser coming up soon. I'm sure Samantha mentioned it. Our annual bachelor auction? Because we have so few single fathers, well," she slid her gaze suggestively up and down his frame, "we're counting on you to be our main event.

Rhyden felt a hot blush creep up his chest and neck to his face. An involuntary shudder swept along his spine. Ew, I need a shower.

He could hear Noah's snide remarks and cackling laughter in his imagination. *No way. No how.* He'd never live that one down. Unless, of course, a certain nurse examiner wanted to bid on him.

Thoughts of sparkling upturned green eyes and messy auburn hair distracted him from the conversation with the girls' high school principal. He wondered what it would feel like to run his fingers through those thick tresses. To release them from their pins and watch them tumble across Mikki's shoulders. *What would her kisses taste like?*

He hadn't been this attracted to a woman since his marriage imploded. *Don't do it.* He headed to the door marked 'Parking.' His steps slowed. *One date, no more. What could the harm be?*

Turning left, determined steps led him

back to the emergency department. He paused at the triage desk and rapped his knuckles on the counter top. "Excuse me. Where can I find Nurse Bubbles? I'm sorry, I mean Nurse Ross?"

Chapter Seventeen

He struggled to slow his breathing, to inhale deeper, but it felt like he couldn't get any oxygen into his lungs no matter how hard he tried. The innocuous tinkling of the brass bell contrasted with the violence of him crashing through the door. His heart pounded in his chest. He felt his pulse hammering at his temples. How much time do I have left?

He'd always heard death from snakebite was rare, but extremely painful. *And with my shit luck, I'll probably be the one in five hundred to die.*

The scent of animals and overpowering lemon disinfectant burned his nose. He stumbled to the front desk, his arm clutched against his abdomen. *Keep it lower than my heart. Don't panic.* The thought circled his brain like a tired mantra, repeating over and over. The tourniquet, hastily made from his brown polyester tie, squeezed his arm. Scraps torn from a white t-shirt wrapped around the actual wound.

A perky voice greeted him. "Welcome to Bennett County Animal Hospital. How may we…?" The lady at the front desk glanced up from her computer screen. She brushed salt-and-pepper bangs from her eyes. Her voice fell flat. "Oh. It's you." She did a double take. "What the hell are you wearing? Headed to a costume party?"

"Yes, yes, it's me. You don't like me. Got it." His eyes darted around the reception area, grateful for the lack of patrons. "Where is he? It's an emergency."

"Isn't it always with you?" She twirled her chair away from the desk and raised her voice. "Dad, your… nephew… is here." She lowered her voice to a mutter and added, "Again."

Noting the swelling of his lower arm,

she inspected him for other injuries. She pursed her lips. "Why do you have scribbles drawn on your arm with a black marker?"

"Where. Is. He?" Sweat gathered at his hairline. A single bead trekked down his temple. The disinfectant odor mixed with the ammonia of cat urine turned his stomach. The ache in his arm throbbed with each beat of his heart. A wave of wooziness passed over him. He wasn't sure how much longer he could remain standing.

She huffed. "He's with a patient. The kind he's trained to treat. You know? The ones with four legs. Why don't you ever go to a regular doctor? I don't care if Uncle Sonny did ask Dad to watch out for you. This is ridiculous."

The room spun. He sagged against the front counter. His pulse beat faster. His throat tightened. *Can't breathe.* "Shut the fuck up and get him," he gasped. "Now."

She opened her mouth to smart off again, but the ice-cold hatred in his narrowed eyes stopped her in her tracks. "Dad? Daddy?" She jumped from the chair and raced down the hallway behind her. "Daddy, help. Please."

"Easy, Lynda." The veterinarian stepped out of an exam room. The high-pitched yelps of newborn puppies were audible behind him. He dried his large callused hands—gentle, compassionate hands that often meant the difference between life or death—on a paper towel. "What's going on here? What has you in such a dither?"

Her cousin collapsed to the floor in the reception room, creating a loud commotion and knocking wormer and tick/flea medication displays off the counter.

A sharp scent brought him back to consciousness. A sensation of cold pressed against the back of his neck. His shirt was unbuttoned and hands fumbled with his belt. He cracked his eyes open to find himself flat on his back on the floor. Several rolled up blankets had been stuck beneath his lower legs raising them six inches or so off the floor.

"There you are, son." Kindly blue eyes met his. "How are you feeling?"

"Uncle Bobby?" The back of his mouth flooded with an acidic taste. His stomach clenched. He squeezed his eyes closed as a gagging noise came from his throat.

Large hands rolled him to his side and shoved a towel beneath his face. "Go ahead. Get it all out." His uncle rubbed soothing circles on his upper back.

After expelling the contents of his stomach, he tried to sit up.

"Easy, there. Not too fast." The vet

looked over his shoulder. "Lynda, sweetie, there should be a couple of Sprites in the fridge. Can you bring your cousin one, please? Maybe a handful of saltines, too."

The younger man held up his swollen arm. He winced with pain. "Rattlesnake bite. Can you help me? Please?"

The veterinarian removed the tourniquet. He peeled away the makeshift bandage and examined the puncture wounds. He motioned to the sharpie marks an inch above the swelling on the younger man's arm. "This the time of the bite?"

He nodded yes.

"Smart boy, but next time, skip the tourniquet. They cause more damage than they are worth with snakebites. Can you stand?" Uncle Bobby helped him to his feet. "Lynda, honey, come clean up this mess while I take care of your cousin."

If looks could kill… Cousin or not, that woman would never like him. He staggered to his feet and followed his uncle to an examining room.

"Son, based on the minimal swelling, this appears to be a dry bite." He tugged on a pair of blue nitrile gloves. "They might not be as rare as a white crow, but without question, you lucked out. Dry bites only occur about twenty-five percent of the time. I usually see bites on noses. Faces swell horribly, but most of my patients survive. 'Course I usually treat dogs, not people, so it's hard to say." The older man washed and disinfected the bite before bandaging it loosely.

"Keep an eye on this and if it swells more, go to the emergency room." Curiosity filled his eyes as he glanced sidelong at his nephew. "Which is what you should have done in the first place." He turned away and began cleaning up the bandaging refuse. His brow wrinkled as he shot a couple of wary side glances at the young man. "What were you up to when the snake got you?"

The old man bit the inside of his lip. "Never mind. Maybe I don't want to know." He stepped to the sink, peeled off his nitrile gloves, and scrubbed his hands. "Look, son, I promised your daddy I would take care of you. You were such a young 'un when he… passed. He never shoulda died that way. And you shouldn't have seen it. Why they put a cop in gen pop with murderers and rapists he'd put away, I'll never understand. I don't care what he did. And why anyone thought it was a good idea for you to visit him—

I tried my best with you, but dammit boy, I was already old enough to be your grandfather. Maybe I should have let a younger family take care of you," he shook his head, "but I promised Sonny. Thought he was crazy when he asked. I had thirty years on him. Always thought I'd die long before he did. The way things happened? It was wrong." Uncle Bobby stroked his snow-white beard and made eye contact with his nephew. "I did my best. You know that, don't you?"

"I do, Uncle Bobby. I really do. And I appreciate it."

"Do you? Then for God's sake, please stay out of trouble." Before his nephew could interrupt, he held up a hand. "I'm not saying you're in trouble or you're doing anything wrong. But I knew my brother. Lord knows I tried to help him, but I couldn't. I tried with you, too. But sometimes, blood will out. Please, son, don't become your old man."

Chapter Eighteen

Sam be-bopped through the kitchen headed toward the back door, curls bouncing on her shoulders and lips tasting of watermelon lip gloss. She paused at the refrigerator and grabbed a can of soda. She continued across the room. Seventies rock music from her phone zipped through her earbuds, flooding her ears. Escape in sight, her fingertips brushed against the doorknob.

"Samantha Elaine Trammell."

Her dad's voice cut through the music. She slid to a sudden stop.

"Is there anything you want to tell me?" Rhyden leaned against the door jamb between the living room and the kitchen. Uncrossing his arms, he pushed off the door frame and moved into the kitchen. He arched a single eyebrow.

Crap on a cracker. What does he know? She turned to face her father. Condensation rolled down the soda can in her hand, dripping to the linoleum flooring. She'd always hated the flooring in the kitchen. *Focus, Sam.* She shook her head. "No, not really."

Storm clouds of disappointment gathered in his eyes. His lips pressed rigidly together. He tapped his fingers against his thighs as he waited.

She sighed and mentally rolled her eyes. She knew better than to let her dad see her actually roll them. Popping one hand on her hip, she asked, "Fine. What do you want to know?"

"Let's start with this 'condition' of yours, why don't we? Then we can move on to where you think you are going. I know Mr. Werner closed the shop for a two-week vacation."

"I'm headed to Jason's house to help

him with that 'Vette he bought. Dang, I wish I could find a 'Vette for $1200."

"No, ma'am. You are not going anywhere. First off, you're grounded for skipping school—"

"Skipping school? Who told you I was skipping school? If Maddie's been tattling, I'm gonna—"

"You aren't going to do anything. And no, it wasn't Maddie." Rhyden's knees buckled. He walked to the kitchen table and dropped into his chair. He traced the scars on the formica tabletop with his fingertips as he concentrated on his breathing. His tight chest labored to expand, to fill with oxygen.

"Dad?" Sam moved to his side and sank to her knees. She grabbed his wrist, checking his pulse. "Are you okay? You look pale. And you're sweating. It's not your heart, is it?"

Rhyden jerked his arm out of her grasp.

Hands trembling, he dug in his pocket for his pill bottle. He thumbed off the lid and shook two pills into his palm. He swallowed them dry before responding.

"The only problem with my heart is the heartache you're causing me." He swept the salt and pepper shakers from the table in a fit of temper before sagging in his seat. Disappointment etched his features. "Damn it, Sam, why aren't you going to school?"

"You don't understand." Hands shaking, she brushed her hair back. Her words rushed together. "School sucks. I'm not learning anything useful, nothing I'll ever use in the real world. I want to build cars. They won't even let me take auto mechanics. Freaking backassward misogynistic school administrators who would rather me waste my time in physics and calculus. When am I ever going to use that shit?"

"Language, young lady."

Sam raised pleading eyes to her father. "Dad… I'm wasting my time. I could make real money working in the shop. Lawrence says…"

"Mr. Walker is not your father. Nor does he give two thin dimes about you or your future. He's looking for cheap labor to help him."

Sam jumped to her feet and spun away from the table. "You're wrong. He does care. He's a good man, and he cares more than you know. Lord knows he cares more than you do. You're never home. Always out on some," she made quotation marks in the air with her fingers, "very important case. Bree's right. You love your job more than you will ever love us. I can't wait to get out of this house."

Rhyden pushed to his feet. "Well, it won't be today. You won't be going anywhere but to school and home. You're grounded. Besides, I need you to take care of Maddie. Grandfather isn't available today."

"Why do I have to babysit Maddie? I never used to."

"No, you didn't. Bree took care of all the heavy lifting around here. She's at college now. It's your turn."

"Why isn't it your turn?"

"Because I'm father and I said so."

"Pfft. Some father you are."

Rhyden raced his voice warningly. "Samantha…"

Maddie walked into the room carrying her well-loved, no-longer-fuzzy teddy bear, Fred. 'Uncle' Noah had given it to her when her mom left years and years before. Seven-years-old and she rarely went anywhere without it. She held the bear in one hand and a book in the other. Holding up the book, she asked, "Will someone read with me, please?"

"AAARGH!" Sam slammed past Maddie, banging into her shoulder, causing her to drop the book. "I hate you." She focused on her father. "I hate you all."

Tears gathered in Maddie's eyes. Fred clutched against her chest, she stooped to pick up her book. Chin quivering, blinking back tears, she peered up at her dad. "What did I do?"

Chapter Nineteen

"Glaucoma? I thought that was when they stole your Glock, shot you with it, and you slipped into a coma."

Doctor Carlson rolled his eyes. Iron-gray, they matched the crew cut crowning his square head. "Well, exchange the Glock for a concrete parking stop and that's damn near what happened to you. Now, like I said, you need to have the pressures in your eyes checked every three months until I tell you it's okay to stop."

Rhyden grinned. "Copy that."

Doc let out a heavy sigh and shook his head. "Please don't tell me you are watching a certain television program involving a family of New York police officers."

"What can I say? My new girlfriend enjoys watching men in uniforms. She's rather fond of Tom Selleck, too."

"New girlfriend?"

Rhyden squirmed. "Well, not exactly. Not yet anyway. I mean, I haven't exactly asked her out yet."

Doc chuckled. His jowls shook. "Well, don't pay too much attention to how they do things, okay? Just remember you're in Texas. Now, let's talk about your pain levels. Any improvement?"

"About that…" Rhyden ran a hand down his leg. "I think we need to increase my dosage. The pills don't work as well as they used to."

The grin slipped from Dr. Carlson's face. A furrow grew between his caterpillar eyebrows. "I know we've talked about this before. It's been long enough after surgery that you should be reducing your consumption, not increasing it." He slid his stylus up the screen of the tablet in his hand, reviewing Rhyden's medical records. Tapping the stylus against his chin, he chewed on his bottom lip.

Doc laid the tablet and stylus on the examination table before spinning on his stool to meet Rhyden's eyes. "On a scale of one to ten, where do you rate your pain?"

"Some days, it's three. Others an eleven. My knee kills me."

"Anything make it better or worse? Prop your foot up here." He patted his knee. "Describe the pain for me, please." He checked the pulse on Rhyden's foot and rotated his ankle.

"No pattern. It hurts. Most days, it hurts a lot."

Grabbing Rhyden's ankle with one hand, Doc placed the other hand on his knee. He wiggled the leg from side to side. "Hmmm."

He released the leg and grabbed his equipment before he patted the examination table. "Kick off your boots and hop up here for me, will you? Lay down on your back and bend your knees."

Rhyden stretched out on the table as instructed.

Doc grabbed his leg below the knee and pushed back. Next, he stretched Rhyden's leg out, held his calf and twisted the knee toward the body. Releasing the calf, he held the knee and the bottom of the foot. He pushed, bending the knee and rotating the leg.

"Okay, you can sit back up." He turned back to his tablet and scrolled through the records again. "I'm sorry, but I can't find any reason your knee should be hurting. Your injuries didn't involve the knee. I can order an MRI, but I don't know if your insurance will pay for it."

Doc grimaced and cleared his throat. He rubbed the back of his neck before meeting Rhyden's eyes. "Are you sure it actually hurts that much? You know opioids can trick the brain into feeling pain so that you take more pills. I think I need to refer you to a pain clinic."

Rhyden's nostrils flared and the muscle in his cheek jumped as he ground his molars. Jerking on his boots, he stormed toward the door. "A referral isn't necessary." He flung the door open and forced the words between his clenched teeth. "I do not have an addiction. I would know if I did."

***

Rhyden limped through the front door. A dark cloud hung over his mood.

"Dad! I found her." Sam danced into the living room, excitement bursting from her.

He bit the inside of his cheek. *Now*

what? He forced a smile to his face. "Hey, kiddo, what's up? Found who?"

"My dream car." She waved her cell phone in his direction. "Can we go get her? Please?"

Taking off his straw cowboy hat, he deposited it onto the coffee table before sinking onto the leather couch. "Slow down, Sam. Aren't you grounded?"

"But Dad," she whined, "I'm going to school. I brought up all my grades. And if I wait, she'll be gone. Do you know how rare it is to find a 1969 Opel GT?"

"A what?" He rubbed his hands across his tired eyes. His mind still lingered on the visit with Dr. Carlson. *Quack. How dare he accuse me of being addicted to pain pills? Why I ought to...*

Sam interrupted his thoughts. "A candy

apple red Opel GT. You know, a poor man's Corvette? She's got a 1.9 liter straight four with a four on the floor. So cool that Grandfather taught me how to drive a stick."

"Sam, please, slow down. A straight what?"

"Dad!" Exasperation tinged Sam's tone. She spoke carefully, over-enunciating every word. "A 1969 Opel GT with a 1.9 liter inline four-cylinder. It's an engine. With a four-speed manual transmission." The tone of her voice said 'duh.'

She continued. "And I can afford it with my savings from working at the shop and what I made selling the truck." She dropped dramatically to her knees in front of her father and clasped her hands together. "Please, Dad?

Please, please, please."

"1969? Sam, that car's older than I am."

"I know, Dad." She bounced back onto her feet. "Isn't it cool? And it still runs. Just look." She held her phone out toward her father. "I mean, I know she's going to need some TLC, but Lawrence—I mean, Mr. Walker said he'd help me with her. Look at her. She's gorgeous."

"Sam…"

"Dad, I'll die without her."

Chapter Twenty

Admiring the curves of Sam's Opel GT in his rearview mirror, Rhyden thought the moniker 'poor man's Corvette' was an apt description. Thoughts of pleasurable curves lured his brain to memories of SANE Mikki Ross.

He dragged his sweaty palm against his denim-covered thigh. Images of her bouncy auburn curls and sparkling aqua eyes contrasted with her tight-lipped glare and jutting jaw. *Which one is the real Mikki—the mean nurse facing me down in the chaotic hallway of the trauma center or the warm woman I caught glimpses of stitching up the young boy who lost a battle with a baseball bat?* He had no clue, but he really wanted to know.

"That's it. I'm calling her," he muttered beneath his breath.

"Calling who, Daddy?" Maddie, his ever-inquisitive seven-year-old blonde angel, piped up from the back seat of the pickup truck where she sat in her booster seat.

"Just a friend, sweetie." He pressed the Siri button on his steering wheel. "Call Nurse Bubbles."

Maddie giggled. "Nurse Bubbles? Is that a real name?"

Rhyden's eyes creased as he swallowed a smile, thoughts of Noah's smartass quip filling his mind. *Acid bubbles.*

Before the call connected, Sam's bright red sports coupe whipped around his truck, beeping its horn as it sped down the road. *Samantha Elaine, you've been spending too much time riding around with 'Uncle' Noah in his precious Challenger.* Or maybe she had inherited her lead foot from Grandfather.

Growing up, Rhyden had heard stories about his grandfather being a speed demon and street racing back in the day. *Hopefully, she can't get into too much trouble. The car was only a four-cylinder.*

Rhyden glanced at his speedometer. *Maybe she doesn't have a lead foot after all.* He was driving eighteen miles beneath the posted speed limit.

A low-pitched, husky voice echoed from the truck's speakers, reminding Rhyden of blues singers and smoky barrooms. "Bennett County ER, Nurse Ross speaking."

"Nurse Ross? Bub… er I mean Mikki? This is Ranger Rhyden. We met at the hospital."

"I remember you, Ranger. Did you catch him?"

"Well, um, no, not yet. But uh, that's not um why I'm calling." *Why am I stuttering like a pimply-faced teenager? Get a grip.* He squeezed the steering wheel. Ask her already. "I'd like—"

"Daddy?" a sweet voice spoke up from the back seat.

"Maddie, Daddy's on the phone."

"But Daddy…"

"Ranger, I'm a little busy here." Ringing phones, sirens, and beeping equipment echoed in the background behind her. "Emergency trauma nurse, remember? What did you need?"

He squirmed in his seat. "Well, um, would you consider maybe—"

"Daddy!" An urgency had entered Maddie's voice.

Rhyden narrowed his eyes at his youngest daughter through the rearview mirror. "Madeline Louise, you are interrupting. Do we interrupt when Daddy is talking?"

A sultry chuckle issued from the speaker. He could see Mikki standing at the nurses' console, one hand propped on her hip and a single eyebrow raised. "Tick-tock, Ranger."

Maddie sniffed back tears. "No, sir. But Daddy, is Sam in trouble?"

"No, baby, Daddy's just driving slow. Sam's not in trouble. Why would you ask that?"

Maddie pointed in front of the truck.

"What the…?"

A Bennett County Tahoe with its distinctive green and yellow markings darted out from behind a large oak tree and chased Sam's car with its red and blue lights flashing.

She eased the Opel GT to the shoulder of the road, with the deputy stopping right behind her. His vehicle kicked up a cloud of dust.

The deputy stepped from his vehicle and checked his reflection in the tinted side window of his unit before he swaggered up to Sam's car with one hand resting on the butt of his gun. Rolled up uniform sleeves revealed 'roided up biceps and a white bandage wrapped around his right forearm.

An overwhelming sense of dread swept through Rhyden. His pulse raced. His eyes locked onto the bandage. Rattlesnake bite.

"Mikki, I need to call you back." Without waiting for a response, he disconnected the call and slid to a stop behind the Bennett County Tahoe. "Maddie, don't move." He snugged his baseball cap on his head and stepped from the truck.

Red dirt and sunburned, dead grass crunched beneath his boots. Struggling to keep his voice calm, he asked, "Deputy? Everything okay here?"

Without looking at Rhyden, the deputy called back over his shoulder. "Sir, I need you to step back into your vehicle. Now." He tapped on the Opel's driver side window and motioned for Sam to roll the window down.

Rhyden continued walking toward Sam's car. He could see her face in the side mirror. Her lips pulled into a thin line and her eyes narrowed. *Uh-oh,* he thought, *Sam-explosion on the near horizon.*

Sam cranked the window down and hollered back at her father. "Dad, I wasn't speeding. I promise."

He held up a placating hand. "I know, Sam. Stay put. Let me talk to the deputy." He approached the deputy, who still had not turned to face him. "Deputy? What happened to your arm?"

"Sir, I ordered you to get back inside your vehicle." The deputy puffed out his chest and spun around to face Rhyden. His eyes widened, and the acrid scent of fear wafted from his body. His hand fumbled with the microphone clipped to his shoulder. "845 to Bennett County. Officer needs assistance." His voice rose with each syllable uttered. "Gun, gun, gun!"

"Bennett County to 845, 10-9 please. You're breaking up. Repeat your radio traffic."

The deputy ignored dispatch and jerked his service weapon from its holster. "Sir, step back." His hand shook as he pointed it at Rhyden. "Drop your weapon on the ground."

"Deputy." Rhyden held his hands out away from his body with the palms facing the deputy. "I'm a Texas—"

Before he could complete the sentence, the deputy jumped forward and shoved his pistol into Rhyden's face. "Remove your weapon, now." His voice trembled. "Don't make me shoot you."

Fucking idiot. A tingling sensation filled his chest. Rhyden stepped back, increasing the space between himself and the deputy.

The deputy started to step forward, but the Ranger stopped him with a hard glare.

"Listen. To. Me. I am a Texas Ranger. I will not remove my weapon. Not for you or anyone else. Not going to happen. Now get your gun out of my face." Rhyden slapped the weapon down, grabbed the man's bandaged forearm, and squeezed.

The deputy screamed and released his gun. It fell to the pavement at his feet.

Rhyden kicked the pistol out of reach, cringing as the stainless steel barrel scraped across the pavement. He shoved the deputy back.

Maddie shrieked hysterically in his truck. He glanced back at the truck and then forward to the Opel GT. Sam was on her cell phone. *Stay put, girls, stay put. Please.*

Eyes wild, the enraged deputy charged Rhyden. He slammed his back onto the hood of the Tahoe and restrained him against the grill guard, yelling, "Drop your weapon, drop your weapon, drop your weapon."

The breath fled the Ranger's chest from the impact. He raised his knee sharply, ramming it into his attacker's bandaged forearm. The coppery scent of blood filled the air as the bandage turned red.

Clutching his injured arm to his chest, the other man snagged the asp from his utility belt with his uninjured hand and flicked it open, extending it to its full length.

Rhyden dropped to his knees and rolled to avoid the metal telescoping baton as it swung past his head. He lunged forward, wrapping his arms around the deputy's midsection, and tackled the man to the ground. Together, they rolled onto the road. Hot asphalt burned Rhyden's exposed skin.

The deputy slammed his weight down on top of the Ranger. Jammed his elbow into his solar plexus.

Sharp pain shot through Rhyden's abdomen. Once again, he struggled to breathe. He heard the deputy scrabbling against the pavement, grabbing for something.

The pistol! The thought entered his head mere seconds before he felt hot metal pressed up beneath his chin and heard the click of a hammer being pulled back.

Click!

The sound of the hammer being drawn back trapped Rhyden's breath in his throat. Dark spots danced at the edge of his vision.

The deputy clambered to his feet,

keeping the gun pressed against Rhyden's neck. "On your feet. Now." He stepped back to allow Rhyden up.

A flood of thoughts overwhelmed the Ranger as he stood. Over them all, a calm voice echoed. His grandfather's voice. "Son, ABC and SING!"

He brushed dirt from his jeans as an image of Sandra Bullock dressed in a frou-frou red-and-black Oktoberfest dirndl exhibiting FBI self-defense techniques for her talent portion of a beauty pageant flashed in his mind. He laughed.

"What's so funny? Are you 10-96?" The deputy shoved him toward the marked Tahoe still idling behind Sam's Opel.

"Nope, not crazy. Just remembering to always be cool and SING."

"What the hell are you babbling about?"

Rhyden jabbed his elbow back into the deputy's abdomen. "Solar plexus," he said as he stomped down on the man's foot. The heel of his boot crushed his instep. "Nose." He slammed his head backwards.

Blood spurted from the deputy's broken nose. The pistol fell to the ground as he grabbed his face with both hands.

"And groin." Rhyden spun around and brought his knee up.

The deputy doubled over, clutching his family jewels.

"You know, Deputy…" Spinning him around, he searched his chest for a nameplate. "Deputy Rudio, if you had stopped for two seconds to listen, we could have avoided all of this." The Ranger snagged the officer's handcuffs from his belt and secured his hands behind his back. "I was never a threat to you."

As Rhyden escorted the deputy back to the Tahoe, a whirlwind of activity erupted. Noah's demon red Challenger and two more Bennett County patrol units skidded around the curve of FM 472. An ambulance pulled in behind them.

Sam jumped from her Opel and raced to her dad. Maddie scrambled out of the truck and did the same. She threw herself into her father's arms, sobbing. "Daddy, that Bubbles lady called back. I told her that bad man hurt you."

"Well, that explains the ambulance." Rhyden glanced at Noah as he walked up. "What are you doing here?"

Noah tousled Sam's hair. "A little birdie called and said you might need help."

Chapter Twenty-One

Rhyden covertly shook a couple of hydrocodone into his hand and, with his back to the room, dry swallowed them. He let his eyes drift closed and stood there for a moment, gathering himself.

Turning around, he handed Noah an ice-cold longneck bottle of beer and grabbed one for himself before shutting his refrigerator. Exhausted and aching, he sank into a chair at the kitchen table, twisted off the cap, and drank deeply. Setting the bottle on the formica tabletop, he sighed and rubbed his hand across the back of his neck. "Thanks for showing up. Appreciate it."

Noah chuckled. "I'm surprised you didn't need more help. Sam's play-by-play had me thinking you were finished a few times. So did she. Took all my powers of persuasion to keep her safe in the car." He tapped his fingers on the sweating brown bottle. "That's a feisty one you have there."

"Tell me about it. Thanks again for keeping her under control."

"So, how did you escape? Sam said he had you pinned to the ground with a pistol shoved up under your chin."

"Fuck." Rhyden cast a look around the room, making sure his daughters weren't there. "I'll confess. At one point in time, I thought I was a goner. He had me dead to rights. Grandfather's voice echoed in my mind. He told me to remember my ABCs and to sing."

Noah's forehead crinkled. "How many of those pain pills have you taken? How does singing the alphabet song relate to staring down the barrel of a gun?"

Rhyden leaned back in his chair and stretched his arms above his head. He rolled his head from side to side on his neck and smiled. Peeling the label from his beer bottle, he met his best friend's eyes across the table. "Not the alphabet song. ABCs. Stands for 'always be calm.' Sing is a self-defense acronym: solar plexus, instep, nose, groin. I just did what I was told."

"Sing? Like that brunette in the feebie comedy with the squeaking wine glasses, right? Miss Friendly or something."

Rhyden shook his head. "Yeah, something like that. What did the LT say when you talked to him?"

"More than you'd expect." Noah took another swig of beer. "Apparently Deputy Rudio is a problem child. He started as a jailer in Bexar County and later became a deputy constable. Can't seem to keep a job. They've had a ton of complaints against him. Everything from being an arrogant asshole to official oppression. They're trying to find a way to dismiss him without being sued. Even tried putting him on the Brady list, but someone higher in the county is protecting him. Personally, I don't know how he passed the psych exam to get into the academy."

"Who knows? He might have been sane back then. Steroids will screw with your head, not to mention your—" Rhyden shut up as Sam wandered into the kitchen.

She opened the fridge. Peeked back over her shoulder at her dad and his best friend. "Are you talking about that deputy?"

"Deputy Rudio? Yes, hon, we are. Are you okay?"

Sam grabbed a soda and shut the refrigerator door harder than necessary. "You mean Deputy Rude-io, don't you?" She shivered. "You wouldn't believe what he said to me before you walked up. Gross!"

Rhyden and Noah exchanged looks across the table. "Honey?" Rhyden pulled out the chair next to him and patted it. "Have a seat. Tell me what happened."

Sam plopped down into the chair. She set her soda on the table and brushed her hair out of her eyes. "He's more than twice my age and so gross. Not just because of his age. Lawrence," Sam blushed and studied the chipped nail polish on her fingernails, "I mean, Mr. Walker is about the same age, but he's not gross."

"What do you mean by gross? Sam, sweetie, this could be very important. What happened before I reached the car?"

Sam shrugged. She chewed on her lower lip. "I mean, nothing really. He asked me how old I was and for my phone number. Wanted to know when we were going to go out. He acted like he had a stick up his butt when I said never. Like I would ever consider going out with a cop, much less an old 'roided up freak. Gross. He just kept asking me why I didn't like him." She picked at her cuticles. Mumbling, she added, "This wasn't the first time he's stopped me."

"Sam, why didn't you say anything?"

"I didn't want you mad at me." Comprehension dawned. Her eyes widened. Her skin blanched with horror. "Oh, my God. You think he's the rapist."

***

Noah tossed his empty longneck into the trash can at the end of the marble counter.

"Score, two points," he said as he stood and stretched, reaching his long arms toward the ceiling. A series of audible pops sounded from his spine. "Oh, that felt good."

Rhyden chuckled. "Sounded like you needed that."

"You sure you're okay, Rhy? I need to

get home to Cat and JW, but I can hang for a wee bit if you need me."

"Nah, I'm good. The girls and Grandfather are here." He shot a glance at Sam. "Besides, I believe Miss Samantha and I need to have a chat."

Sam groaned. She sank lower in her kitchen chair, folded her arms across her chest, and chewed on the inside of her bottom lip. She avoided her father's eyes.

Noah tousled her hair as he walked past her to the back door. "Good luck, kiddo." He turned his attention back to Rhyden. "Well, you know where to find me if you need me. I'll try to get to the office early in the morning so we can do a bit more digging on Deputy Rudio. I wonder what size shoe he wears? Oh, and don't forget we have a tux fitting day after tomorrow."

As the door closed behind Noah, Sam hopped to her feet. "I'm going to go say hi to

Grandfather, then get started on my homework."

Rhyden pointed at her recently vacated chair. "Sit."

"Damn, Dad. I'm not a dog."

"Language," he warned.

"Fine." Sam plopped back into the chair. She tapped her foot against the linoleum. Scuffed the side of her shoe against a torn spot under the table. "I hate this flooring. Why can't we replace it?"

"Samantha Elaine, we need to talk. You are spending too much time at the mechanic's shop. Your grades are suffering. You're never home. Maddie misses you, and it's unfair to ask Grandfather to babysit all the time. Do you realize how old he is? Maddie wears him out."

"D-a-a-d—" she said as she sat up straight in the wooden ladder-back chair.

Rhyden raised a hand, palm facing Sam. "I'm not finished."

Sam huffed and slouched back. She rolled her hand in a 'please proceed' motion.

The muscle in Rhyden's cheek twitched as he ground his molars. He closed his eyes and took a cleansing breath. "This attitude of yours is just the beginning of the problem." He made direct eye contact with Sam. "It ends. Now. Do you understand me?" He waited.

Sam nodded.

"Good. Effective immediately, you will cut your hours at the shop in half. Be grateful I'm not making you quit completely."

"But Dad, Lawrence—"

"Yet another reason to limit your exposure to the shop. Mr. Walker is an adult male more than twice your age. You should not be spending so much time alone with him, and you absolutely should not be calling him by his first name."

A heavy silence, broken only by the ticking of the cuckoo clock hanging near the refrigerator, filled the room. A rosy color crept up Sam's neck to her face. Her eyes darted around the room as she avoided her father's eyes.

"Sam?"

"What? You just don't like," she emphasized the words, "Mr. Walker because you are too much alike. He's a good man. If you took the time to actually talk to him, you'd see how much you have in common." She glared at her father. "He likes me. And unlike some people, he doesn't treat me like a little kid."

Starbursts exploded behind Rhyden's eyes. Pain surged through his entire body from the beating he had just endured. *What I wouldn't give for a hot shower.* He glanced toward his office, knowing his favorite little 'friends' waited in an orange prescription bottle in the middle drawer of his desk. Wincing, he rubbed circles on his temples. "What exactly do you mean he doesn't treat you like a little kid?"

"He just doesn't. That's all. Did you know his dad was a police officer, too? And that he was killed in the line of duty when Law—Mr. Walker was young. Like you. Only he didn't have a grandfather. His dad's older brother raised him. He wanted to be a cop, too. I don't know why he isn't." She trailed off. Stared into space. Refocusing, she shook her head. "Maybe he's better with cars or likes them more. I don't know, but I do know he doesn't have a criminal record. Unlike Uncle Noah and you, he doesn't even have a speeding ticket."

"I don't think it's appropriate for your supposed boss, a grown man, to be sharing so much personal information with you, a teenage girl. It needs to stop. Maybe it is time you quit work and focused more on your studies."

Sam blushed, looked away. She scratched the back of her neck. "Um, he didn't exactly tell me all these things. I might have done a little research on him."

"Samantha—"

"Da-a-a-d, you always tell me what a good detective I'd make." She shrugged. "Besides, you're the one that left the computer in your unit logged on. I just put some of my God-given talents to work."

"Well, now I'm putting some of my God-given parental rights to work." Heat flashed through Rhyden's body. He clenched and unclenched his fists. "You're grounded. Samantha Elaine, using state equipment and accessing information you have no business accessing violates CJIS regulations. You could cost me my badge."

Chapter Twenty-Two

Sam stomped into the shop. She stubbed her toe on a transmission sitting on the floor in her usual pathway. The relentless whir of the heavy-duty oscillating fan and the deafening sound of air tools masked her scream of frustration. Storm clouds filled her eyes. She could feel her temper rising. *I hate my life.* Everything angered her.

She flung her backpack onto the top of her large, red, roll around toolbox. Placing her palms over her ears to block out the noise, she wrapped her fingers in her hair and pulled. Hard.

"Who pissed in your cheerios?" Her boss stepped into her line of sight, wiping his greasy hands on a dirty red shop rag.

The sulfuric scent of burned differential oil caused her nose to wrinkle. She glowered at him.

"Whoa, just asking." Throwing his hands into the air in a symbol of surrender, he stepped back.

Sam ducked her head. Heat crept up her neck to her high cheekbones. She felt like her ears were on fire. "I'm sorry. I'm just so—angry."

Lawrence walked over to his workbench, grabbed another rag and began cleaning tools. He picked up a ⅜ inch socket and sprayed it with degreaser. He rubbed it with a clean red rag in a circular motion, turning the socket left to right. Setting the socket down, he picked up the can of degreaser and repeated the process twice more before moving on to the next socket. "Want to talk about it?"

Sam watched him as he cleaned the tools. *Every time,* she thought. *He does it the same way every time. Smallest to biggest, three times each.* The repetitive motion of the rag soothed her, but the pungent odor of the degreaser turned her stomach. She exhaled. "Why are fathers always so unreasonable?"

She threw her hands up in the air before popping them on her hips. "Can you believe he wants me to cut my hours here? He's knee-deep in some investigation and wants me to stay home and watch Maddie. Me? I don't even like kids. I'll probably never have any of my own. Jeez. Why would I, right? If I point out it's not fair I should have to sacrifice my dreams because of his job, he gives me that superior look and says," she lowered her voice into a deeper octave and in a sing-song manner mimicked her father. "Samantha Elaine, how many times do I have to tell you life and fair are both four-letter words, but that's all they have in common? Aargh!"

Sam scrubbed her hands up and down her face. Dropping her arms to her side, she leaned against the workbench. "And then there's this wedding thing. Oh my God, that dress.

Layers and layers of lace. Lace upon lace upon lace. I feel like I'm wearing the wedding cake, not a bridesmaid's gown. I hate lace. Don't misunderstand me, I love Cat. I do. She's the only one around here, except you that is," she paused and a blush crept up her chest to her cheeks, "that ever listens to me."

Lawrence placed the sockets into the appropriate cutouts in the foam-lined toolbox drawer. "I can't help you with the wedding, but come on, kiddo, cut your old man some slack. He's got a demanding job." He closed the drawer and turned to face her. "You know, I always wanted to be a cop."

Sam narrowed her eyes. Tightened her jaw. *Don't call me kiddo. I'm not a freaking kid.* Consciously relaxing her facial muscles, she changed the subject. "So, did you enjoy your vacation? Where did you go?"

"Vacation?" He absently rubbed at a red mark on his forearm. "Um, okay, I guess. More of a staycation."

She moved closer. "What happened to your arm? Did you burn it?"

He jerked away from her. "Yeah… burned it. On a muffler." He rolled down his sleeves, covering his wound. He slipped his hand into his pocket and pulled out his Zippo. He ran his fingers over the worn surface, flipped it over and over in his hand. "Hey, I need you to make a parts run for me."

Chapter Twenty-Three

Rhyden leaned back in his black leather office chair and ran his fingers through his hair. Staring at the ceiling, he let his thoughts wander. *What am I missing?*

He dropped his hands onto the stacks of paper covering his desk. Toe tapping, he swiveled his chair back and forth in front of his desk. *It's got to be here somewhere.* He began shuffling reports separating them by location. He spun around to face the map covering the wall behind his desk. *Think, Rhy, think.*

Chatter, jangling keys, and the sounds of a minor scuffle in the hallway drifted through his open door. He stuck his head out. Two officers half-carried and half-dragged a handcuffed detainee toward the interview room. The suspect twisted in their grip, trying to break free. "Everything okay out here, guys? Need a hand?"

One deputy grinned. "We got this, Ranger. Just another fun day, Monday."

The fiery smell of pepper spray burned his eyes as they escorted the prisoner past. His eyes watered. "I'll leave you to it, then." Closing his door, he turned his attention back to the map. The deputy's words tickled in the back of his mind. *Fun day Monday, indeed.*

Rhyden swept up the reports he had separated by location and re-sorted them by day of the week. He grabbed a multicolored handful of pushpins. For every attack on a Monday, he placed a red push pin on the map approximately where it happened. He repeated the process using a different color push pin for each day of the week. When he finished, he stepped back and observed the map. *Where's the pattern?* There has to be a pattern.

He settled into his office chair. Drummed his hands on the arms of it. He tried squinting at the map. It didn't help.

A hot electrical jolt shot down his femur. He ground his molars. *Not now.* He jumped to his feet and paced the ten by ten space that comprised his work space. Wall to wall, back and forth, he stalked the room while letting his brain run free. *Damn it! What the fuck am I missing?*

In a pique of anger, he swept the papers and file folders from his desk. They fluttered to the floor.

A tap on the door drew his attention. Noah peeked around the doorjamb. "Snow often in here, does it?"

Rhyden growled and bent to pick up his mess. "Hey, if you're going to be a smart ass, I can do without it."

"Okay." Noah held a manila file folder in his right hand and tapped it against his left palm. "If you don't want a copy of the deputies' duty schedule…"

Rhyden snatched the folder from Noah. He flipped it open. Sat back down in front of his computer and opened a blank spreadsheet. "Sorry, man. Thanks."

He began titling columns with dates and rows with duty districts. Opening the schedule, he filled cells with the last name of the deputy covering each area. His fingers flew over the keyboard.

Noah walked around the desk to see what Rhyden was doing. "No worries."

"Anything else I can do to help? Please say yes. If not, I have to go pick out tuxes with Cat." His shoulders sagged. "I am seriously wedding'ed out."

"Sorry, can't get you out of that." Thoughts of his and Cara's wedding day crashed into his thoughts. A restless ache swept through Rhyden. His heart skipped a beat.

After finishing with the schedule, Rhyden color-coded the attack dates and locations from the map on the wall into his spreadsheet. *There it is! Rudio, you bastard, I've got you now.*

He slammed his hand against the desk in victory. "Do you see what I see?"

"Well, son-of-a-bitch. Could there be two of them?"

"What?"

Noah pointed to the screen. "Look, here, here, and here. Every time there's been an attack, Deputy Rudio and T. J. Ross have been on duty in that sector."

Ross? No way. Can't be. Rhyden looked where Noah pointed.

Noah's gaze narrowed on Rhyden. "You okay, man? Your face is the color of curdled milk."

A cold sweat rolled down the Ranger's temple. He blew out a noisy breath, inhaled but didn't feel like he could catch his breath. He felt like he had just finished a marathon. His heart sped up. He sucked air. *Can't breathe.* "Fine. I'm fine. Go, please."

Throbbing pain surrounded his eye, radiated across his cheekbone. Fire shot through his leg. *How long? How long since my last pill?*

"I don't know, bud. I think I should call—"

"Please, get out. Now." Rhyden fumbled with his desk drawer, jerked it open, and swept his hand through the contents. His fingers searched for that smooth plastic cylinder. "Go, Noah. I mean it. I need you to leave."

"Rhy—"

"Damn it, Noah. Leave. Now."

"Fine." The slam of the office door

reverberated, slapping up against Rhyden's aching head.

Where is it? His hand wrapped around the pill bottle. He popped the bottle open and shook two pills into his hand. Cracked them with his molars before choking them down, bitter taste and all. He squeezed his eyes closed. *Breathe, two, three…*

The Ranger returned his attention to the computer screen in front of him. Nothing had changed. T. J. Ross. Sergeant T. J. Ross, suspect in the rape case. T. J. Ross, ex-husband of one sexy Nurse Mikki Ross—his dinner date for tonight. Rhyden slammed his head onto his desktop. *Well, fuck my life.*

Chapter Twenty-Four

Sam smiled as her Opel GT purred into the parking lot at the auto parts store. She put the car in park and revved the engine a time or two just to listen to it. *I love you, Liza Jane.* Stepping out, she ran her hand down the curves of the hood. She hummed the old David Bowie song to herself. *Oh yeah, love my little Liza Jane.* The shiny red paint sparkled in the sunlight. "You're such a good girl," she murmured to the car.

"Motherfucker!"

The sound of flesh hitting metal jerked her attention to the other side of the parking lot. A denim clad butt stuck up over the fender of an older Monte Carlo, a much older Monte Carlo. She licked her lips. *Gotta love Wrangler butts.* Sam fluffed her hair and sauntered over to the car. "Cool Monte dog. What's wrong with her?"

"Fuck if I know." The boy straightened

up and turned to face Sam. He scraped his gaze up and down her slender figure. "What do you care, anyway?"

Sam ran a loving hand down the curves of the car. She shrugged. "This baby's a classic. 1979 Chevy Monte Carlo SS. Dark carmine, one of my favorite colors for this model." She peeked in the open window. "Manual transmission. Three speed or four? Which engine? 267 or 305? I'm assuming she's a V8. She deserves a bit of respect, don't you think?"

The boy took a second look at Sam. "You know your shit, don't you? Four speed, 305. Top of the line in '79. Piece of shit now." He kicked the front tire on the car.

"Nah, she just needs a little TLC. What's she doing?"

"No power, stalling out, rough idle, and now the bitch won't start." He blew an upward breath that lifted coal-black hair from brilliant blue eyes. "Thought maybe I had a clogged whatchamacallit—catalytic converter—when I first started losing power, but she passed the back pressure test."

"You cuss a lot, don't you?" She slid a gaze up and down his frame. Attitude aside, she liked what she saw.

He shoved his hands into the back pockets of his jeans. Shrugged. "What of it?"

Sam leaned into the engine compartment. She tapped the distributor cap. "Does she struggle under load? Like going up a hill?"

"How'd you know? She loses power on hills and feels like the tranny's not shifting."

"Hang on a sec." Sam darted back over to Liza Jane and popped open the passenger-side door. Leaning in, she reached behind the seat and removed the small shelf that held up the fold-up panel blocking the trunk space. *Liza*

Jane, why couldn't you have a trunk lid like a normal car? She removed the panel and tugged out a small toolbag and carried it back to the Monte Carlo. She gestured under the hood. "Mind if I poke around?"

With a shrug, the boy stepped back, giving her space. "Knock yourself out."

In her element, Sam pulled out her multimeter and placed a lead on the distributor cap's center terminal. She moved the other lead to each spark plug terminal, one after another. "I'm getting continuity in a couple of places. That's not good. You obviously need a new distributor cap. And of course, you don't want to replace the cap without replacing the rotor."

"Of course," the young man echoed drily.

Irritation etched on her face, Sam scowled up at him. "Do you want my help or not?"

With a flitting wave of his hand, he said, "Please, by all means, continue." He leaned against the front quarter-panel and shook a cigarette from a crushed soft pack. He patted his jeans pockets, followed by the pockets on his chambray work shirt. "Damn. You wouldn't have a lighter, would you? Or a match?"

"Why would I?" Sam crinkled her upturned nose. "Cigarettes are nasty." Sam removed the spark plug wires from the engine, laying them out in order so she would know which one went back where. After physically inspecting each wire for cuts, cracks, or burn marks, she tested them for resistance.

Returning her multimeter to her tool kit, she grabbed a spark plug swivel socket and a ratchet handle. She began removing spark plugs from the engine block. She held one plug out to the young man. "Look..."

"Zane." He took the plug.

A frisson of excitement danced up her spine as his fingers brushed her palm. *Nice name. Fits him.* She checked him out from the corner of her eyes, lingering on the fit of the well-worn, faded denim. She loved the way they molded themselves around his muscular thighs.

He chuckled.

When she realized he had caught her checking him out, she felt a hot flush rush up her chest. "Listen, Zane, the porcelain on this plug is cracked, and the center electrode is worn almost completely away." She gestured to the spark plug wires still laying on the asphalt of the parking lot. "At least half of your wires are bad, too. You need plugs, wires, a distributor cap and rotor at a minimum. Probably need fuel and air filters, too. When's the last time you had a tune up?"

Zane shrugged. "I don't know. My dad picked up the car at the police auction last month and gave it to me a few days ago." He skimmed his gaze from her head to her toes and back up again. "Damn, girl, you actually do know your shit."

"Why do you sound so surprised?" Sam pursed her lips. Her jaw ached as she clenched her teeth.

"Well, I mean, you know."

Her temperature rose. Her chin jutted out as she crossed her arms over her chest. She narrowed her eyes. Her fledgling attraction to him evaporated. "No, actually, I don't know."

"Sure you do. I mean, you're a hot chick. I just didn't expect..."

"What? Because I'm attractive means I have to be stupid? Is that what you're saying? God! Men!" She threw her socket wrench back into her toolkit and scooped the bag up from the pavement. "You can figure out how to put this back together yourself." She pretended to bat her eyelashes at him and waggled her fingers in front of his face. "I mean I'd hate to break a fingernail or strain my poor, little female brain."

Zane looked at her hands covered in the tiny wounds that come from working on cars, and her fingernails chewed down to the quick. He snorted.

"Oooooooo!" Sam stomped her foot, turned and stormed away from him, muttering under her breath. "Never fails. Try to help someone and..."

"Hey!" Zane grabbed her shoulder.

She threw an elbow back, catching him in the gut. Spun around and buried her fist in his solar plexus. "Get your hands off me." Panting hard, she said, "Never touch me without permission. Never. Do you hear me?"

He doubled over. Gasped, tried to catch his breath. In a strangled voice, he pleaded with her. "Please. Wait." He placed his hands on his knees and struggled to breathe. Straightening up, he said, "I'm sorry. Please, just give me a sec."

She narrowed her eyes at him. "Why the hell should I?"

Still trying to catch his breath, Zane straightened up. He raised a hand in a placating manner. "Please."

She waited with her arms crossed over her chest and her toe tapping on the pavement. She tilted her head to the side and considered him. *Why does he have to be so cute?* "I'm waiting."

"Listen, Sam. I think you're cute and smart and amazing with cars. I'm sorry you got the wrong idea. I don't think females are helpless or stupid or any of that other stuff. My mom's a single mom and she's the smartest, toughest woman I know." He paused. Brushed his hair out of those eyes that reminded her of the pictures she had seen of the Caribbean ocean. "I want to get to know you better. There's a party tomorrow night. Do you want to come with me? Or meet me there?"

Chapter Twenty-Five

Rhyden and Noah walked into the interrogation room carrying three folding chairs. Paint crawled away from the walls, flaking onto the floor. Well, that's welcoming, now isn't it? Rhyden rubbed the back of his neck.

A metal table crouched in the middle of the room, bolted to the floor. A stainless steel loop was welded to the center of the table. The Rangers placed one chair on the far side of the table. The other two they set up on the side of the table closest to the door.

"Damn, it's cold in here. You could hang beef." Rhyden tossed the yellow legal pad he carried on the metal tabletop. He rubbed his hands up and down his arms to tame the goosebumps popping up.

"Are you sure you want to do this?" Noah asked. He shoved the chairs nearest the door right up against the table.

"What choice do we have?"

"You know the gossip's going to fly. The peacocks don't have any press conferences to plan their attire for at the moment."

Rhyden sighed. "I know, but it's got to be done. Can you unplug the camera, please?"

Noah smirked, "Sucks to be short, doesn't it?"

Rhyden gave him the hairy eyeball. "Just take care of it. Please." He dragged a hand through his hair. A heavy weight settled on his chest. He hated investigating other officers. Gave the whole profession a bad name. He took a seat on the far side of the table. Tapped his pen against the pad of paper. Stretched his legs out and tried to appear relaxed. He nodded at Noah. "Okay, go get him."

Noah escorted Deputy Rudio into the

interrogation room.

"You!" The deputy backed out of the room, but Noah blocked the door.

Rhyden kicked one of the spare chairs out from under the table. "Have a seat. You're not under arrest. Being a deputy, you should know that. All we want is to have a friendly chat."

Head shaking from side to side, Deputy Rudio placed his back against the wall. "Stay away from me." He dragged his hands down his uniform pants to dry his palms. "I have nothing to say to you."

"You know you can walk out of this room any time you want, but I would highly recommend you have a seat and talk to me."

Noah guided the deputy to the metal folding chair. With a hand on his shoulder, he shoved Rudio to a seat.

Rhyden grabbed his chair and moved around the table to sit next to Rudio. "Can I get you anything? A soda? A snack?"

Rudio scoffed and scooted away from him. "I'm not falling for this. Interrogation 101, get on eye level, pretend to be friends. How was I supposed to know you were a Ranger? I was conducting a traffic stop and saw a gun coming up behind me. I reacted." He jutted out his jaw and raised his chin. "You're lucky I didn't shoot you."

"Over-reacted is more like it," Noah muttered. He slid his chair up to the other side of the deputy. "Look, buddy, we can clear this up right away. What happened to your arm?"

"What?" Bafflement creased his facial features. "What does my arm have to do with anything?"

"You tell me." Rhyden glared at Rudio. "What were you doing on the Kyote corridor two weeks ago?"

Rudio whipped his head from Rhyden to Noah and back. "What the fuck are you two trying? I didn't stop that Opel on the Kyote corridor. This is some kind of trap, isn't it?"

Rhyden moved closer, sandwiching the deputy between himself and Noah. He leaned closer to his ear and whispered, "Answer. The. Fucking. Questions."

The deputy reeked of fear-sweat. Perspiration dotted his hairline. His hands trembled. Eyes widened, his gaze darted back and forth between the Rangers.

Noah leaned in closer over his other shoulder. "You like young girls, don't you?" He licked his lips and leered. "I mean, who doesn't, right? All that untapped... potential."

Rudio shot to his feet, knocking the folding chair to the ground. "What the fuck?!?"

He glared at Noah. "You are one sick fuck. I don't know what you are trying to pin on me, but I didn't do it. You wanna see my arm?" He shoved his uniform sleeve up. "Here." He ripped the bandage off. "I got some new ink. Big deal. If I didn't work for such a backwater county, I wouldn't have to cover it up. Don't like it? Arrest me."

Fuck. Unequivocally not a rattlesnake bite. Rhyden waved a weary hand toward the door. "You're free to go. Please don't mention this to anyone."

"Don't mention it to anyone? Like hell. I'm going straight to my union rep. You'll be hearing from me." He stormed from the room, cursing a blue streak.

Noah picked up Rudio's chair and collapsed into it. "That went well, didn't it?"

"What was up with that comment about young girls? You kinda freaked me out, too."

Noah shrugged. "Hey, it worked on television."

Chapter Twenty-Six

Head buried under the hood of the car, Sam stretched an arm out behind her. She wiggled her fingers. "Hey, Zane, can you hand me that socket wrench, please?"

Zane playfully slapped the tool into her outstretched hand like an operating room nurse handing the surgeon a scalpel. He moved around beside her and scrutinized the engine compartment. "How's the patient doing?"

Sam turned her head and looked over at him. She brushed her hair out of her eyes with the back of her hand. "She'll live."

He laughed.

Sam narrowed her eyes at him. "What's so funny now? Haven't we been down this road before?"

Zane stepped back in mock surrender. "Nothing like that, I promise." He tugged a red rag from his back pocket. "You look like you're wearing war paint. You've got stripes of grease on your cheeks and forehead."

Sam took the rag and rubbed at her face. She walked to the driver's side of the car, bent down, and checked her reflection in the side-view mirror of the Monte Carlo. "Yeah? Well, be careful I don't decide to scalp you." She patted the pink pocket knife peeking out of the front pocket of her jeans. "Grandfather, well, he's actually my great-grandfather, taught me how. His grandfather taught him."

"Family tradition?" Zane laughed. When Sam didn't, he raised his eyebrows and tilted his head to the side. He studied her face. "You're not kidding, are you?"

She turned her attention back to the car. "Nope. Hey, hand me those wires, please. In order. Starting from left to right." She stroked the top of the front quarter panel. "We'll have you purring again in no time."

"I thought you called her a Monte Dog. Dogs don't purr. Cats do."

"This dog will purr. She'll roar, too. Just you wait and see."

Zane handed her a spark plug wire and watched as she fitted one end over the terminal on the distributor cap before attaching it to the spark plug in cylinder one. "How did you learn how to do all this?"

She smirked. "Scalping isn't the only thing Grandfather taught me. He taught me to hunt, fish, throw knives, and work on cars."

"What did your mom think of that? Didn't she want you to learn girly things? Like cooking and putting on makeup?"

A shutter slammed down behind Sam's eyes, masking the twinkle that had just been present. She opened her mouth to say something, but stopped herself, pressing her lips together in a flat line. She bit the inside of her cheek. Her knuckles whitened as she tightened her grip on the spark plug wire gripped in her left hand.

"Hey, I didn't mean to—"

Sam returned her attention to the Monte Carlo's engine compartment. She exhaled shakily and lowered her voice. "It's okay. You didn't know. I don't have a mother. She died a few years back, but I lost her a long, long time before that."

After installing all the spark plug wires, she gestured toward the passenger compartment of the car. "Fire her up and let's see how she sounds."

With a doubtful expression on his face, Zane climbed into the driver's seat and placed the key in the ignition. The engine started on the first turn of the key. Disbelief flashed across his face, followed by a giant grin. "Thank you."

Sam shrugged. "No biggie."

"Hey, do you want to grab a bite to eat? It's the least I can do to pay you back."

Sam glanced at the clock on her cell phone. "Shit. I wish I could, but I gotta get back to work. The boss sent me to pick up parts. He's probably pitching a hissy fit right now because I've been gone so long."

"Man, I'm sorry. Didn't mean to get you in trouble. I'm grateful you helped me. Without you, I'd still be kicking tires and cussing."

Sam smiled. "You do cuss a lot."

"Hey, now..."

"You mentioned a party? Why don't you text me the information?" she winked as she walked away. "I might meet you there."

"Wait. I don't have your number."

She grinned as she continued to walk away. Tossing a look at him over her shoulder, she said, "You'll figure it out if you really want to see me again."

Chapter Twenty-Seven

Rhyden tugged the door to the restaurant open. Laughter, chatter, and the clinking of dishes slipped through the opening surrounding him and his date. The scent of seared beef tickled his olfactory nerve. His stomach grumbled. *Dang, that smells good.*

"After you, please." He held the door open for Mikki. Grandfather would have his hide if he didn't hold open doors and pull out chairs for a lady. He took a moment to enjoy the view as she passed in front of him. He loved the way her jeans lovingly cupped her butt. *Something about how she looked...that woman had the best butt denim had ever cupped. And sass? My God, I love her sass.* "Has anyone told you how beautiful you are tonight?"

Mikki looked back at him, a bemused smile teasing her lips. A blush graced her cheeks. The surprise bubbling in her eyes said she thought he was crazy.

"No?" He leaned in and whispered in her ear. "Then let me be the first."

She scoffed. "How often does that line actually work?"

He feigned being struck in the chest. "Ouch." Placing a hand in the small of her back, he guided her to the table where Noah and Cat were already seated.

Cat hopped up and hugged Rhyden. "So glad to see you back at work." Releasing him from her embrace, she patted his shoulder. "I was worried about you. Extremely worried."

"Noah, Cat, I'd like you to meet—"

"Mikki! What are you doing hanging around with this old polecat? I thought you had better taste than that?" Cat enveloped Rhyden's date in a friendly hug.

Mikki returned the hug. "How's JW? Is

he sleeping through the night yet?"

Rhyden pulled a chair out for Mikki and exchanged a worried look with Noah. "You two know each other?"

She slid gracefully into the chair, placing her purse on the floor beside her feet. She raised a single eyebrow. "Really?" She pointed to Cat. "Paramedic." She pointed to herself. "Trauma nurse. What do you think? Do we know each other?"

The ladies locked eyes and laughed. Cat grinned an evil grin. "And I told her what you and my knucklehead future husband call her."

Rhyden feigned ignorance. "What we call her?"

"Does acid in fact bubble?" Mikki asked.

Heat crept up the back of Rhyden's neck. He cleared his throat and felt his ears growing hot. At that moment, he envisioned his face like a brilliant red tomato. He grimaced. "About that." He dipped his chin and peeked up at Mikki through his thick black eyelashes. "That was before I knew you."

"Really?" Mikki picked up her cell phone and dialed a number. Rhyden's phone rang. "Care to show me the screen on your phone right now?"

Noah cracked up laughing. "Busted, buddy. Better apologize now before you dig the hole any deeper."

Cat slapped her soon-to-be husband on the back of the head. "The way I understand it, you started the nickname. I think you need to be apologizing about now as well."

"Hey," Noah rubbed the back of his head. "That hurt, you know?"

Cat rolled her eyes. "It was supposed to. *You know?*"

Laughter danced around the table. Time flew as the couples enjoyed a delightful meal and good fellowship.

"Excuse me. I need to step into the little boy's room for a moment." Rhyden turned to Noah. "If the server comes back by, would you order me another whiskey and water?"

"Sure thing, buddy, but we might want to call it quits after that one. I think we've both reached our three drink limit for the night. Tomorrow's a workday."

Rhyden glowered at Noah. "Who are you? My daddy?"

Noah waved him off. "Hey, just a suggestion. You're a big boy."

The Ranger nodded and turned to the ladies. "Excuse me, please." He walked away from the table, slipping his hand into his front pants pocket. He fished around until his fingers closed around the smooth, oval pill tucked away in the pocket's corner. *There you are. Now where's your brother?*

He stepped into the restroom and walked to the sink. Turning on the cold water, he slipped the pills into his mouth and bent to drink from the faucet.

"Hey, you know they have glasses for that in the restaurant? If you want a glass of water, all you have to do is ask?"

Rhyden raised his head and met the stranger's eyes in the mirror. Whatever the other man saw seemed to frighten him off. He left without even washing his hands.

The Ranger slumped against the cold ceramic tiles lining the restroom wall. *What the fuck? Why won't anyone leave me be?* Forcing a smile to his face, he headed back to his table. The ladies' discussion had turned from Cat and Noah's upcoming wedding to hobbies.

He sat down and picked up his dessert

fork.

Mikki smiled over at him. "What about you? If you could do anything, what would it be?"

Rhyden took another bite of the delicious German chocolate cake. He looked around the table, judging the mood of his audience. He put his fork down on his plate. "Actually, now that you ask, I think I'm about ready to ride bulls again. We've got a benefit ride for autism coming up before too long. I need to get back in shape."

Cat's fork clanged against the plate as it slipped from her hand. "Are you a freaking lunatic? Don't you remember your last ride? I thought the girls were going to have to come live with us."

Mikki wisely stayed silent.

Noah wasn't that smart. "Hey, I understand it. Bull riding gets in your blood. It's addictive. I mean, while you're riding, you get super like hyper focused. You deal with what you've got going on. I know the announcer says the crowd helps the cowboy, but honestly, you don't even know they are there. Yeah, sure, you might glimpse something or have a conscious thought, but, for the most part, you're living in the moment. You don't have time to think. Like they said in Top Gun, if you think, you're dead."

Cat turned on Noah. "Really? And you know this how?"

Noah said, "Well, it wasn't a real bull, just one of those mechanical things, but I rode it at that strawberry festival thing in Poteet a few years ago. Luckily, I had ridden horses as a kid because it took every bit of strength I had in my legs to grip on. I did well. Held myself upright, taking the greatest bucking force with my hips. Like they told me to. Well, until I got tossed too far forward. In that instant, all I could see were two enormous metal horns as my face slammed closer with every heave."

"Um," Rhyden cut into Noah's story, "you know those mechanical bulls don't have heads, much less horns, right?"

"Shh." He flipped his hand toward his friend, waving him away. "Don't interrupt. This is my story." He propped his elbows on the table, folded his hands, and leaned into them, resting his chin on his entwined fingers.

"Now, where was I? Oh right, I pushed back against the neck with one arm while still gripping the pommel with white knuckles on the other hand. Of course, now I'd reached forward, and didn't have an arm free to catch my balance. I panicked. Let me tell you. My heart raced. I couldn't catch my breath. These were my last moments. I knew it. This was it. I was about to have my face smashed, my eyes gouged out, or something broken for sure with the next buck. Then just as suddenly as it started, the careening below me stopped."

Noah paused and took a sip of his whiskey. "A wave of relief sent chills over my sweating body. Then I realized my legs had gone to jelly. Didn't matter how hard I tried, I could not climb off that mechanical bull. They helped me down but my legs were shaking so bad I couldn't stand up." His face reddened at the memory. "They asked me to please not come back."

He leaned back in his chair, turned to face Rhyden. "On second thought, why the hell would you ever want to climb onto the back of a real bull? That one wasn't even real. I survived my brush with death, but I can promise you it will never, ever happen again. I'm too damn old to get a chiropractic treatment like that again."

Laughter swirled around the table. *Leave it to Noah to break the tension.* Rhyden turned to Mikki. "What do you think?"

"You truly want to know what I think?"

"Yes, I do."

"I went to a rodeo once with my friends. You know, a group of teenage girls wanting to flirt with cowboys. A bull rider went off the back end of the bull and came down perpendicular to the ground, head first. Kid did a handstand but without the hands. The boy, because he was just a boy, was unconscious long enough for the rodeo clowns to get the bull all the way out of the arena. He was safe from the bull, but he didn't know it. When he woke up, he jumped to his feet and made a mad dash for the arena wall. He acted like he was going to climb the wall before he collapsed and passed out again. Paramedics swept in and took him to the hospital. To this day, I don't know whether that kid lived or died. You want to know what I think? I think you're flakier than a southern biscuit to want to climb on the back of a 2,000 pound hate-filled beast ever again. Especially with the injuries you've already sustained."

***

A tiny touch of cool tinged the night air. Rhyden loved the feel of Mikki's hand, warm and firm, wrapped in his larger, callused one. She swung their arms between them. Reminded him of walking the halls of the high school with his girl of the week. *So long ago.*

"This is enjoyable."

The gravel pathway crunched beneath their feet. Large oak trees threw shadows on the edges of the park. The stark black lines of a towering swing set were silhouetted against the pink-orange glow of the setting sun. Fading sunlight sparkled off the chains holding up the wide, black rubber seats.

"Mm-hm." He glanced down at her, pulled her in closer, wrapping an arm around her waist. She fit right up against his shoulder. "I'm glad we did this."

Mikki pulled away and walked backwards in front of him. A mischievous smirk danced in her eyes. She grinned. "Race ya?"

Before he could answer, she spun around and sprinted toward the swing set. Her laughter floated on the evening breeze. He lengthened his stride and caught her as she reached the swings. Rubbing the scar on his thigh, he said, "Damn, I'm getting old."

"I hear you." Mikki sat on one swing and pushed off the black dirt with her toe. Gently swinging back and forth, she said, "I forgot how relaxing swinging can be."

Rhyden perched on the swing next to her. He twisted the chains until he faced her. Her auburn hair blazed like fire in the setting sun. He reached over and swept his thumb across her cheek. *So soft.* He pulled his hand back. *I could drown in her eyes.* "You have the prettiest eyes."

She tilted her head down, then gazed up

at him through her lashes. A pretty pink blush crept across her porcelain skin. "Thank you." Mikki turned away from him. Her shoulders curved inward. "Been a while since anyone said that to me."

Rhyden raised his eyebrows. He twisted back and forth on the swing. The motion caused his stomach to churn, but he ignored it. His boots dug a hole in the ground beneath the swing as he continued to rock from side to side. Giving up on the swing, he stood and walked over to stand in front of her. Tenderly, he lifted her chin until their eyes met. The pain in hers stabbed him in the chest. "I'm sorry. You should hear that and more every day. Your ex is an ass."

She pulled away. Shrugged and shook her head. "It is what it is. My ex is a good man. He's an okay dad. Could he be more involved with our son? Sure, but if I didn't work such crazy hours, so could I." She licked her lips and bit her lower one. "I mean, yeah, he's a teenager now and doesn't need me, not like he used to, but I wish we were closer." She met Rhyden's eyes. "You know what I mean?"

Thoughts of his last argument with Sam flitted through his brain. He sighed. "Yeah, I know what you mean." He gripped the chains of her swing in his hands and tugged her towards him before pushing her back in a slow, swinging motion. *Crap, might as well get it over with.* "Can I ask you about your ex? He's T. J. Ross, right?"

She furrowed her brows. Tilted her head to the side. "Do you know him?"

Rhyden shook his head no. "Just by reputation. What's he like?"

"He's a good man, a great boyfriend, but a shitty husband." She crossed her arms over her chest and narrowed her eyes. Suspicion rolled off her. "Why?"

A wave of nausea swept over him. He pressed a hand against his stomach. Closed his eyes. His chest rose and fell with rapid breaths. "Do you have a mint?"

"A mint? What does a mint have to do with T.J.?"

"Nothing. I'm just feeling a bit queasy. Probably something I ate."

Mikki raised one eyebrow. "Something you ate? More like the pills you were mixing with alcohol." She pushed the swing backwards out of Rhyden's grasp. Wrapping her arms around herself as if cold, she stood and said, "I think it's time to go home."

"Wait, please?"

She turned to face him. Tilted her head back to meet his gaze. "Why are you asking about my ex-husband?"

Fuck, I don't want to do this. He

dragged a hand down his face. "You really want to know?"

"I wouldn't have asked if I didn't."

"We think he might be the rapist."

"What? No fucking way." Mikki shoved him out of her path and stormed toward the parking lot.

Rhyden cut in front of her. Grabbed her hands. "Hey, stop. Just for a minute. Let me explain. Please?"

Anger flashed in her eyes, but she stopped. Crossed her arms over her chest and jutted out her jaw. "I'm waiting."

"Hey, it was your theory in the first place—"

She interrupted him. "My theory, as you call it, was that the rapist was a sheriff's deputy. Not my ex-husband. T.J. may be a shitty husband, but he would never hurt anyone. Not like that."

"The evidence paints a different picture."

Mikki crowded into his space and jabbed a finger into his chest. "Well, you can take your evidence and shove it—"

Damn, she's fiery. I always thought 'beautiful when angry' was a cliche, but damn. Without thinking another thought, Rhyden swept her into his arms and kissed her.

After a moment's struggle, Mikki kissed him back. Passionately.

At the sound of applause, they came up for air. Rhyden glanced around the park. A group of teenage boys loitered on one of the picnic tables. "Maybe we should move this—"

The words stuck in his throat. A cold sweat dripped down his sides and spine. The back of his mouth filled with burning, acidic saliva as his stomach clenched. *No, oh please no.* He took a deep breath in. Blew it out slowly. Repeated. It didn't help. He fell to his knees and heaved his stomach contents onto the ground.

Mikki helped Rhyden to his feet and led him back to the parking lot. She unlocked her car and pulled out a rag and a couple of bottles of water. She handed one to him, opened the other and soaked the rag. "Here, you can use this to clean up."

Rhyden took a swig of water and rinsed his mouth. He used the rag to wipe his face. Collapsing to the sidewalk, he drew his knees up to his chest. He bowed his head. "Thank you. I am so embarrassed."

Mikki dug through her purse and found a couple of mints. She handed them to him.

He fumbled with the wrappers, finally tearing them open and popping them in his mouth. "Thanks again."

She sat beside him and rubbed comforting circles on his back. "Hey, it happens. Do you want to talk about it?"

"Talk about it? I just ate—"

She jerked her hand away from his back. Stood up. "Don't. Don't even. You realize I'm a trauma nurse, right? Do you know what that means? You aren't the first addict I've dealt with." A far away look filled her eyes. "And not only at work."

He grabbed her hand and tugged her back down next to him. Reluctantly, she sat beside him. Avoiding his eyes, she stared off into the distance. In a voice so soft he had to strain to hear it, she said, "My dad was an addict. That's why I grew up with my grandmother."

"I'm sorry. I didn't know."

She gave a half-hearted shrug. "Not your fault. I guess it's a hot button for me. My dad died a few years back, but I lost him probably twenty years before that. I couldn't compete with the alcohol. Or the drugs. Or the other women." She swiped at her eyes before turning to face him.

Rhyden caressed her cheek. "You deserved better. From him and your ex."

She brushed his hand away. "And what about you? Do I deserve better from you?"

He froze. His thoughts swirled so quickly he couldn't make sense of them. He opened his mouth to speak.

She held up a hand to stop him. "Before you say anything else, don't lie to me. I think I could like you. I mean like-like you, a lot, but I won't tolerate lies. Do. Not. Lie. To. Me."

He snapped his mouth shut and dragged his hand across the back of his neck. A feeling of heaviness settled over him. *I'm going to screw this up. I don't want to screw this up.* "I like you, too. And yeah, I probably take too many pills, but damn it, I hurt. All the time. I can't even explain the pain to you. I'm not an addict. I've got it under control."

Mikki scoffed. "That's what they all say. Did you know that opioids cause rebound pain? They trick the brain into thinking it needs more pills than it actually does."

Rhyden's jaw tightened. "I've been told."

"Do you think maybe some of your emotional trauma might have something to do with it? Can I tell you a secret?"

Intrigue warred with irritation. *I don't have any emotional trauma.* His own brain snorted in laughter at that thought. He could almost see his brain rolling its eyes, if it had eyes. *Sure you don't have any emotional trauma.*

Pigs fly, too. "What's your secret?"

"My son is not my ex's biological son."

"Really?"

"Nope. That's how I know T. J. is a good man. But that's not all of it." Mikki bit the inside of her cheek and turned her attention to her hands resting in her lap. She picked at the cuticle on her left thumb. She grimaced, shook her head, and threw her hands up. She looked over at Rhyden. "Sorry, bad habit. I pick at my hands when I'm nervous."

He reached over and clasped her hands. "You don't need to be nervous." He brushed the hair from her eyes. "You also don't have to tell me your secret if you don't want to."

She tugged her hands free and examined his face, searching for something. Apparently satisfied, she continued, "Yes, I do. For two reasons. One, so you know I understand addicts and two, so you know why T. J. couldn't possibly be the rapist. I was pregnant when we got married."

She squared her shoulders, and said, "Let me tell you a story." She squeezed her eyes closed. Rubbed the bridge of her nose. Opening them, she made eye contact with Rhyden. "I was in nursing school. A bunch of us, including my brother and some of his friends, met up at a bar after class one night. T. J. was fresh out of the academy. He was my first serious boyfriend, but he was on shift that night and couldn't come." She shook her head. "I probably should have stayed home, but we'd just finished finals and needed to blow off some steam."

Mikki rose to her feet and paced in a circle. She blew out a shaky breath and twisted her hands together. "Damn." She frowned at Rhyden. "This is harder than I thought it would be."

"You don't have to tell me anything."

"Yes, actually, I do." She put a hand on

his shoulder and eased herself back onto the sidewalk beside him.

He took her hand in his and held it between both of his. "No, you really don't."

A sad smile graced her face. She laid her on his shoulder. "You know every girl grows up being told to never leave your drink unprotected. You hear stories about drinks being spiked and what not. So when I went to dance, I asked my brother to watch it for me." A single tear slid down her cheek.

Rhyden leaned in and wiped it away with a callused thumb. "Hey, now…"

She sniffed. Swallowed loudly a time or two. "I'm okay. It was a long time ago. You feeling okay? Mind if we walk?"

Without a word, he stood and held out his hands. When she placed hers in his, he tugged her to her feet.

Red blotches covered her face from trying not to cry. Wild strands of hair lifted in the breeze and blew across her face.

Rhyden tucked the strands behind her ear. He leaned forward and placed a kiss on her forehead. "Whatever you want, Nurse Bubbles."

She choked out a laugh. "Ha. Ha." She waved him back, entwined her fingers with his, and began walking toward the lake. A flock of ducks quacked and waddled out of their path. They walked in silence until they reached the water's edge. Releasing his hand, she bent down and scooped a flat stone from the ground. She drew her arm back and flicked her wrist. The stone skipped across the surface of the black water.

He mimicked her movements. For the next little bit, they stood without talking, watching rocks dance across the lake. A wind picked up bringing a chill off the water.

Mikki shivered. She dusted her hands off on her jeans. "I knew my brother dabbled in drugs, but I didn't realize how deep he'd gotten." She rolled her shoulders inward and wrapped her arms around herself. "I trusted him." Her voice lowered to a broken whisper. "I trusted him."

"Oh, baby—"

"Don't. Just don't."

Rhyden wrapped his arms around her shoulders and held her close.

She buried her face in his chest. "When I woke up, my clothes were gone, and I hurt all over. That son-of-a-bitch, my own brother, gave me to his dealer to pay off his debts."

He stroked her hair but remained silent. *That bastard. I will hunt him down and castrate him.*

She forced out a laugh. "I can hear you

thinking. There's nothing you can do. He OD'ed six weeks later. About the same time I discovered I was pregnant."

Mikki stepped out of the protective circle of Rhyden's arms. She searched his eyes. "My son is the result of rape. T. J. knows the destruction it causes. He could never be a rapist."

Rhyden reached for Mikki, but she pulled away. He slipped his hands into his back pockets and rocked back on his boot heels. Nodding toward the trail, he asked, "Care to walk?"

Mikki rose. The rattle of the swing chains followed her. A cloud drifted across the moon, blocking its silver glow. She wrapped her arms around herself. Lifting one shoulder, she let it drop. "Now, you know my deepest, dark secret." She stared at the ground.

He stepped closer to her as they

wandered down the path. "I guess we're both hauling around a bit of baggage. My youngest daughter was three when I discovered she wasn't biologically mine. It stung… hard."

"I guess that's one good thing about being female. You know whether you're the mother or not. No doubts." She stopped walking and turned to face him. Wrapped her arms around him and hugged. "I'm sorry."

He shrugged. "It is what it is. It doesn't matter what her genetic code says, Maddie is my daughter, plain and simple."

She grabbed his hand and pulled him toward a cast iron bench sitting beside the path. They sat together, thighs touching. "Tell me about your ex."

"Why?"

"Hey, I showed you mine. Show me yours."

Rhyden rubbed the back of his neck. Dropped his hands to his lap. He stood and paced in front of the bench. He glanced at Mikki, then dropped his gaze. Guilt tightened the back of his throat. "I don't know where to start."

She grabbed his belt and tugged him back down onto the bench. She shook her head. "I'm sorry. You don't owe me anything. Dang, I seem to be apologizing a lot tonight. Not the best way to end a first date. Let's talk about something else."

Rhyden loosened his clenched hands and ran them through his hair before turning to face her. He studied her face. Blowing out a noisy breath, his shoulders slumped. "Can we walk, please?"

Shadows danced across the path in front of them as the breeze ruffled the leaves on the oak trees. Mikki slipped her hand into his. They walked in silence.

In the distance, a lone coyote called out to its pack mates. No answering yip-yip-yips filled the air. The coyote howled again. The haunting sound sent chills down Rhyden's back. Goosebumps raised on his arms. Memories, unhappy memories, slammed into him.

"Hey, are you okay?"

He stopped walking. Staring into the dark, he said, "I had just turned eleven when my dad died."

Mikki squeezed his hand, but stayed quiet.

"It happened on a night like this. Late summer. Just a hint of fall creeping into the air. I went camping with my grandfather. The coyotes had been yipping and barking all night, but suddenly they stopped." He shuddered. "A bad feeling, like a dark wind, swept through our camp. Grandfather stopped the story he was telling me mid-sentence. Started putting out the fire and gathering up our supplies. At first, I didn't know why. Then in the distance, a lone coyote let out a mournful howl—like the one we just heard. None of the others responded."

He met Mikki's eyes. "I don't know how, but I knew. Dad was gone. When we got home, Doc had sedated Mom. She'd lost it and attacked the officers who came to notify her." He started down the path again.

"His partner—Dad was Magellan PD— waited in the living room. They'd responded to a domestic assault. Frequent flier address. The husband had beaten his wife bloody—again. They arrested him, and when they were loading him into the back of their unit, the wife flipped out. Started screaming 'don't take him' and 'he loves me.' I don't get it. I really don't." He tightened his grip on Mikki's hand. Looked away and swallowed hard. "She grabbed a shotgun from behind the kitchen door and opened up. Dad should've been okay. He was wearing his ballistic vest, but a stray pellet ripped through his carotid artery. He bled out on the scene. Nothing anyone could have done to save him."

"Oh, Rhy, I am so sorry."

Rhyden closed his eyes and shook his head. He waved off her words. "It happened a long time ago. It shouldn't still hurt this much, but sometimes, particularly when I hear a lone coyote, it slips back up and bites me in the butt."

She nodded. "Grief is like that."

"My whole life is like that." He let go of her hand, turned to face her, and widened his stance as if afraid the wind would blow him over. "You want to know the true reason why I don't want to talk about my ex-wife?"

She studied his eyes. "Yes, I do."

He squared his shoulders. "Because I killed her."

Rhyden watched as the color drained from Mikki's face. Her eyes widened. Her jaw opened and closed like a guppy. A myriad of expressions chased one another across her face—fear, confusion, disbelief. As quickly as they flashed, they were gone.

She steeled her spine, shoulders pushing back, strengthening her posture. She moved into his personal space. "I don't believe you."

He leaned away from her. A bitter edge tinged his words. "I didn't physically murder her, but it was still my fault." He took a deep, pained breath and closed his eyes. Opening them, he raised his chin and faced Mikki fully. "Have you ever heard of Palo Mayombe?"

She reached to take his hand in hers.

He pulled away and shoved his hands into his back pockets. Nodding to a picnic table beneath the picturesque street lamp reminiscent of the Victorian whale oil lamps that lined the streets in the early 1800s, he said, "Join me?"

She settled on the picnic bench. Craning her neck to meet his eyes, she patted the space beside her.

He shook his head no. "So, Palo Mayombe? Santeria?"

"Santeria? Voodoo witchcraft, right?"

"Not exactly. Santeria is a religion that developed in the late 19th century. A combination of the traditional Yoruba religion of West Africa, Catholicism and Spiritism. Roughly translated, 'santeria' means 'the way of the saints.' Palo Mayombe, according to some, is the exact opposite of Santeria. Santeria is light. Palo Mayombe is dark. Or at least, some people have twisted it to become an evil thing."

"O-kay. Thanks for the history lesson, but what does that have to do with you killing your ex-wife?"

Rhyden collapsed on the bench next to her. He buried his face in his hands before scrubbing it with his palms. "About four years ago, I was investigating a drug cartel from deep Mexico. Talk about horrible timing. Cara and I had recently started divorce proceedings. Things were getting nasty—at work and at home."

Cara slammed the folder onto the kitchen table. "There's your proof. What judge in their right mind would give a little girl to a man who isn't even related to her? You don't want the girls separated? Want to keep the older ones out of boarding school, boarding school you will have to pay for, by the way? Get me my money by the end of the week."

Rhyden's vision tunneled. His pulse pounded in his ears. Grabbing a knife from the butcher block on the counter, he advanced on Cara. "You cold-hearted bitch."

She stumbled backwards, tripping on her fancy stilettos.

"Hey, are you okay?" Mikki slid her hand up and down Rhyden's arm.

He patted her hand. "Sorry. Got lost in the past."

"I get it."

Rhyden faced her. Tilted his head to the side. He took in her expression, the concern in her eyes, the understanding. He caressed her cheek. "You know, I think you really do."

She leaned her head against his hand for a moment before pulling away. "Continue, please."

"This crew was nasty. They believed human sacrifice would protect them and make them invisible on their drug runs. Tourists had been disappearing from around South Padre Island. The numbers increased if they crossed the border into Matamoros." He wrapped her hand in his and absently rubbed his thumb across her wrist. He felt her pulse increase. "You know how spring break is to begin with—kids never turned loose without parental supervision before, crazy drinking, partying, the drugs."

She murmured, "No, I have no idea." She rolled her eyes. "You do remember what I do for a living, right?"

He forced a grin for her sake. Shook his head. "Anyway, a local kid went missing. Not even a college kid. Just a high school senior."

She pulled away from him. "I remember that. The craft store sold out of yellow ribbon. You couldn't pass a tree, telephone pole, or sign post anywhere in the county without seeing a big yellow bow wrapped around it. They found his body…"

"Yeah. They found his body across the border. What remained of it."

"I still don't understand. What's that

have to do with your ex?"

"I got too close to the cartel without stopping them. A CI warned us they were going after one of my girls. Maddie was a baby. Sam and Bree were barely teens. We moved the girls and their mom to a safe house." Rhyden gazed into the past. "She should have been safe. I should have stopped her."

"I refuse to be confined like this," Cara declared as she slammed her bag onto the double bed in the biggest bedroom of the tiny safe house. "I'm not your prisoner. You can't keep me here. I won't stay here." She glared at him. "I won't."

Rhyden leaned against the doorjamb. "Cara, be reasonable."

She shoved past him, her shoulder pushing him out of the way. "Get out of my way."

"You could be in danger."

"Danger?" She tossed her hair over her shoulder and popped her hands on her hips. "The only danger I'm in is from you."

His limbs tingled with fatigue. He slumped forward, forearms resting on his knees as he stared at the ground. He lifted his head to make eye contact with Mikki. "That was the last time I saw her. She snuck out to meet up with Maddie's sperm donor."

Anger flared in his eyes. "I refuse to call him Maddie's father, biological or otherwise."

Mikki placed a hand on his shoulder and stroked, offering him comfort.

"We launched a massive manhunt. Both sides of the border. They even arrested me on suspicion when that douche accused me of kidnapping her." Rhyden swallowed hard. He wrapped his arms around his stomach. "We found her… remains… in a hole fifteen feet from the kid. She'd only been dead for a few hours. If I had been faster…"

"Don't." Mikki stood and tugged Rhyden to his feet. She wrapped her arms around his waist and held him close. "Just don't. She made her choice. And she paid for it. There's no need for you to continue paying for it."

Rhyden sagged in her embrace and sobbed. For the first time since Cara's disappearance, he allowed himself to grieve.

Chapter Twenty-Eight

The cool plastic slipped smoothly through his fingers. Leaning back in his chair, feet propped on top of his metal desk, Lawrence held the driver's license to the light. *Crystal Davis, 5' 3", brown over brown.* A shiver danced down his spine as he remembered the delicious tone of her screams. She had been a fighter. He chuckled. *Stupid cops. If I was a snake, I'd have bitten them on the ass by now.*

The door slammed behind him. Scrambling, his feet hit the floor. He gathered the stack of driver's licenses and slipped them back into his orange metal pencil case. He quickly shoved the pencil case into his drawer and covered Groucho's slightly rusty face with a stack of work orders.

"Hey, boss man." Sam dropped her backpack onto a blue towel covering the grease-stained workbench across the room from his desk. "What are we working on today? Do you mind if I pull the Opel in for a little work?"

That was close. Lawrence concentrated on slowing his heart rate. "Shouldn't be a problem. Not much going on today." He waved at the marked Tahoe up on a red hydraulic lift. "Just a little maintenance for BCSO."

"Cool. Bay three okay?" At his nod of approval, Sam grabbed her keys and headed out the roll-up bay door to the parking lot.

Fuck! I need to be more careful. Gloating could end him up in a hell of a lot of trouble. Especially with the Ranger's kid working for him. *Speaking of...* Lawrence walked over to where Sam climbed out of her poor man's Corvette. "What are you doing to her today?"

She blew her bangs out of her eyes. "I need to check the timing. She's got a little stutter-step thing happening. I'm hoping the timing is just a little off, but I don't have a timing light at home. Mind if I borrow yours?"

Lawrence went to his toolbox and counted down four drawers, tapping each drawer as he went. He repeated the process two more times before tugging the drawer open. Nestled in its perfectly shaped foam cutout rested his timing light. He knew how to take care of his tools. The timing light, actually his grandfather's, was older than Lawrence himself, but looked brand new. He handed it to Sam. Before relinquishing his hold, he said, "Make sure you clean it and put it back where it belongs."

"Yes, sir. Pinky promise." Sam grinned and hooked the power cables for the timing light to the battery terminals. She linked the pickup for the light near the number one spark plug wire. "Have you heard the crazy theory circulating between the chief deputy, my dad, and Noah?"

She pulled the vacuum hoses off the distributor and stuck bolts into the ends of them to plug them off. After loosening the hold down at the base of the distributor, she straightened up and looked over her shoulder at her boss.

He shook his head no.

Sam removed a hair tie from her wrist, scraped her curls off her face, and twisted her hair back into a messy bun, securing it with the tie. She climbed into her car, set the parking brake, shifted into neutral, and started it. "You won't believe it. No wonder people get away with so much in this county."

"Are you going to share or leave me in the dark?"

Sam crossed back to the front of the Opel's engine compartment. Picking up the timing light, she pointed it at the little window behind and below the carburetor and pulled the trigger. The tip of her tongue hung out the corner of her lips as she concentrated. She leaned forward and twisted the distributor until the ball and pointer lined up. She tightened the distributor, dusted off her hands, and shut off the engine.

Walking back to the workbench, she cleaned the timing light and replaced it in the proper drawer.

Lawrence followed her to the toolbox and repeated his counting ritual before making a minute adjustment to the way the tool sat in its foam housing. He raised an eyebrow. "Well?"

Sam swallowed a sip of soda and rested her hip against the workbench. "So... you've heard about the serial rapist, right?"

"Serial rapist?" His pulse throbbed in his ears. *Did I hear her right?* "What serial rapist?"

"Crap, that's right. No one is supposed to know. Okay, so I didn't tell you this, but apparently we have a rapist targeting the Kyote corridor. He's attacked three women, young girls actually, so far."

Only three? He hid a sigh of relief. *They're not nearly as smart as they think they are.*

"Anyway, so now Dad thinks Zane's father is the rapist. The chief and Noah seem to agree with him." She waved the words a way with a flip of her hands. "Can you believe these stupid people? Just because someone wears a uniform doesn't mean they are a cop. I could buy a uniform and a badge at the uniform place, and no one would bat an eye. Hell, you can order badges and uniforms online. Next thing you know, they will think you're the rapist because you have the keys to different patrol cars. Wouldn't that be a hoot? I bet you've even got your dad's old uniform hanging in a closet somewhere, don't you?"

Lawrence's stomach clenched. His chest

tightened, restricting his breathing. He blanched. *Fuck, fuck, fuck! She thinks she's being funny, but what if they think about me?* He grabbed onto the workbench as his knees buckled at the thought.

Sam reached out to steady him. "You okay, boss man?"

He stammered, cleared his throat and tried again. "Fine. I'm fine. Just got a little overheated."

She guided him to his desk chair and helped him sit. "Let me grab you some water or something. I'll be right back."

He watched her as she left the shop and headed into the LEC lobby where the vending machines sat. *What am I going to do?* Perspiration prickled his hairline. He swallowed the excess saliva building in his mouth and fought to slow his breathing. Rubbing his palms on his jeans, his gaze bounced from place to place in the shop. He pulled his zippo from his pocket. The smooth metal sliding between his fingers calmed him.

Sam returned with an ice-cold bottle of water. She held it out to him. Concern pinched her forehead in the middle, worry clouded her eyes.

He smiled, tucked the lighter away, and accepted the bottle. He rolled its sweaty exterior across his forehead and the back of his neck before cracking it open and taking a big swallow. "Thank you. I just got a little dizzy. The heat. Who is Zane? Why do they think his dad is a rapist, and what does being a cop have to do with anything?"

Sam blushed. "Oh, Zane. Um, remember the other day when you sent me to the parts store? I-uh, well-I kinda met him in the parking lot. He was having a hard time with his Monte Dog."

Lawrence chuckled, forcing his external demeanor to seem calm and collected while his insides were a nuclear mess. "You mean the parts trip that took four times as long as it should have?"

"Um, well," Sam turned away, her normally olive complexion glowing with embarrassment, "yeah, that trip."

She looked back at Lawrence. He could tell she was desperate to change the subject. He let her dangle on the hook a bit longer before asking, "What's the latest on the wedding and your frou-frou dress?"

Relief at the change in subject crossed Sam's face. "Oh my God, it gets worse every day. You should see the flowers..."

Lawrence tuned her out. His pulsed raced until it felt as if his heart would explode in his chest. Images of himself in cuffs and being shoved into a cage raced through his head. He could hear his long-dead father berating him for his stupidity, telling him he knew he would end up behind bars, calling him a useless waste of flesh.

Lawrence stared at Sam as a plan formed in his mind. *Damn, I liked the girl, too.* He pushed his sleeves up and nodded to himself. *But not as much as I like my freedom. I will never go to jail. No matter what.*

***

Lawrence lugged the heavy case up the shaky fire escape stairs. *What the hell? Why couldn't she keep her crazy thoughts to herself? She just had to go and open her mouth.* He wiped the sweat off his brow before it could drip into his eyes.

Breathing hard, he stepped onto the rooftop of the building across the street from St. Mary's Cathedral. He stared down at the cathedral doors. Huge white ribbon bows adorned the doors, their tails flapping in the light breeze. *Excellent. Wind markers.*

Pacing across the roof expanse, he settled on the perfect spot and opened his case. He pulled out a yoga mat and spread it out a foot back from the building's edge. Removing a spotting scope, he checked distance and range. Setting the scope aside, he assembled his rifle and double-checked the bolt action on the gun. Balancing it on a bipod attached to the front of the barrel, he peered down the scope, making minor adjustments.

He draped an emergency blanket across himself to break up his profile and reduce his infrared heat signature, not that anyone would suspect he waited on the roof, much less be searching for him with infrared sensors. *This is downtown Magellan, not Iraq.*

Time ticked past. He pursed his lips and played with the dog tags he always wore. It didn't matter that the dog tags were no more his than the uniform and badge he often wore. In his mind, he'd earned them. *Living with the old man should have earned him combat pay as well.* His internal temperature rose with his temper.

Breathe, two, three. He took a small sip of the bottled water he carried with him. Settling further back into his hide, he reminded himself that patience was a virtue. *Not one I have in abundance, but a virtue to be sure.*

Sweat trickled down his temples, dampened his palms. He rubbed his hands together to dry them. Hours had passed since he'd first climbed up here. He blew out a breath and waited. Based on the position of the sun, the action should kick off soon.

As if summoned by his thoughts, two long white limousines pulled to a stop in front of the church. *Right on time.* Six women of a variety of shapes climbed out of the front limo, laughing. Each woman wore an A-line, v-neck asymmetrical lace dress in a different pastel color. If he had been a guest invited to the wedding, he might have thought the effect was gorgeous.

A seventh woman, dressed in a sage green version of the same dress, stepped from the second limo. She held her hand out to assist a young girl decked out in white lace from the limo. Based on the flowers woven into her platinum curls and spilling from her basket, she must be the flower girl. His target followed the flower girl.

Despite Sam's frequent complaints about the dress, he still wasn't expecting the abundance of layers and layers of off-white lace. *She did resemble the layers of a multi-tiered wedding cake.* He huffed out a chuckle. *Damn, I'm going to miss that girl.*

He smiled. The flimsy fabric of the dresses worked better than drifting smoke for gaging windage.

Grinding his molars, the sniper's lips flattened against his teeth. The wood of the rifle cool against his cheek, he snugged the stock tighter to his shoulder and waited. Adrenaline cascaded through his body, flooding his limbs with a low-voltage electrical hum.

Finally, the seven pastel-clad ladies lined up in front of the double doors and, one by one, disappeared into the interior of the church. After the cathedral doors closed again, the bride's father stepped from the limousine. He held out a hand for his daughter. She stepped from the limo, face glowing. She hugged her father. The flower girl skipped around them, spilling a trail of crimson rose petals.

The quartet gathered in front of the door. Sam fidgeted with her dress. She wiggled her weight from one foot to the other. Impatience rolled off of her.

Faintly, the swell of music reached the sniper's ears. Hidden in the shadows of the opposing building, he peered through the scope. Adjusted the magnification. As the night stole the light from the day, he settled the crosshairs on a cluster of pearls on a hairpin in Sam's hair dangling in front of her temple as she stood facing the flower girl. *Inhale, exhale, hold.* He squeezed the trigger, sending his bullet flying toward his soon-to-be former employee.

Chapter Twenty-Nine

Toes pinched in brand new shiny black boots, wearing pressed black tuxedo pants, a crisp white shirt, and a tux jacket, Texas Ranger Rhyden Trammell felt like the peacock he always accused the sheriff's investigators of being. He tugged at his collar and dusted off the spit-shined tips of the boots on the back of his pants. Nervous energy hummed through his veins. Heat flushed his body. *Come on, come on, come on.*

Instrumental music floated delicately in the air. Standing in front of the flower-bedecked altar, the scent of roses struck his nose while need crawled up his spine. His hands itched. He clenched and unclenched his hands.

Rhyden's muscles twitched, and bones ached. A stabbing pain throbbed in his right temple. The vision in his right eye tunneled, blackening around the edges.

He rolled his neck on his shoulders. The shirt collar felt like it was tightening, strangling him. The flash of heat intensified, consumed him. *Fuck! Can't breathe.* Fidgeting, shifting his weight from foot to foot, he gazed out across the sanctuary, trying to distract his thoughts from the little white pill nestled at the bottom of his pants pocket. A myriad of perfumes mixed with the overwhelming scent of roses threatened to swamp him, adding nausea to his growing headache.

Rhyden's oldest daughter, Bree, gorgeous in a deep emerald lace sheath, sat in the front pew of Saint Mary's Cathedral holding Noah and Cat's four-month-old son, John Wyatt Morgan. His youngest two daughters waited out front in the limousine with the bride. He grinned, remembering how Maddie's chest puffed up when Cat asked her to be the flower girl.

Ranger Noah Morgan leaned over and

whispered to him. "You okay, man? I'm supposed to be the nervous one. I'm the groom, after all."

"Just a headache." Rhyden squeezed the bridge of his nose, rubbed his temple, and glued a fake smile to his face. "How are you holding up, bud? Ready to run out the back yet?" He scanned his partner from head to toe. Polished boots peeked from beneath black tuxedo pants. A black cumberbund circled his waist beneath a black tuxedo jacket with tails, but the tie. Oh my God, the tie... eye-searing yellow with neon green stripes. "Really, partner, you couldn't wear a normal bow tie like any other self-respecting groom would wear?"

Before Noah could answer, the music swelled. The sanctuary doors opened. One by one, seven bridesmaids minced their way up the aisle, taking their assigned places at the front of the church. The doors closed behind them, giving the bride time to settle and adjust her dress before making her grand entrance.

Noah inhaled a stuttery breath. He blew it out and bounced on his toes.

Rhyden chuckled beneath his breath, thoughts of the pill momentarily forgotten. He leaned toward his partner. "Too late to run now." He winked.

The music changed, and Mendelssohn's Wedding March rang out. Rustling filled the sanctuary as the congregation rose and turned to face the back of the church, awaiting the appearance of the bride. The music reached its crescendo, but the doors never opened.

Rhy couldn't resist teasing Noah. "Maybe she ran away instead."

The processional music ended, but still the doors remained closed. The crowd shuffled in place and whispered, growing restless. With a nod from the minister, the organist played the piece again.

"Something's wrong, man," Noah said.

"I'm sure it's okay. Maybe she's having a costume malfunction? Want me to send Bree to check on her?"

"No, man. Something's wrong. I can feel it in my bones. Something is way wrong."

The left door to the cathedral slammed open. Shrill cries for help reached Rhyden at the altar. "Daddy!" Her white dress drenched in red, Maddie raced toward the front of the church, screaming.

Maddie flung herself at her daddy, wrapping her arms around his leg and clinging for dear life. Rhyden's heart stopped. Beside him, Noah staggered on the altar steps before lunging toward the back of the church. Rhyden dropped to his knees and swept Maddie into a tight hold as Noah surged past him.

"Are you okay? Maddie, what happened? Are you hurt?"

"S-S-Sam..." Maddie turned her tear-stained face to her father. "Help. Help, help, help. Sam." She gasped for air and waved toward the door. "Da-da-daddy, please. Sam, please." She buried her head against his chest and stuck her middle two fingers into her mouth, regressing to an early childhood comfort gesture.

He checked her for injuries. Not finding any, he held her tight to him. The need to protect her fought with the need to see what had happened to Sam. Dread churned his gut. *Not Sam, please, not my fiery, beautiful girl.*

Bree stepped up, placed a hand on her father's shoulder as he kneeled in the aisle, arms wrapped around Maddie. "I've got her, Dad. Go do what you do. Sam needs you."

Rhyden squeezed Maddie to him once more before he passed her over. "Keep her here.

Make sure she's okay." He made eye contact with each of his daughters. "I love you."

"Go, Dad. We've got this. We'll be right here waiting for you."

He hesitated for a moment before pushing his way through the congregation to reach the front door. "Please, people, stay here. Stay put and stay down."

Fortunately for Mr. Ramos, his daughter was popular with her co-workers and her bosses. Half the congregation were paramedics, and several had driven their units to the wedding because they were on duty. By the time Rhyden made it to the sidewalk, Cat—her wedding gown soaked in blood—held pressure on her father's gunshot wound as her partner started an IV. She alternated between barking orders at those around her and sobbing. Sam was nowhere to be seen.

Rhyden squeezed Cat's shoulder. When

she raised her head, he asked, "Sam? Where's Sam?"

Cat nodded to the parking lot. "She's grabbing the jump bag from the ambulance."

Rhyden's knees buckled as Sam raced up to the sidewalk carrying a red bag of trauma supplies and dragging a backboard. He took them from her, handing them off to a waiting paramedic. He grabbed Sam and held her tight. "You okay?" He pushed back from her so he could check for injuries. "What happened?"

Sam gestured at the building across the street. "Gunshot, Dad. From over there." Her gaze skipped feverishly around her, canvassing the sidewalk. "Maddie. Dad, where's Maddie?"

"She's good. She's with Bree." He nudged her toward the cathedral doors. "Why don't you go help Bree with Maddie and JW?"

The law enforcement half of the congregation swarmed out said doors and spread out working the crime scene and searching for the shooter.

Noah tugged on Cat's arm. "Come on, sweetie, let them do their jobs. Let's go. We'll meet them at the hospital."

"I'm going in the ambulance with Dad."

"Cat." Gingerly, he tried to pry her away from her father so the medics could load him up for transport. "Babe,think about it. In that dress, you'll be in the way. No room for the medics to work. You work with these guys every day. You trust them. Let them do their jobs. I've got you. We'll get you changed and cleaned up and to the hospital, okay?" He noticed Rhyden standing there. "Rhy, need your help here. And can you bring John Wyatt?"

Rhyden slid his hands beneath Cat's, holding pressure on her father's gunshot wound. For a split second, blood pulsed as the switch took place. He applied more pressure. "You got it, partner. Get her out of here." He applied more pressure. "Go with Noah, Cat. The medics have your dad. The girls and I have JW."

Chapter Thirty

Hands shaking with anger, Lawrence efficiently broke down his weapon, stowing it away like he'd done many times before. *Crazy old fool. You just had to lean in for a kiss, didn't you? Serves you right. Blocked my fucking shot.* He knew he couldn't blame the miss all on the bride's father. He was the one who jerked the rifle. Maybe killing Sam wasn't the answer after all. Down deep, relief flooded his system. *Damn it. Now what?*

Easing back from the edge of the rooftop, Lawrence tried to keep his thoughts from spiraling. He knew he had to hold it together, or he would go to jail. Sticking to the shadows and moving slowly so as not to attract attention from the guests rushing out of the cathedral, he eased his way over to the back side of the building where the fire escape led to the ground. Out of sight, he scrambled down the ladder.

Heart pounding, he sprinted through the narrow alleyway. Shadows danced along the graffiti-covered walls, concealing his desperate escape. The sound of his own ragged breath echoed in his ears, fueling his determination. Adrenaline coursed through his veins, pushing him faster, harder.

His feet skidded on the slick pavement as he rounded another sharp corner, narrowly avoiding collision with a startled pedestrian. Ignoring the startled shouts, he surged forward. *I can't get caught. Not now.*

Sirens wailed in the distance, their shrill cries growing louder with each passing second. Panic threatened to engulf him, but he pushed it aside, using the fear as fuel. He darted through narrow alleyways and leapt over obstacles.

A flicker of movement caught his eye, and he ducked into a dimly lit doorway, desperate for a moment of respite. Chest heaving, he pressed his back against the cold brick wall, his senses on high alert. He had to stay hidden, had to catch his breath. Time to escape was slipping away.

He caught a glimpse of his pursuers, police officers and sheriff's deputies in dress uniform.

Idiot, idiot, idiot. He hadn't thought this part through. *What the hell did you think was going to happen, firing a rifle at the wedding of a Texas Ranger and a paramedic?* Every other guest was a first responder of one type or another. All of them trained to watch for danger. Most of their families had also received training. He could hear his father's voice echoing in his head, berating him for his stupidity.

As the footsteps of the officers searching for him grew faint, he knew he had to seize this moment. Pushing himself off the wall, he silently emerged from his hiding place, eyes scanning the surroundings.

Taking a deep breath, he sauntered down the sidewalk fighting the adrenaline rushing through him—adrenaline telling him to run. *Easy. Walk.* He knew running would just draw attention to him. Monitoring the activity in front of the church, he slipped into the darkness and disappeared.

***

Pacing the halls at the hospital waiting on word concerning Mr. Ramos's condition, Rhyden locked eyes with an auburn-haired nurse. Time froze for a moment until she whipped the privacy screen shut between them, protecting the bruised teenage girl huddled in torn clothing on the gurney. *Mikki. Crap, I forgot to call her after our date. Damn it.*

The craving which had fled during the chaos slammed back into him with a vengeance. Hand shaking, pain eating him alive, he reached for his pocket to find it soaked in blood and the contents missing.

Impotent rage swept through his body. Pain intensified, shooting through his leg, stabbing his head. Rhy pounded his fists against the hospital wall before dropping his forehead against it. Tears stung his eyes.

"Dad? You okay?" Bree stood behind him, bouncing a crying infant in her arms. The baby flailed, waving his arms frantically in time to his screams. "I can't get JW to stop crying, and I can't find Cat or Noah anywhere. I don't know what I'm doing. Can you help?"

Rhyden spun to face Bree. He took JW from her and headed into the waiting room. Laying the boy on a chair, he snatched a thin receiving blanket from the diaper bag and swaddled him snugly. He placed the baby on his shoulder and patted his back. The raucous cries quieted to an occasional sniffle. He paced the width of the waiting room, gently bouncing the child on his shoulder. JW succumbed to sleep.

"Wow. That was magic. How did you

do that?" Bree asked.

"Swaddling makes babies feel more secure. I guess it reminds them of the tight quarters in the womb or something. All I know is it worked with all three of you girls."

"Dad, are you okay? I was talking to Sam, and she said—"

Cat followed closely behind Noah as he came out from the back of the emergency room, interrupting Bree. "They are taking him back to surgery," Noah said before anyone could ask.

Cat ran a jerky hand through her hair, pulling pins loose. Her elegant wedding updo had long since fallen. She took her son from Rhyden and cuddled him close against her chest. Tears left streaks of black mascara cascading down her face, cutting through her meticulously applied makeup.

"Here." Rhyden handed her a pocket handkerchief. He nodded toward the door of the ladies' room on the other side of the waiting room. "You might feel better if you clean up a little. Remove that paint-for-what-you-ain't as Grandfather calls it."

Swollen, red-rimmed eyes met his. Gratitude swept through them. "Thank you." Cat handed JW to Noah. "Here. Don't wake him up or you get to deal with him."

Noah feigned fright. "Heaven forbid." He accepted the child and cradled him in his arms like a football.

JW squirmed in his father's arms. He fussed.

"Ch, ch, ch." Noah rocked his weight from side to side, soothing his son back to sleep.

Rhyden glanced at the ladies' room door as it swung closed. "Now that Cat can't hear us, how is he?"

Keeping his voice quiet to avoid waking

the baby, Noah explained. "The doctors are worried. They tried to hide it from Cat, but when she visited with him they talked to me. The bullet missed his heart by mere inches. It didn't exit, so they have to attempt to remove it. They're afraid of nicking something and causing him to bleed out. If he survives the surgery, his recovery will be long and hard. Like needing around-the-clock care hard. I guess I didn't realize it, but Cat was a late-in-life surprise baby. I mean, I knew her father was older, but I didn't know how much older. The man is in his late seventies. This is going to be rough on him and rough on Cat. With her mom gone, she feels like she has to do all the caretaking. I don't know how we're going to work it."

"If you need anything, buddy, call me. And I'm not just mouthing platitudes. I mean it."

Footsteps approached. Noah raised his chin in acknowledgement before whispering to his best friend, "Here comes Trouble with a capital T."

Rhyden whipped around. Mikki headed straight to him.

"Are you okay? You're covered in blood."

He looked down at his tuxedo shirt. *Well, hell. Guess I'll be buying this shirt instead of returning it.* Dark crimson fading to brown blood stains covered his sleeves and the front of his shirt. "I'm fine. It's not mine."

The nurse's eyebrows shot to her hairline. Her lips pursed.

"I promise, the blood's not mine. A sniper shot Cat's father at the wedding."

"Wait. What? Sniper?" Her hand flew to the base of her neck. Long, graceful fingers wrapped around her throat. "Is he okay? Oh my God, poor Cat. At the wedding? I can't..."

Rhyden placed a hand on her shoulder.

"He's in surgery. It will be a rough haul, but he's strong."

"But still—at the wedding? I can't imagine how traumatized Cat must be." A thought occurred to her. "Oh, crud monkeys. Weren't your daughters supposed to be in the wedding? Were they there when he got shot? How are they holding up? Is there anything I can do?"

"They're pretty shook up but seem okay." Blood soaked through his shirt and stuck to his skin. "You wouldn't happen to have a spare set of men's clothing sitting around here in my size, would you? And a place to clean up? This blood is drying and starting to itch."

"I can probably grab you a set of scrubs if you want to change. You can use the nurse's shower."

"You wouldn't happen to have a spare hydrocodone with those scrubs, would you?" At the appalled look Mikki threw him, Rhyden threw his hands up in surrender. "I'm joking."

He pulled Mikki into a tight hug inhaling that unique ocean breeze scent she always carried on her. He held on longer than propriety allowed. "You are a lifesaver. You know that? I mean that literally as well as figuratively. Thank you. And I'm sorry I haven't called. Things have been crazy." Thinking of T.J. Ross's parting shot during the interview, he said, "Hey, when you have a spare moment, I need to ask you something."

Bree interrupted. "Who is this? Is there something you need to tell me?"

He swallowed nervously. "Bree, this is Mikki. She's a sexual assault examiner here at the hospital and has been helping me with a case. Mikki, this is my oldest daughter, Bree." He narrowed his gaze on Bree. "Quit bristling. You're not a porcupine. There's nothing you need to know."

Both women turned to him with matching expressions of disbelief.

"Nothing?" Mikki asked.

Bree raised a single eyebrow. "Really? Nothing? You always hug your coworkers like that?"

Crap, crap, crap. I'm on thin ice, and I can hear it cracking. Fortunately, Cat emerged from the ladies' room and provided a much needed distraction.

"Dad." Bree cleared her throat. She wrapped her hair around her finger. "Dad, I need to talk to you."

"Baby, can it wait? The smell of this blood is getting to me."

Bree shrugged helplessly and turned away. She walked to Noah to see if she could help with JW in any form or fashion.

"Rhy, if you'd like to follow me, I can

help you get cleaned up." A crimson blush raced from her chest up her neck into her face. "That didn't come out right."

"I don't know." Rhyden smirked. He leaned down and whispered in her ear. "Sounded pretty good to me."

Mikki tossed a glance over her shoulder at his daughter to find her glaring at the couple. She straightened her spine. Speaking loud enough for the entire waiting room to hear, she said, "Ranger Trammell, if you will follow me, I can show you the facilities and find you some scrubs to wear. I'm sure you won't need any help after that."

He chuckled and gestured for her to lead the way.

As they turned a corner in the hallway, she asked, "What did you want to talk to me about?"

"Oh, that." Rhyden pulled the tuxedo

jacket closed. A quiver tickled his stomach. He slipped his hands into his pants pockets while casting a sideways glance at her. "Well, um, so I was talking to T.J."

She stopped walking and turned to face the Ranger. She widened her eyes. A flare of anger flashed across her face. Her expression quickly shifted from anger to wariness. "And?"

"So, he um... well, I need to know 'cause you know."

"No, I don't know."

Rhyden squirmed beneath her no-nonsense glare. His Adam's apple bobbed as he swallowed hard. "T.J. led me to believe you are still married."

"That son-of-a-bucket-kicker said what?!?"

Chapter Thirty-One

"Thanks for coming to dinner with us. I wanted the girls to meet Mikki before Bree spills the beans. I thought it might help if we had a buffer. Mikki's bringing her son, Benjamin, too," Rhyden said as he, Noah, and Cat followed Maddie and Sam toward the restaurant. "I miss Bree's cooking. Hell, I miss Bree."

Cat juggled the diaper bag and her purse on one shoulder while holding a wriggling John Wyatt balanced on her other hip. Noah relieved her of the blue denim diaper bag and her purse.

"Thanks, babe. And thank you, Rhy, for inviting us. Hospital food every day is getting old," Cat said. "How is Bree liking college? She enjoying the freedom of not having to baby-sit all the time? John Wyatt misses her. Don't you, JW?" She directed the last comment to the infant in her arms.

"She's loving it. Although she calls

home every few days to make sure I'm remembering to take care of Sam and Maddie. Like I'm not the father, right? I do worry about her being on her own, though."

Noah and Cat laughed. "She knows you, partner. What can we say?"

"Speaking of hospital food, how is your dad doing, Cat?"

"He's improving. Hopefully, Doc will release him soon."

Rhy continued the conversation. "And when's the wedding?"

A wolf whistle echoed across the street as Sam and Maddie made their way past a crew of construction workers building a convenience store across the road from the restaurant. Sam whipped both hands to her hips. "Put your eyes back in your freaking head and close your mouth before you trip over your tongue." Sam flounced inside the restaurant, pushing Maddie before her.

Rhyden chuckled. "It's so nice knowing at least I don't have to worry about Sam. That girl can take care of herself."

"Maybe you should be worried," Noah muttered, partially under his breath.

"What the hell do you mean by that?"

Cat grabbed the diaper bag from Noah. "I think I'll just go change little man here." And ducked into the restaurant after the girls.

Rhyden turned to face Noah. "I asked you a question. I'm waiting for an answer."

Noah squirmed, looking a bit like his son, before firming up his spine. "Rhy, all teasing aside, you're a wonderful dad, the best. You've done an amazing job raising those girls on your own. And I know you love the girls more than life itself, but it seems lately, I don't know. I think you need to pay a little more attention to what's been going on. Take a closer look at who Sam's been hanging out with.

Primarily that Zane punk and his buddies. You seem out of it a lot of the time over the past month or so. Like you're not even here.."

Now Rhyden squirmed. His mind flashed to the little white pill waiting in the bottom of his pocket. "Not sure what you're talking about, buddy." Changing the subject, he asked, "So, when's the wedding rescheduled for?"

"Forget that. I don't think I can talk her into another wedding. Her dress is ruined—ripped from stem to stern, soaked in blood. The mere mention of the Wedding March brings back memories of fucking sniper fire. Every time I mention it, she bursts out in tears. She thinks it's her fault her dad got shot. She says we're cursed even though her dad is going to be fine.

"I did use her guilty feelings to talk her into taking him on a cruise to the Bahamas next month after he finishes physical therapy. She doesn't know it yet, but I'm paying the ship's captain to marry us on the boat. Her dad thinks it's a fine idea."

The men hushed as they joined the rest of their party at a table set for eight.

"Dad, who else is coming?" asked Sam.

Before he could answer, Mikki approached the table with a lanky teenage boy in tow. She patted Noah on the shoulder, leaned down to hug Cat, and tickled JW beneath the chin before turning to face the rest of the crew. "Rhyden, Sam, Maddie, this is my son, Benji."

The sullen teenage boy huffed out a breath and slouched over to the table. Arms folded across his chest, he said, "My name is Zane. Benjamin Zane Ross. If you will not call me Mr. Ross, I will respond to Zane, but not Benji. Never Benji. I am not a shaggy dog from a seventies movie."

"Benjamin! Manners. Now, sir."

He plopped down into a chair at the table. "Do they even have anything decent to eat in this roach-infested hellhole?"

Sam pointed at Zane. "I know you. Monte Dog, right?" She turned to face Mikki. "But who the heck are you?"

Before anyone could reply, Maddie tugged on Sam's hand. "Sam, will you go to the ladies' room with me?"

"What is it with females traveling to the bathroom in packs?" scoffed Zane.

Maddie's eyes filled with tears.

Oh, shit. Rhyden opened his mouth to respond, but Sam beat him to the punch.

She rose to her full height, which on the stiletto heels she wore was quite impressive. Towering over Zane, she pointed at herself, then made a circle with the finger. "Do I look like I travel in a pack? Do you see a large group of females surrounding me?"

"Come to think of it, I never see you around any other girls. You're always hanging out with the motor heads." Zane smirked. "Are you sure you are female?"

"Just because I can kick your ass on or off the football field and know more about the inner workings of a Chevy 350 V8 engine does not mean I'm not female." She ran a hand up and down her side from shoulder to hip. "Or hadn't you noticed with all your staring from across the cafeteria?"

"Noticed what, string bean?"

Sam launched herself across the table, but Maddie grabbed her hand. "Sam, please? I gotta go... bad."

"Still don't see why she needs a chaperone to go pee." Zane examined his short, grease-stained fingernails.

Sam raised her chin in a regal motion as Maddie hopped from foot to foot. Staring down her nose at Zane, she said, "She's seven years old, douchebag." Taking Maddie's hand in hers, shoulders and back straight, she swept from the table.

Maddie scowled back over her shoulder. "Yeah, I'm six years old..." she obviously searched her limited vocabulary for a suitable insult. Apparently not finding one, she settled for sticking out her tongue before whipping her face back to the front and strutting away with her big sister.

Mikki wrinkled her nose and held back a smile. She arched a single eyebrow. "Douchebag? Really?" she asked.

Rhyden shrugged. "Well, he did start it."

***

After dropping the girls at home, Rhyden met Mikki at the park where their first date concluded. Walking hand in hand down the path, they headed toward the empty playground. Rhyden tugged on Mikki's hand, pulling her closer to him. He wrapped an arm around her waist and pulled her to his side.

She snuggled against him and laid her head on his shoulder. They continued walking in silence.

A fresh breeze blew across Bennett Lake lifting strands of her auburn hair and blowing them into his face.

"That tickles," he said as he smoothed her hair down, tucking the loose strands behind her ears. He pressed a kiss to her forehead. "So... dinner went well, don't you think?"

Mikki snorted before bursting into laughter. "Oh, yeah. Real well. I'm grateful Cat and Noah were there. I thought the kids were going to disembowel one another with their soup spoons."

Rhyden laughed. "Yeah, probably not the best start. Did you know Zane and Sam had been hanging out?"

"Zane mumbled something at dinner the other day about some girl he met at the parts store when I pinned him down about where he had been spending all of his time, but he never told me her name." She dropped onto the strip of rubber making up the swing's seat.

Rhyden grabbed the chains in both hands and gave her a gentle push. "Well, that's more than I got. I'm not sure they'll spend any more time together after that dinner."

"Who knows with teenagers? They hate you one day, love you the next. Lord, save me from hormones."

He chuckled. Sitting in the swing next to her, he pushed off with his toe in the dirt and lightly rocked the swing back and forth. Silence filled the air for the next few minutes as they each relaxed, lost in their own thoughts.

"Mik—"

"Rhy—"

They both laughed. Rhyden gestured for her to go first. "Ladies first."

Mikki looked down at her hands folded in her lap. She raised her chin and grabbed the chains for her swing. She twisted to face him. "Rhy, I like you. I really like you. With time, this may evolve into something big, something real. But I'm not sure I can continue seeing you."

"Wait, what?" His head flinched back slightly and his chest tightened. "Why?"

"I feel you've got some things to work through first. It's like you've locked your heart behind walls thicker than the Alamo. I'm not asking you to throw the door wide open, not yet at least, but if you can't crack a window a smidgen, I don't see how we can get anywhere. I don't think you're ready."

"Mikki, please." He held a hand toward her. He dropped the hand when she didn't take it. Stepping in front of her swing, he grabbed the chains and stopped her from moving. Waiting until she met his eyes, he continued, "Please. You're the first woman I've let this close. Hell, you're the first person, period. I want to keep seeing you. What do you want me to do?"

She hesitated.

He watched a myriad of emotions chase across her face. "Mik, seriously. Anything."

Taking a deep breath, she said, "I think you need addiction counseling. Maybe go to a Narcotics Anonymous group."

Heat flushed through his body. His nostrils flared. Dropping the chains, he stepped back and crossed his arms over his chest. "What the fuck? I don't have a pill problem. I'm in pain. My doctor prescribed those pills. I don't sneak around to a scumbag drug dealer. I'm a fucking Texas Ranger. Believe it or not, I know right from wrong."

"Rhy—"

He held up a hand, stopping her from speaking. Turning his back to her, he clenched and unclenched his fists. He visibly relaxed every muscle in his body. He inhaled deeply, held it, and blew the breath out completely. Repeating this several times in a row, he could feel the tension leaving his body.

Squatting on the heels of his boots in front of Mikki, who waited, perched on the swing, he asked, "Why do you think I have a pill problem?"

Mikki sighed. "You know I'm a trauma nurse. Dealing with injuries is a daily occurrence for me. Dealing with junkies is something I face daily as well." This time, she held up a hand to stop him from interrupting. "I'm not saying you're a junky. I'm just saying you should be taking fewer pills by now, not more. Your judgment feels a bit off lately." She shook her head sadly. A single tear tracked down her cheek. She didn't bother to wipe it away. "I've been married to an alcoholic. I have no desire to become involved with another addiction."

Rhyden rocked back away from her. A thousand thoughts raced through his brain. His mind and heart battled. He rubbed a hand across the back of his neck. "If I get help, go to these meetings, will you continue seeing me?" Seeing the refusal on her face, he added, "Please?"

Chapter Thirty-Two

Digging around in his desk drawer, Rhyden snagged the transparent orange prescription pill bottle from the back of it. He opened the child safety cap and dumped the pills on his desk. Spreading them out on the mahogany surface, he counted them. *That couldn't be right.*

Anger masked the fear boiling beneath the surface. He couldn't have taken that many pills already. *If Sam and that punk friend of hers, Zane, had been in his meds...* Another thought chased that one. *What if he ran out too soon?* He couldn't breathe. No matter how deep he inhaled, his chest felt tight, like no oxygen was getting in. *Calm down, Rhy.* He concentrated on slowing his breath. *It's got to be a mistake. Check again.*

He counted the pills again. Same number. *What the fuck?* Doc and the insurance company kept a close eye on opioid consumption. No early refills allowed—period. He had already tried breaking the pills, taking half a pill at a time, but they didn't work that way.

Damn it. He'd been shot. In the line of duty, no less. Didn't anyone care? A bullet had shattered his shoulder. He had multiple pins and rods in his leg. Pain like that doesn't disappear overnight. And the headaches. Don't they realize he'd tried to stop taking the damn pills?

He hated being tied to a clock, always watching, waiting, and counting the minutes until he could take the next pill. But the headaches—blinding, excruciating headaches like someone was stabbing an ice pick through his right eye—kept coming. Indescribable pain. Lord knows he'd tried to find the words to get the doctor to understand the pain. Doc couldn't feel it, so why would he care?

"Daddy, what are you doing?" His

youngest daughter, Maddie, wandered into the room.

Cursing beneath his breath, he swept the pills back into their container. In his haste, they scattered, rolling all over the desktop. He scooped them up and dumped them back into the pill bottle. Brushed the chalky residue off his hands on his denim-clad thighs.

One fell to the floor and bounced to Maddie's feet. She picked it up. "What's this?"

"Give that here, sweetie." Rhyden struggled to keep the pain and emotions from his voice. "Please. That's daddy's special headache pill."

She handed him the pill. "Do you have a headache, Daddy? If you want to, you can hold Fred." She offered him her threadbare teddy bear. "He always makes me feel better."

Rhyden dropped to his knees beside his

daughter and gathered her close. Tears clogged his throat. "No, thank you, sweetie. You hang on to Fred. I'll be fine."

Her lower lip trembled. "Are you sure, Daddy? I don't want you to go back to the hospital. Last time, that mean lady next door told Grandfather you were never coming home. Not ever. She called us poor orpins. What's an orpin, Daddy?"

"Oh, Maddie-girl." He hugged her tighter before pulling back so she could see his face. "An orphan is someone without parents, but I will always come home to you. Always. I promise. Okay?"

"Pinky promise?"

He solemnly linked pinky fingers with her and shook. "Pinky promise."

"Good." With the capricious nature of a seven-year-old, she changed the subject. "Can we please order pizza for supper? With lots of pepperoni? But no pineapple. Pineapple is yuck. I don't want Sam to cook. She burns everything."

Rhyden chuckled. He ruffled Maddie's long, platinum hair. *Child of my heart, what would I ever do without you?* "Let's go see what Sam's doing. I'll take you both out to dinner. How does that sound?"

Maddie tilted her head. "What about Fred? Can he come, too? And Grandfather? I bet he's hungry, too."

Shoving the pill bottle into his jeans pocket, he decided he could worry about the missing pills later. "They can all come, sweetie. Let's go find everyone."

Chapter Thirty-Three

Fwap, fwap, fwap. *Fucking boots.* Lawrence stepped out of his father's boots. He would never grow into his father's footsteps— literally. The man wore a size fifteen. Grabbing two rolled pairs of socks, he shoved one pair into the toes of each boot before slipping them back on.

As he buttoned the uniform shirt and shoved the miles of extra fabric into his pants, he could hear his father's voice rumbling in his head. *You'll never measure up to me, little boy. Why do you keep trying?*

Lawrence was by no means a small man, but his father had been a giant. He cringed as he remembered being swatted by hands that felt like they were the size of tennis rackets and made of stone. He shook his head to dislodge the memories. *I'm no longer a child. I am in control now.* He grinned as he thought of what he had planned for his next victim. *Very much in control... of everything... except this itch.*

It had been too long since his last "outing" if he didn't count the failed sniper attack. Which he refused to do. *Bad idea from the beginning. Target a Ranger's kid? What the hell was I thinking?*

Again, he heard his father's gravelly voice echo. *Think? You never think, do you, boy?*

Blocking the voice from his mind, he polished the badge pinned to his shirt with his sleeve. He double checked the weapons on the duty belt wrapped around his waist. Settling the felt cowboy hat on his head, he left his crappy apartment behind.

As Lawrence made a left turn onto Kyote highway, red and blue flashing lights caught his attention. His pulse ratcheted up. It throbbed in his temples. *What the hell?* He hit his brakes, slid to a stop in the loose gravel on the shoulder of the road, and double checked the mapping app on the dashboard of the sheriff's office Tahoe. There shouldn't be any on-duty units in this area. He gripped the steering wheel—hard—to stop his hands from trembling. The acrid scent of fear-induced sweat filled his nose. He rolled forward.

The familiar black and white of a Texas Department of Public Safety officer's Dodge Charger pulled away from the sports car sitting on the side of the road and shut off its flashing lights. Pulling even with Lawrence, the DPS officer lowered his driver side window. "How's it going?"

Lawrence didn't recognize the officer. "Um. Good, I guess."

The baby-faced trooper opened his door and looked behind his vehicle, which still blocked the road. Seeing no traffic coming, he stepped up to the Tahoe. He stuck his arm through Lawrence's open window and extended a hand to shake. "Trooper Rory Anderson. I'm new to the area." He chuckled. "Actually, I'm new to the force. Just finished field training last week. I want to become a Ranger."

A wave of relief passed over Lawrence. He took the proffered hand. "Deputy—" His mind scrambled for a name. "—Morgan. Nice to meet you." He cast about for something else to say, but his brain drew a blank. Dampness gathered inside the band of his hat, causing his head to itch. His mouth was dry as sand. He swallowed hard, trying to force moisture into his mouth.

"Is it always this quiet at this end of the county?" asked the trooper.

"Uh-oh. Now you've done it." Lawrence laughed uneasily. He repeated what he'd heard the deputies and paramedics say all the time. "Didn't anyone ever teach you not to use the Q word on shift? It's a surefire way to get all hell to break loose." As if in response to his words, the radio began squawking loudly in the background.

"Shots fired. Officer needs assistance. 3876 Old Wild Rock Road. Repeat shots fired."

The young trooper whooped in excitement, raced back to his vehicle, and jumped inside as he hollered over his shoulder at Lawrence, "I don't know where that is. I'll follow you."

Fuck! Now what? This was emphatically not how Lawrence had his evening planned, but he didn't have many options at this point in time. The pressure built in his gut. If he wasn't able to release it soon, he worried his tightly held control might snap. *What to do? What to do?* He definitely couldn't show up in a county vehicle at a crime scene.

He slipped the Tahoe into gear and flipped on his flashing lights. Engaging the siren, he raced down the road, kicking up dust and rocks behind his wheels. *Maybe I can lose him.*

Chapter Thirty-Four

Rhyden handed Mikki an ice-cold glass of coke. He dimmed the lights, walked around the back of the sofa, and dropped beside her. "I'm glad you gave us another chance."

Mikki took a sip of her soda, tucked her sock-clad feet up under her legs. "How are the meetings going?"

Rhyden shifted in his seat. He reached up and pulled on his left ear before nodding. Speaking faster than normal, he replied, "Good." He nodded. "Really good, but we're not supposed to talk about it. It's right there in the name. Narcotics Anonymous." He cleared his throat. "So tell me more about yourself. Where are you from?"

She quirked an eyebrow at him. "You okay?"

"Yeah. I just like to know family

histories. My great-great-great-grandfather was a Comanche Power Possessor or, as you round-eyes liked to call them, a medicine man. He passed his healing skills down through the family until they reached my grandfather. Grandfather was already an outcast for marrying a red-headed Scots woman, but Dad really split the blanket by becoming—gasp—a Texas Ranger. Great-great-great-grandfather must be spinning in his burial cave."

"And you added injury to insult by following in your father's footsteps." She placed her glass on a coaster resting on the coffee table in front of her. She turned to face him. "My family probably fought with yours. My grandma always told us we had been in Texas since before there was a Texas." She chuckled. "My third-grade teacher sent me to the office once for telling her to call my grandma her own darn self if she didn't believe me. Of course, this was after she called me to the front of the classroom and told me no one was from Texas. That we were all from somewhere else."

Rhy kept his eyes glued to her, watching every emotion that played across her face. Her thick, silky cap of auburn hair showcased lowlights and highlights that vied with the colors of the fire in the fireplace. Middle of the summer in south Texas and he had cranked the air conditioning all the way down as cold as it would go so he could light the fire and watch the way its glow caressed this woman who fascinated him.

With the room lights dimmed, the light and shadow from the flickering flames played across her face. Shadows emphasized her sharp cheekbones, the full bottom lip, thin upper lip, and round eyes that seemed oversized for her face. Her large Roman nose kept her from being considered conventionally beautiful, but the mischief, spark, and energetic enthusiasm for life lit her from within, making her looks compelling to Rhyden.

A soft smile graced her lips, soft until it turned downright wicked. Her eyes gleamed. "Man, I wanted that teacher to call Grandma and tell her we weren't from Texas. Grandma was a fine hand with an ax, but she had no weapon sharper than her tongue." Mikki caught Rhy watching her closely. "What?" A brilliant pink flush covered her from the tips of her ears, across her cheeks, and down her chest.

"What what?" he asked before leaning in to steal a kiss.

"What about you? Why did you follow your dad into law enforcement?"

Rhy pulled back, shrugged. "What can I say? It gets in your blood. If we don't have a sheepdog to protect the herd from the wolf, the herd gets eaten. The sheepdog is still a wolf down deep in its DNA, but it's using that aggression to protect instead of harm."

"Yeah, I get that. But why you

specifically? Why did you want to become not just a cop, but a Ranger?"

He shrugged. "My dad was a Ranger."

"So it's a legacy thing?"

Rhy stood, paced around the room, clutching his glass before placing it beside Mikki's glass. "Not exactly. I told you my dad was gunned down in the line of duty a few weeks after my eleventh birthday. I rebelled. I hated anything and everything to do with law enforcement." He reached down and rubbed the side of his thigh. His fingers tracing the rough ridge formed by the scar beneath the denim of his jeans. "I was heading down the wrong road. I don't know what would have happened to me if Grandfather hadn't stepped in."

"Grandfather? The Native American man who drove the nurses in your unit nuts burning sage?"

"That sounds like him. He's a

Comanche, but I already told you that. He was brought up by his great-grandfather in many of the old ways. His name means Spirit Talker, and if you ask him, he'll tell you the spirits talk to him. He believes a warrior never dies. He comes back as a spirit. The warriors surround him and protect him, but occasionally, an evil spirit will try to come back. He uses sage to cleanse his surroundings of negativity. And he would definitely believe the 'white man's hospital' would be full of negative energy and evil spirits."

Mikki patted the sofa beside her. "Sit down, please? You make me nervous pacing around like that. Is your leg hurting?"

Rhy dropped back onto the sofa beside her. He turned her so her back snuggled against his chest and they could watch the flames together. "You're not laughing?"

"Why would I laugh? I've seen enough to know that some wolves are hairy on the inside. There's evil everywhere. If sage will keep it away, sign me up for weekly—heck fire, daily—cleansings. What's the wildest thing you've ever done in the line of duty?"

"Who me? Mr. Straight and Narrow? Why would you think I had ever done anything wild?"

Laughter burst from Mikki's lips. "I didn't believe it until now. 'Fess up. What did you do?"

"Well, I'm not saying if it's true or not," Rhy shifted, turning Mikki, pulling her into his lap, "but they sent a group of us to the border to deal with the cartel. We may or may not have invaded Mexico." He brushed a lock of her wild, fire-kissed hair from his face before he leaned forward and pressed his lips against hers. His tongue tangled with hers.

The lights flashed on.

"Eew, gross! Could you please not do

that in the living room? What would you do if Maddie walked in?" Sam stormed into the room. "What the hell, Dad?"

"Maddie is in bed asleep. Has been for hours."

Mikki slid from Rhy's lap and slipped her feet back into her shoes. She stood. "Um... I've got to be going. Early morning. See you tomorrow, Rhy?"

Rhyden walked Mikki to her car before returning to the house. Sam sat on the couch with her feet propped on the coffee table. "What are you doing home? I thought you were spending the night with what's her name, your friend from school."

"Tanya, Dad, her name is Tanya. Her dad came home drunk. I felt safer coming home... until I walked in on that. Is this one going to break your heart, too? Cheat on you like the last one?"

"Samantha Elaine! The 'last one', as you so elegantly put it, was your mother. I'll ask you kindly not to refer to her in that manner."

"Jeez, Dad, in that manner? You sound like a dried up prune of an old lady, like one of those stereotypical spinster aunt cat ladies. I asked a simple question. Is this one going to break your heart like the incubator did?"

"And you sound like a young lady who has gotten too big for her britches. Consider yourself grounded for two weeks. Go to your room."

Sam slammed her hands down on the coffee table. "Jeez. All I did was ask a question. Who peed in your cereal?"

"Want to go for four weeks? Go to your room—now." As she swept from the room, Rhy muttered to himself, "Sometimes I wish I believed in spanking when she was younger."

He walked into the kitchen and began

cleaning up.

"Dad..." Sam called from the bedroom.

"Sam, I've had about enough of you for one night."

"Dad, hurry." Sam's voice was fraught with fear. "It's Maddie. I can't wake her up. She's not breathing."

Glass shattered in the sink as Rhyden dropped the plate he held and raced to Maddie's room. Flipping on the light, he saw her lips were turning blue. He checked for respirations and a pulse. "Call 911. Tell them we need an ambulance. Now."

He swept Maddie from her bed and placed her on the hard floor. Checked her airway and gave her two rescue breaths. He pressed her chest to make her blood circulate. To keep it moving to her brain. After fifteen compressions, he checked for a pulse. Still nothing. He resumed CPR.

Chapter Thirty-Five

Rhyden slumped into the hard plastic chair in the pediatric intensive care unit treatment cubicle. Beeps and whirs filled the room. Maddie looked like a small wax doll, her normally rosy complexion porcelain pale and clammy. Her lips still carried a tint of blue. A strangled sob escaped his throat as he clung to Maddie's limp hand.

Cat and her partner, Jim, responded to the house and were able to resuscitate Maddie, but his little girl wasn't out of the woods yet. As if thinking the words caused the worst to happen, alarms began blaring.

Rhyden leaped to his feet and stuck his head out of the curtain. "Help! Please, help."

A pediatric ICU nurse brushed past him. She checked the monitors, grabbed a rigid plastic backboard and shoved it beneath Maddie.

She climbed on top of the bed and yelled, "I need a crash cart! Someone get this father out of the room." Without waiting to see if anyone responded, she began chest compressions.

A herd of stampeding footsteps converged on the cubicle, a crash cart towed behind the lead nurse. The doctor shoved Rhyden out of the way. "You heard her. Nurse, remove this man."

A registered nurse grabbed Rhyden by the arm and tried to tug him out of the way. "This way, Sir."

He dug in his heels. "That's my baby girl. I'm not going anywhere."

She motioned to a burly orderly. "A little help here."

The orderly, his massive biceps barely contained by his green scrubs, approached. Rather than try to strong arm Rhyden, he lowered his voice and spoke calmly. "Sir, do you want what is best for your daughter?"

The Ranger glared at the other man. "Of course, I do. What the fuck kind of question is that?"

Wrapping a gentle hand around Rhyden's upper arm, the man replied, "Then let's get out of the doctor's way so he can do his job." When it appeared he might be met with resistance, the orderly tightened his grip. "Sir, we can do this the easy way or the hard way. Completely up to you, but you will leave this space."

Rhyden allowed himself to be led away and settled into a waiting area with a lukewarm cup of coffee. His throat tightened. His eyes burned hot. Stomach churning, he flung the scorched cardboard cup of coffee into the waste bin. He paced from corner to corner of the small waiting area, grateful to be alone.

He strained his ears, trying to hear what was happening in Maddie's cubicle. Minute after minute ticked by. More personnel and equipment swept into his daughter's treatment area. Occasionally, a harried-looking nurse darted out, grabbed something, and darted back in, but no one came to speak with him.

He collapsed onto the tiny sofa in the waiting area. He leaned forward, his shoulders drooping with the weight of the world on them while his hands dangling limply over his knees. The salty taste of tears slipped past his lips at the corners of his down-turned mouth. He swallowed his sobs.

Closing his eyes, he spoke to God. *Lord, please do not take my baby from me. I know I'm a sinner. I've failed as a father. I beg your forgiveness and your guidance. Please don't punish my little girl for my mistakes. I would gladly give you my life for hers. Give us another chance. In Your Son's Holy Name. Amen.*

Rocking in his seat, he stared at the clock. *Please, Lord, please.* The prayer played in his mind on repeat as he watched the minute hand creep around the face of the clock.

The brisk sound of footsteps approached the waiting room. Rhyden jumped to his feet as the exhausted doctor rounded the corner. As the doctor's words penetrated his skull, Rhyden dropped to his knees.

***

Sam's footsteps echoed on the pale gray tile as she walked down the white-walled, antiseptic-smelling hallway toward the waiting room. Splashes of color on the walls in the form of floral photographs broke up the sterile feeling of the hospital.

She stared blankly at the bag of chips rattling in her hands. *Why did I even get these?* She searched for a trash can. A hair's breadth before she turned the corner into the family waiting room, she heard Mikki and Noah arguing. She skidded to a stop and darted out of sight behind a curtain.

"I'm afraid he has a problem." Stress filled Mikki's voice. "He's addicted to those blasted pain pills. By this time, he shouldn't need them anymore. At least, not as many as he's taking daily. Where is he getting them? Do you know?"

"Mikki, first, now is not the time to have this discussion. I only called you about Maddie, in case he needed you. Second, I've known Rhy for a long time. He's not an addict. He's one of the strongest men I've ever known. What do you think he's doing? Sneaking around with his badge and gun and stealing them from drug dealers? His doctor prescribes them for him. The doctor wouldn't do that if he didn't think Rhy needed them."

The air conditioner kicked on, sending a shiver across Sam's skin. The noise made it harder for her to hear. She inched forward, not wanting to miss a word. This conversation shed a light on a lot of strange behaviors she had noticed in her dad.

Mikki raised her voice in frustration. "Look, Noah, I know he's your friend. But I know addiction. I deal with it every single day. Strength has nothing to do with it. Do you know how many people come to the emergency department with phantom pains, taking up our time and resources, chasing narcotics? I'm just saying I know a problem when I see one. And Rhyden has a problem."

Anger roughened Noah's voice. "Ranger Trammell is as solid as they come. He wouldn't take the pills if he thought he would get addicted to them. His plate is too full. Rhy loves his girls more than anything. He would never endanger them. If he thought he was developing a problem, he would stop taking them in a heartbeat, pain be damned."

Sam peeked around the corner. She watched as her dad's girlfriend tugged on her auburn hair and growled.

"Freaking Y chromosome." Mikki muttered under her breath. She dropped her hands to her hips and spoke up. "I get it. I really do. He's a good man. A good man who's been through a lot of bad things." She shrugged. "If you drop a frog into boiling water, it will immediately jump out. But if you put a frog in a pot of cold water and then turn on the burner, the frog gradually adapts to the temperature until it's too late. Addiction is like that."

"Mikki, if you want to talk to him, talk to him. I'm not going to. I don't think he has a problem. He would tell me if he did. If we're trading platitudes, Plato said wise men speak because they have something to say; fools speak because they have to say something. Rhy is my friend, and I'm not a fool."

"Aaargh, men! Will you please pull your

head out of your fourth point of contact and talk to him before it's too late? You've been partners and friends for a long time. He will listen to you way before he will hear me."

Sam stepped out from behind the curtain where she had hidden. She made eye contact with Noah. Nodding toward Mikki, she said, "She's right, you know. It's bad, and it's getting worse. You don't see the things I do."

Noah blew out a heavy breath. "Well, hell."

An exhausted, bedraggled Rhyden chose that moment to enter the waiting room. Sam raced to him. He folded her into his embrace. "She's going to be okay. They're keeping her overnight in the pediatric intensive care unit to be safe, but they promise she's going to be fine."

Sam's courage abandoned her. She sagged against her dad's chest. "What happened?" Tears streamed down her face.

"Why did she stop breathing like that? Dad, her skin turned blue!"

Rubbing a soothing hand on Sam's back, he held her tight. The thickness of unshed tears in the back of his throat caused his voice to crack. His chest tightened. Self-loathing consumed him. He made eye contact with Noah over Sam's head. "She said she had a headache, so she took two of my 'special' headache pills."

Sam shoved away from her father. Eyes wide, she glared up at him. "Special headache pills? Is that what you told her those fucking pain pills were? How did she even get a hold of them? Why were they where she could reach them? I told you that you needed to get rid of them, that they were going to ruin your life. I guess I was wrong, wasn't I? They almost took Maddie's life instead. Is that what you wanted? You want to get rid of all your kids so you can screw around with that stupid nurse?"

"Sam—" He reached for her as she

raced across the room and slammed her fist against the wall.

Noah stopped him. "Give her a minute. I didn't want to believe the girls about those pills. I stood up for you. But Sam's right. It's time you do something about it."

"You think I haven't tried? Do you have any idea what it feels like to have pain chewing you up from the inside out, twenty-four seven? To feel your body flayed by need? The constant wanting? I don't take the pills to get high. I take them to quit hurting. There's a difference."

"Says every addict everywhere. I should have seen it sooner. Rhy, you need help. Maddie could have died. Think about that. Your daughter could have died...dead. Gone forever. And it would have been your fault. What do you think that pain would feel like?"

Chapter Thirty-Six

Lawrence circled the hospital parking lot, searching for Sam's Opel GT or her dad's F150. Listening in on the BCSO radio traffic as he worked late at the shop, he overheard the ambulance call to Sam's house. He arrived at the hospital to search for her. They needed to talk. He needed to ensure he was still free from any negative law enforcement attention. Her comment about the Rangers suspecting him because he had access to county vehicles kept circling inside his head on constant repeat. He knew she didn't know he had a uniform and badge. Nor did he believe she suspected him. After all, she still showed up for work. *Her father wouldn't let her do that if they had any suspicion he was the serial rapist. Would he?*

Tonight, he drove one of the investigator's unmarked pickup trucks. With the light bar installed in the grill, the truck wasn't obviously a county vehicle. According to the investigator, the truck would stop running during a pursuit. *Little shit probably just chickened out and wants to blame it on the truck.* Lawrence had taken it up to 120 miles per hour with no problems other than a slight front end shimmy. *Time for new tires. Focus, Lawrence. Get back to the problem at hand. Come on, girl, where are you?*

***

Sam stormed out of the hospital. Worried about her baby sister, she couldn't stand to be in her father's presence for another minute. Her hands shook as she tried to insert the key into the lock on the Opel's door. The keys fell from her hand. She bent down and scooped them off the pavement.

"Sam! Where are you?" Her dad walked out of the emergency department entrance, calling for her. "We need to talk this out."

She stayed ducked down beneath the window of her car. *Don't see me, don't see me, don't see me.* Still hidden behind the car, she reached up and unlocked the door. For once she was glad that she hadn't gotten around to replacing the interior bulb in the car. She slipped into the car without catching her father's attention. Once in the driver's seat, she started the car and fled from the parking lot. She watched him in the rearview mirror as he chased after her, trying to flag her down. *Good luck with that. I know you can't run sixty miles per hour.*

Taking a deep breath, she blew it out as she cruised out of town heading to Bennett Lake. She needed to clear her head and bodies of water always helped. She would prefer the ocean, but she refused to drive two hours away from the hospital. She might have to return in a hurry. Part of her didn't believe her father when he said Maddie would be okay. *If she's going to be okay, why are they keeping her overnight? And in the pediatric ICU?*

Her dad had already lied to her about the pain pills and attending Narcotics Anonymous. *Why should I trust him?* He lied to Mikki, too. *I wonder how she will handle finding out he's a big fat liar?*

She rolled down the window, letting the sultry night air brush her face. Despite the wind whipping her hair into knots, it felt good. Necessary even. She needed the moving air to breathe. Her throat felt swollen. Her eyes burned from unshed tears. She blew out another deep breath. *Deep breathing is therapeutic, or at least that's what everyone says.*

Her head spun. The more she worried, the heavier her foot became on the accelerator pedal. She didn't even realize how fast she was going until the red and blue lights flashed in her rearview mirror. She glanced down at the speedometer. Liza Jane zipped along way above the posted speed limit. *Oh shit! I can't let that deputy catch me. He'll drag me back to Dad. I bet he pulled his Ranger card and put out a BOLO for Liza Jane.*

Sam pressed the accelerator pedal into the floorboard. Turning right at the first crossroad, she skidded around the corner. Hopefully that truck isn't as easy to handle as her Opel. She kept the accelerator floored and took the next left turn, followed by another right. When the truck disappeared from her sight, she darted into the nearest driveway, turning off the lights and engine. *Please don't let anyone be home.* She looked in the rearview mirror. A red glow lit the driveway behind her little car. *Dummy!* She jerked her foot off the brake pedal. *Nothing like making an awesome escape and being caught because your foot on the brake pedal gave away your location.*

Red and blue flashing lights came around the bend on the road. She sank down into the driver's seat until she was invisible to passing vehicles.

***

What the hell? Lawrence slammed his hand on the steering wheel. Pressure built behind his eyes. His heart pounded like it was trying to escape from his chest. The chase always invigorated him. So did playing hide-and-seek. "Olly, olly, oxen free," he whispered as he looked from side to side along the road. *Where did she go? I'll make her sorry she ran from me when I catch her.*

Chapter Thirty-Seven

"Looks like we found some nasty feathers." Maddie jumped on the bed, her platinum tresses flipping up and down with each bounce. She and her best friend from school giggled and sang, using wooden spoons as microphones. She grinned and strummed air guitar before the two girls screamed out the final lyrics "There's a bathroom on the right." Both girls collapsed onto the mattress in a gale of laughter.

Grandfather applauded. "Wonderful performance, Ladies." He wrapped Maddie in a tight hug. "I'm so glad you are feeling better, *Ebikuyuutsi.*"

Maddie wrinkled up her face. "Ebiku-what? Why do you call me that, Grandfather?"

He tapped her on the tip of her upturned nose. "It means roadrunner. I call you that because you are clever and fast."

Rhyden stormed into Maddie's room. "What the hell is going on in here?" He snapped at the girls. "Is all that screeching necessary?" He squeezed the bridge of his nose. The throbbing in his skull threatened to liquefy his brain. Or at least that's how the migraine felt to him.

"But, Daddy, we were putting on a show for Grandfather. You always let us..."

"Madeleine Louise Trammell, do we talk back in this house?"

Embarrassment stained Maddie's cheeks crimson. She tossed a glance over her shoulder where her friend huddled hiding behind the pile of stuffed animals adorning the bed. "But, Daddy..."

Rhyden glared a warning.

Behind him, now seated at Maddie's toy table with a tiny china tea set in front of him, Rhyden's grandfather, Daniel, shook his head at

Maddie, placing a finger over his lips in a shushing motion.

She bit her lip and dropped her head, hiding tears behind her mass of messy platinum ringlets. "No, sir," she muttered as she grabbed her friend's hand and tugged her from the room.

"That was a bit harsh, Grandson. Don't you think?"

"Grandfather," a warning tone entered his voice, "stay out of it."

Daniel stood from the chair at Maddie's tiny round table and patted his grandson on the shoulder. "Son, you know I am here when you are ready to talk." Quietly he slipped from the room.

Rhyden stood in silence for a moment before he shook his head. *What in the hell is wrong with me?*

Hours later, head still pounding,

darkness surrounded Rhyden. A small glow tried to creep into the room beneath the closed door. He leaned back in his desk chair. Small white oval pills spilled across the desk. He counted them one more time. *Damn it, that can't be right.*

A shiver chased the heat that danced up his spine. He reached for a full shot glass of whiskey. Set it back on the coaster on the corner of the desk. "Thanks, but no thanks," he muttered as he swept the handful of pills back into the prescription bottle.

The pain, like a dark creature, writhed inside his body. Wrapped itself around his bones. He felt as if he were being devoured from the inside out until nothing remained.

A door slammed in the other room. Laughter spilled through the house. To Rhyden, it felt like taunting laughter. He squeezed the prescription bottle in his hand, placed it reverently back into the bottom desk drawer, hidden by the file folders. Grabbing the shot glass, he threw the whiskey back. Swallowed the burn. Flipped on the overhead light in his home office.

"Samantha Elaine, I need to see you in here right now."

The door creaked open. Sam peeked her head into the room. "You wanted to see me, Dad?"

With a sharp movement of his head, he gestured for her to come into the room. "Where have you been?"

She shrugged. "Out. With friends."

Rhyden narrowed his eyes. "Which friends?"

"Jeez, Dad, just friends. Okay?"

"No, it's not okay. Come closer."

Gingerly, Sam stepped closer to her

father. Held her breath.

Rhyden sniffed the air. The scent of cheap beer tickled his nose. "Have you been drinking?"

"No, Dad, I haven't been drinking." She hiccuped. Giggled. "Well, not really drinking. We just had a couple of beers, that's all."

"And driving?"

"Just home. That's all. It's not like I'm drunk or anything. I've got a tiny buzz."

"Give me your keys. You're grounded."

Sam hid her keys behind her back. "No. That's not fair. It's my car. I bought and paid for it."

"You know what we say about fair in this family."

In a sarcastic, high-pitched pissy voice, Sam quoted, "Life and fair are both four letter words but that's all they have in common." Returning to a normal voice, Sam tried again, "Dad, no one was hurt. What's the harm in having a drink or two?" Her eyes lit on the empty shot glass sitting on the corner of the desk, a single drop of whiskey clinging to the inside wall of the glass. "You do it."

"I am not a minor. Nor am I driving. You're grounded for two weeks. Open your mouth again, it will be a month."

"But, Dad..."

"Want to try for two months?"

"You know what? At least I'm not popping pills and hiding the bottles in the back of a file drawer. I'm not the one with a substance abuse problem, am I?" Sam flung her keys at her father before she fled the room, slamming the door behind her.

The door opened again. Grandfather leaned against the doorjamb, a glass of iced sweet tea in his hand.

Rhyden shook his head and held up a hand. "Please. Not now."

Grandfather walked into the room and took a seat in front of the desk. "You know, Grandson, I knew this man once. Mean old man. He spent his entire life pushing everyone who cared for him away. And it worked. He fell in the pasture one day and broke his hip. He couldn't move. Didn't have a cell phone. Hell, no one to call even if he had had a phone. He lay in that field for days being devoured by fire ants. Those ants ate him alive. Killed him, they did. No one even knew he was missing. Wouldn't have cared even if they had known it. Vultures circling the pasture were the only reason anyone ever found his body.."

Grandfather stopped and took a sip of his sweet tea. Stared into the glass, rattled the ice. Finally, he looked up at his grandson. "Do you want to be that man? 'Cause if you keep pushing everyone away, that's what's going to happen to you." He set the glass on the corner of the desk and rose to his feet, grasping the back of the chair to steady himself. He lowered his voice. Shadows flirted through his eyes, whispering of ancient violence, almost forgotten evils. "I know it's the pills, son. For me, it was the alcohol. The Indian and firewater is a stereotype for a reason. I almost lost it all—your grandmother, your father, you. Get help, grandson. Get help before it's too late."

"Why won't anyone leave me alone about those damned pills? You were in the hospital. You saw what happened to me. I can't sleep. My brain whirls a million miles a minute. The fractured bones almost stole my vision. Every minute of every day it feels like someone is taking a fireplace poker, holding it in the flames until it glows red-hot, then shoving it down the marrow channel of my long bones. After they clean out the channel, they fill it with termites. Leave them there to chew their way out through my bones. And we haven't even gotten to the ice pick stabbing headaches yet. If you felt like that, you'd be reaching for pain pills, too."

"Death smiles at us all, grandson. All we can do is smile back… and choose how we want to live."

Rhyden clutched his hands in anger. He respected his grandfather more than any man alive, but Grandfather just did not understand. He never would. No one who hadn't lived his life could ever understand.

"Grandson, I know losing your father as young as you were hurt. I know having your wife murdered hurt worse, even after the way she treated you, abandoning you and those precious babies, but the way you're living now? Those secrets you're trying to keep are putting a callus on your heart. You're hurting yourself, and those girls, more than any of the rest. I know you think you are trying to keep Coyote the Trickster away from Sam by keeping his attention squarely on you, but it's not working. He's getting two for the price of one without even having to try."

"Grandfather..."

"You think I'm wrong?" Grandfather drew himself up to his full height, no longer clinging to the back of the chair. "I am Daniel Mukwooru Trammell, spirit talker of the Comanche tribe. Coyote whispers to me and laughs."

Chapter Thirty-Eight

Lawrence tapped his fingers impatiently on the leather-wrapped steering wheel as he waited for an opening in traffic. He flipped on the seat heater, enjoying the soothing heat on his lower back. *These investigators travel in luxury. No wonder the deputies all strive to join their ranks. Shame the people who do the most work reap the fewest rewards.*

"Shit." He reached beneath the dash and disconnected the GPS tracker on the truck before pulling out of the law enforcement center. "That could have been bad."

Pulling into the west-bound traffic, he turned the truck toward Old Kyote Road. Humming under his breath, he clicked on the radio mounted under the dash to listen to dispatch. He wanted to make sure he didn't stumble into any 'secret squirrel' shit sometimes thrown together by the wanna-be SWAT team.

He chuckled aloud. *SWAT. Right. Those idiots couldn't swat a lethargic fly in a tiny box.* Now his old man? That man didn't need SWAT. He was an old time badass. Cruising toward the lake, he let his memories drift.

His old man stretched out in his cracked leather recliner. It creaked beneath his weight. A drag race blared on the television set. He snapped nicotine-stained fingers and pointed at the refrigerator. His dad's flavor of the week—they rarely lasted more than a week, two at the most—jumped and fetched him a beer. The girl, barely out of her teens, waited beside his chair, staring at the floor and waiting for more instructions. He waved his hand in dismissal. She slunk back to the kitchen table where her own beer sat next to a cigarette smoldering in a thick, amber-colored glass ashtray. Close enough to jump when called, far enough away to not be in the way. Stringy blonde hair fell into her face, hiding the most recent black eye and bruised cheek from the last time she didn't maintain a proper distance.

Cracking the top of the beer can, he took a long swallow and belched. Gesturing to the girl huddled in the kitchen, he told his son. "That right there is how you treat a woman, boy." He looked his son up and down and snorted. "Not that you'll ever be man enough to do it."

The blare of a horn jerked Lawrence back to the present. He whipped the truck's wheel to the right, correcting his course and narrowly avoiding a head-on collision. The muscle in his cheek jumped as he ground his molars. Pulling to a stop on the shoulder of the road, he blew out a noisy breath. "Fuck!"

He glanced over at his "unique" toolkit sitting on the passenger seat. The duct tape had fallen off the seat and rolled around on the floorboard. Zip ties were scattered from hell and back. *Damn it! How would I explain all that?*

With shaking hands, he gathered his equipment and secured it in the tool bag. As he finished zipping the bag closed, the text notification on his phone sounded. He pulled back onto the road and resumed cruising speed.

His thoughts drifted to his plans. He imagined a helpless blonde. A flutter danced in his stomach quickening to match his increasing heartbeat. He licked his lips and smiled. He'd show his old man. He could too treat a woman the way she was meant to be treated.

The notification on his phone dinged again. Glancing at the home screen, he saw a text from Sam. He unlocked the phone and opened the text app.

'Hey boss. Sorry. Can't make it to work today. Paternal unit is forcing me to watch the brat.'

He responded. 'No worries.' A thought

occurred to him. 'What's your dad doing?'

'Some stupid stakeout.'

'Oh?'

'Yeah, him and the secret squirrels are hiding on Old Kyote Road. Even got one of the new female jailers pretending to be broken down on the side of the road.'

Lawrence slammed on his brakes. A cloud of dust boiled up behind the truck as the tires locked up and skidded on the shoulder of the county road. *Fuck! Fuck! Fuck!* He rocked back and forth in the driver's seat. Tremors raced down his arms into his hands. His breath caught in his throat. *I didn't even know they had a new female jailer.* He drove around planning an attack less than two miles from where a team of law enforcement hid out, waiting for him. Of course, they didn't know who they were waiting for. Nevertheless, this was way too close for comfort. *Bless you, Sam.* If it hadn't been for her text, he would have been busted.

Making a U-turn, he racked his brain trying to think of another hunting ground. Tilting his head against the headrest, he let out a heavy sigh. His eyes darted from side to side as he searched his memory for a deserted country road that would fit his requirements. Nothing came to mind. At least, nothing safe.

Lawrence slammed his hand against the pickup's dash. Climbing out of the truck, he slammed the door. He paced back and forth beside the truck, his steps jerky. Muttering to himself, he threw his hands around, talking with them. He paused and observed his surroundings. *Thank God no one is here.* Anyone seeing him would think he was off his rocker.

His hands slid up his temples into his hair. He grabbed clumps of it and tugged hard. This was all Ranger Trammell's fault. His nostrils flared. Cracking his knuckles, Lawrence swore he would make the Ranger pay. The beginnings of a plan flickered to life in his mind. *Sorry, Sam.*

In the meantime, he didn't know how much longer he could control the monster inside of himself. His hands twitched. The demon need raked its claws through his brain. A sharp pain stabbed above his left eye. He needed release—now.

Chapter Thirty-Nine

"Grandfather, are you sure you don't mind watching Maddie?"

Sam placed her compact of purple eyeshadows on the vanity, picked up her eyeliner, and leaned closer to her magnifying makeup mirror. With the precision and concentration of a professional, she closed one eye and skillfully traced it with black eyeliner, her mouth twisted open in concentration. She repeated the process with her other eye, leaving each with a slightly winged outline.

She turned towards the door, and her heart warmed at the sight of Grandfather leaning against the jamb, his eyes twinkling with affection. "Dad should be home before too long."

He crossed his arms over his chest. "Granddaughter, why do you bother with that paint for what you ain't? You should let your natural beauty shine."

Sam shook her head. Her curls bounced on her shoulders. "Mother Nature doesn't mind a helping hand now and then." She winked at her great-grandfather and turned back to the mirror to apply a light coat of midnight black mascara to her lashes. After she finished, her eyes appeared so blue that one could dive into their depths and become lost forever.

She skipped foundation and blush, opting to let the sprinkling of freckles across her nose stand out. A quick swipe of clear gloss over her full lips completed her look. "Besides, it's not like I wear a lot of makeup. Just a touch. For emphasis."

She took a step back from the bathroom mirror, her eyes scanning the reflection of her great-grandfather standing behind her. The harsh light of her makeup mirror illuminated the delicate lines on his weathered face.

"Are you absolutely, positively certain you don't mind?" she asked, her voice laced with a hint of uncertainty. As she bit her lower lip, she could taste the faint hint of her watermelon lip balm. She hoped Zane liked watermelons. He waited for her by the lake. She knew its shimmering surface would mirror the vibrant hues of the setting sun. She imagined the feel of his arms surrounding her as they cuddled by the crackling bonfire. The sparks of young love flared hot.

"I can always call Tanya and cancel." She shrugged. "It's not that big a deal." *Please don't make me cancel.*

Grandfather opened his arms and pulled Sam into a gentle hug. "Your sister and I will have a fine time. Go. Enjoy yourself. You're only young once."

Yes! In her mind, Sam triumphantly punched the air, the whooshing sound echoing in her ears. A sly smile curved her lips as she arched one eyebrow, feeling a surge of satisfaction coursing through her veins. "If you're sure…"

Suspicion entered his eyes. He released her from his embrace and held her by the shoulders at arm's length as he studied her face. "Is there something you aren't telling me? Some reason you are hesitant to attend this… " he waved his hand in a circle. "…fiesta?"

She fidgeted, rocking her weight from foot to foot. She twisted a curl around her finger, wrapping it around and around. An empty feeling swept through the pit of her stomach. She looked over her shoulder as if expecting her dad to be standing there. *I can't lie to Grandfather.* She didn't believe in his spirits, but he did. And somehow, he always knew when she lied to him.

"Samantha…" He let go of her and stepped back.

She straightened her spine, squared her shoulders, and raised her chin. Making firm eye contact with Grandfather, she confessed. "Dad grounded me." She took a deep breath, and the words rushed from her. "But it's not fair. I didn't do anything wrong. He took my keys. MY keys. I worked hard to earn the money to buy Liza Jane. She's my car. But it's okay. Tanya will give me a ride. It's those freaking pills. His entire world revolves around taking pills. And I promise I won't drink. Not a drop." Tears threatened to smear her makeup. She blinked repeatedly, holding them back from falling. She dropped her chin and lowered her eyes to the floor.

"I see." Grandfather rubbed his chin. He stared off into the distance as if listening to voices only he could hear. Finally, he nodded. "So be it."

He puffed his cheeks with air, much like a chipmunk hiding nuts, before blowing it out.

"Granddaughter, you know I would never countermand my grandson."

"But…"

He raised a hand, stopping her speech.

Sam's shoulders slumped. "I'll go upstairs and call Tanya. Tell her I can't make it."

He continued speaking. "However, the spirits are speaking to me." He held his hands in front of him as if they were a scale. "I must weigh your father's wishes against what my guides say."

He continued to raise and lower his hands alternately before tightening them into fists. He curled his fists toward his chest and then released them, dropping his arms to his side. "Just this once, I will help you defy your father. According to the ancestors, you will be needed."

Lines of worry etched his face. A

shadow haunted his dark eyes. He scrutinized her face and added, "But be aware. There will be a hefty price to be paid."

Chapter Forty

"I can't believe your grandfather helped you sneak out of the house. How cool is that?" Tanya squealed and bounced in her seat as she gleefully clapped her hands. "My grandparents would never go against anything my parents said."

Sam rolled her eyes. "As if your parents would ever ground their precious princess." She pulled the truck door closed and slipped on her seatbelt. As the latch clicked into the buckle, she glanced back at the doorway where Grandfather still stood, silhouetted by the lights inside the house. A sense of unease at his last words washed over her. She shrugged it off and turned to her best friend. A grin turned up the corners of her mouth and lit her eyes. "He's one of a kind. That's for sure."

Tanya put the truck in gear and pulled away from the curb. Within a few minutes, they left the populated area of town and turned onto a deserted county road. She motioned to the super-size sodas sitting in the cup holders on the center console. "Coke," she said. Pointing to the glove box, she added, "Let's introduce it to our friend, Jack."

"I can't. I promised Grandfather I wouldn't drink tonight."

Tanya shrugged. Her fuzzy, cream-colored sweater slid from one shoulder. "How's he going to know?"

"His ancestors will tell him."

"What?" Her best friend gave her a look filled with disbelief, eyebrows raised and mouth slightly agape.

"Never mind. He just will. He always does. So who's going to be at this party? Is it a big one?" *Not that I care who's there as long as Zane shows up.*

"I've never known you to care who comes to a lake party." Tanya wiggled her eyebrows. "Are you expecting anyone in particular? Like maybe a certain long-haired Monte-Carlo-driving gear head?"

Heat rushed up Sam's chest to her neck and face. She imagined she glowed vibrant red with little flames of embarrassment shooting from the top of her ears.

Her best friend gasped. "Oh my guacamole! You do like him." Her voice raised into a sing-song pattern. "Samantha and Zane sitting in a tree k-i-s-s-i-n-g." She wrinkled her brow. "But wait a minute. I thought the last time you saw him, you called him a misogynistic douche?"

"That was not our finest hour. I mean, how would you like it if your dad announced he was dating your boyfriend's mom? Add in a nosy little sister and a bunch of other people butting in, and neither of us handled it very well." She examined her fingernails with exaggerated casualness. "Soooo, is he going to be there?"

Tanya grinned. "Hand me the bottle from the glove compartment, and I'll tell you. I've already dumped part of the soda on the ground to make room for the good stuff. I'm not wasting it."

Sam cocked her head. "Um, aren't you driving?"

Tanya arched her eyebrows. "Weren't you driving the other night?"

With a snort, Sam said, "You win." She opened the glove box and reached for the bottle. As her fingers brushed the cool glass, red and blue lights lit up the rear windshield. Coming from the absolute darkness around them, the lights were stark and blinding. "Fuck me!" She slammed the door of the small cubby space closed and ducked below window level. She glanced at the time on the dashboard. "What do you want to bet my dad sent that deputy after us to drag me home? Overbearing control freak."

"Quick, before I stop, I'll turn the flashlight on my cellphone on, stick it out the window and wave my hand around to distract him. While he's watching me, you can lower the passenger seat all the way down, slip into the back seat, and hide on the floorboards. There's a blanket back there you can cover up with."

A weight settled in her stomach. She bit the inside of her cheek. Indecision caused her to hesitate.

"Come on, hurry and get ready." She watched the unmarked truck with the flashing lights close the gap between them. "Unless you have a better plan? Or want to deal with your father? No? Okay then, I'm rolling the window down now."

Sam ran alternate scenarios through her

mind. None had a snowball's chance in hell of succeeding. This one was at least a plan. *What the hell. If I'm busted, I'm busted. Maybe this will work.*

She squirmed over the console, trying to stay as flat as possible and avoid being seen. Tugging the blanket over her head, she stifled a sneeze. The blanket smelled of stale beer and mold. She squeezed her eyes closed and concentrated on making herself as small as possible.

The deputy pulled even closer to the tailgate and hit his siren. He lit up both sides of the county road with his spotlight.

Tanya gave a half-hearted shrug, engaged her turn signal, and eased to the side of the road. As her truck rolled to a stop, she slumped forward and let her head fall against the steering wheel with a solid sounding thump. In a stage whisper, she said, "My dad is going to kill me. I've already gotten three tickets, and that's just this month."

Before Sam could respond, a powerful white light flashed through the cab of the truck. "Ma'am, do you know why I stopped you?"

The light skimmed over the backseat. Sam held her breath. She kept herself perfectly still, not daring to peek out from under the blanket to see which deputy had stopped them. Something about his voice, even muffled by the heavy blanket covering her, was familiar but wrong, out of place. She knew that voice, but didn't think it belonged to an officer. *Who is that?*

A shiver of fear rattled down her spine. She strained her ears trying to hear more, trying to figure out why his voice bothered her so much.

"No, sir. Was I speeding?" Her best friend sounded breathy, flirty.

Oh, Tanya, don't. That doesn't work. Most of the time, it just irritates the officer and then you get a P-O-P ticket. All a 'pissing off the police' ticket accomplished was jacking up the fine. No wonder you've gotten three tickets in less than a month. Tucked away as she was in the back seat, she couldn't even nudge her friend to get her to shut up.

"Are you alone tonight? Where are you headed? Expected anywhere soon?"

Warning bells blared in Sam's head. *Deputies shouldn't be asking questions like that.*

"I need your license and insurance card, please." The truck door hinge squealed. "Please shut off the engine and step out of the vehicle."

The engine sputtered to a stop. A muffled rattling noise suggested Tanya was digging through her purse for her wallet. The click of a seatbelt being unfastened followed the crunch of gravel beneath boots barely reached

Sam's ears. "Sir, may I ask why you stopped me?"

No, Tanya, don't do it. Didn't your parents ever tell you to request a female officer before getting out of your vehicle? Sam's dad had always told her to remain polite but firm and not to get out of the car in an isolated spot with a male officer. She could hear his voice in her head as if he were in the truck beside her. 'Offer to drive to a well-lit, well-populated area or to the law enforcement center but never, ever get out of the vehicle until a second officer, preferably female, arrived on scene.'

Tanya giggled uncomfortably. "Oops. I guess I need some WD-40 on that door. Sounds like a haunted house. Um, excuse me, why did you put my license in your shirt pocket?"

"Shut the fuck up," the officer growled. The sound of flesh hitting flesh followed by a high-pitched scream split the air.

Sam heard a struggle outside the truck door. *Crap, crap, crap. What do I do?* Adrenaline pumped through her system. She had seen the previous crime scene photos when her dad forgot to lock his home office. Fear paralyzed her, but she couldn't let that happen to her best friend.

Hands shaking, she flung the blanket off and scrambled out of the back seat. She tripped over Tanya's oversized handbag, scattering its contents on the shoulder of the road. She fell onto the road, hitting her head against the open edge of the door. Gravel ground into her palms and knees. Warm blood dripped into her eyes from a cut on her forehead. She swiped the back of her hand across her face, clearing her vision. *Not that it did any good.*

Dark thunderheads covered the sky. Not even a hint of the moon shone through. The emptiness of the road and lack of light made her feel like she was drowning in a room void of windows, with no escape and no glimmer of hope. Dread soaked through her pores. "Tanya? Where are you?"

Muffled screams and ripping fabric reached her ears. She darted into the brush, pausing to listen for anything that might lead her to her friend. The impenetrable darkness blinded her. She patted her pockets, looking for her cellphone or anything she could use as a weapon. *Nothing*. The fall must have jarred the phone from her grasp when she hit the ground.

"Stop! Get off me."

Sam darted toward Tanya's voice. A meaty thwack followed by a man's voice cursing pulled her up short in her tracks. She dropped to her knees. Her hands scrabbled across the ground, searching for a big rock or a broken limb—anything she could find to protect herself.

A running figure brushed past her. She held her breath, praying he didn't turn back. He continued to crash through the brush, stumbling and cursing. When she couldn't hear him, she inched forward following the path of broken branches he had left in his wake.

A breeze whipped up, scooting the clouds across the sky. The moon's feeble light broke through, illuminating a scrap of Tanya's cream-colored sweater. She sprawled face down across the path.

Sam gasped, struggled for breath. No matter how much she inhaled, her lungs felt empty. Hands trembling, she pressed two fingers against her friend's icy skin. *Was this the price Grandfather's spirits referred to?*

Tanya blindly flailed her arms. "No! Get off me." With a wild motion, she kicked out with both feet, knocking Sam onto her butt in the dirt.

"Oh, thank God!" Tears streamed down Sam's face as she clung to Tanya. She wrapped her best friend in her arms as the other girl continued to fight against her hold. "Shhh, shhh. It's me. You're okay. I've got you. You're safe."

The girls pressed closer together, quivering with fear. Tremors swept through them both as they huddled together in the brush, sobbing.

She's alive. She's hurt, but she's alive. Sam tried to stand, but her legs wouldn't support her weight. Her muscles shook fiercely. She collapsed back onto the dirt. She leaned her forehead against Tanya's, blood from their respective wounds and their tears ran together and intermingled. Lifting her head, she brushed her friend's hair from her face and examined her.

Reddish-purple bruises were beginning to emerge on her cheek. Deep scratches encircled her throat, a visible sign of the ordeal she'd experienced. Her torn clothing—covered in prickly mesquite thorns, entwined twigs, a layer of dirt, and dried blood—provided evidence of the chaos she had faced.

Sam draped Tanya's arm across her shoulders and helped her stand. "Can you walk?"

The girl stumbled and swayed, but stayed on her feet. She nodded.

Carrying as much of her friend's weight as she could manage, Sam guided her out of the brush and toward the road. They stumbled, tripped over fallen mesquite limbs. With each step, Tanya leaned on Sam more. *Where is the truck?* Sam struggled to half-carry, half-drag her friend to safety. The headlamps were a welcoming beam in the oppressive darkness.

Sam propped Tanya against the side of the pickup as she struggled to open the door. *Thank God, it's unlocked.* Maneuvering her friend the best she could, she shoved her into the passenger seat and pulled the seatbelt across her chest, securing her in place before slamming the door shut.

Sam bolted around the truck bed, flinging herself into the driver's seat. Keys jingled in the ignition. Her hands trembled as she turned the key, the engine roaring to life. Gravel sprayed from beneath the truck's spinning tires; the vehicle lurched and fishtailed, but Sam wrestled it under control. Heart pounding, she tore off towards the nearest hospital emergency department.

"Tanya. Tanya! Are you still with me?" Sam tore her eyes away from the road to check on her friend. Tanya slumped forward in the seat, unresponsive, her seatbelt the only thing keeping her upright. *Is she breathing?*

Sam leaned over and used her hand to guide Tanya into an upright position in the truck seat. The unconscious girl slid sideways just as the truck hit a huge pothole. The impact jerked the steering wheel from Sam's grip. She turned

her attention back to the road in time to swerve,
narrowly missing a black cow that had wandered
into the roadway.

Breath caught in her throat, tried to claw
its way out of the tightened space. Spots danced
in front of her eyes. *We're gonna die.* Her hands
tightened on the steering wheel. *I'm going to flip
this truck, and we're going to die in a fiery
crash.* An involuntary whimper escaped her
throat. Nausea swamped her. Her skin prickled
with a cold sweat.

In the distance, the lights of the
hospital's ambulance bay cut through the gloom.
She skidded the truck to a stop in front of the
large glass doors. She stumbled from the
driver's side door and made her way around the
truck, clinging to the hood. Tugging the
passenger door open, she waved her arms and
yelled for help.

A passing orderly saw her and darted
out the door. Interpreting the scene in mere

seconds, he took charge, calling for additional help and a gurney.

As medical personnel carried Tanya from the front seat of the truck, Sam slid down the door until she collapsed on the ground. She curled into a ball, her arms wrapped around her knees, buried her face and wept.

A warm, soft blanket draped her shoulders. "Hey, you okay? Let's get you inside."

Sam raised her head to see her father's girlfriend kneeling in front of her. She drew back, shaking her head. "Please. No, you can't please. You can't tell him I was here."

Mikki raised her hands in a calming gesture, palms facing the panicked teen. "Easy. Easy now. Just breathe." She stepped back to give the girl room to stand. "Come on. Your friend is asking for you. Let's get you inside and sort this out."

Sam shook her head. The pounding of her pulse in her ears drowned out Mikki's words. She squinted her eyes, trying to read the nurse's lips, all the while repeating, "Please. Don't call him. You can't tell my dad I was here."

Running boots echoed through the hallway. A frantic male voice called out. "Where is she? Where is my daughter?"

Chapter Forty-One

"Whooooo!" Lawrence slammed the front door open and strutted through it. Adrenaline still pumped through his veins as he stood in the middle of his decrepit living room, panting heavily. Beads of sweat trickled down his flushed forehead. The room, cluttered with old furniture and worn-out belongings, was now filled with an air of triumph and satisfaction.

With a mischievous grin on his face, Lawrence surveyed the small space. The front door, now ajar, creaked softly on worn hinges in the aftermath of his forceful fling. The room itself seemed to have come alive, as if awakened from its slumber by Lawrence's exuberant entrance.

His tool kit, a battered and well-used companion, landed on the threadbare sofa with a thud. The worn-out cushions barely absorbed the impact, causing a cloud of dust to rise from the old fabric. Lawrence paid no mind to the mess he had created; he was too busy reveling in the thrill of his recent adventure.

As he sauntered further into the room, his footsteps echoed against the faded linoleum floor. The sound reverberated through the small space, intertwining with his racing heartbeat. Lawrence's body language oozed confidence and satisfaction, his shoulders thrown back and his chest puffed out.

The room itself seemed to respond to Lawrence's energy. The dim, flickering light bulb hanging from the ceiling appeared to burn a little brighter, casting a warm glow on the worn-out walls. Walls covered with warped paneling, once dull and lifeless, seemed to shimmer with newfound vitality.

Lawrence couldn't help but let out a chuckle, a mixture of adrenaline and contentment. His eyes darted around the room, taking in every detail, as if imprinting the memory of this moment in his mind. His crappy efficiency, once a place of monotony and boredom, had transformed into a canvas of his triumph.

In that moment, Lawrence relished the feeling of accomplishment. The rush of excitement still coursed through his veins, fueling his sense of self-assurance. He couldn't wait to embark on more exhilarating adventures, leaving his mark on the world one fake traffic stop at a time.

He dropped down beside his kit and kicked off his boots. He floated on the high from dominating and controlling that girl. Digging into his shirt pocket, he plucked out her driver's license and skimmed the front of it. *Tanya, sweet blonde Tanya.*

He flipped the license between his fingers. Noticing a splotch of blood on his knuckles, he flicked his tongue out and licked it off.

Stretching his arms over his head, he felt his spine pop. He rolled his shoulders and stood. He unbuttoned his shirt as he headed into the kitchen. Dropping the license onto the top of the chipped formica table, he shrugged off the shirt and draped it over the back of a cracked red vinyl-covered kitchen chair. He scrubbed the remaining blood spatters from his hands.

Da-yum, that felt good. He poured a slug of whiskey into a crystal lowball glass. His dad's glass and beside his nine-millimeter pistol, most likely the most expensive thing in the apartment. He raised the glass in a toast to the ghost of his father. "See, Dad, you aren't the only 'real man' in the family."

"You call that being a real man. Boy, you don't have the first clue how to be a real man. A real man wouldn't have let the little whore go."

Lawrence shook his head, trying to dislodge his old man's voice from his head.

"Pansy. The only women you can get are little girls that you grab off the side of the road. A real man reels them in like a bass on a lure, gets them hooked, and then shows them who's boss."

"Stop it. Shut up!" He flung the glass across the room. It bounced off the wall and rolled into the bedroom area. Whiskey ran down the paneling adding yet another stain.

"Can't even break a glass, can you? And what about that other girl?"

Lawrence rubbed his fingers up his nose between his brows. "What other girl?"

Haunting laughter echoed inside his head. A bright aura flashed behind his eyes. The pressure of a migraine built.

"What other girl?" He spun in a circle. His eyes bounced from spot to spot around the room. "What girl?" White noise echoed in his skull. He grabbed his temples and dropped to his knees. Banged his forehead against the carpet.

"You know what girl. That sassy little pet you keep around the shop. The one who laughs at you behind your back, your so-called apprentice."

"Pet? Sam?" He raised his head from the floor. Sitting up, he leaned back against the wall. He blinked his eyes. Squeezed the back of his neck. "What about Sam? What does she have to do with anything?"

That laughter filled his mind again.

Lawrence stumbled to the bedroom and collapsed face-down across his unmade bed. He squeezed his eyes closed. Acid roiled in his stomach, trying to escape up the back of his throat. The room spun. He tried breathing exercises to stave off the nausea—blowing out completely emptying his lungs, inhaling shallowly. At a snail's pace, he regained control of his body.

Rolling onto his back, with an arm draped across his eyes, he replayed the events of the evening through his mind.

The feel of the gravel beneath his tires as he slid to a stop behind the silver pickup truck. The flash of motion in the front seat as a light blazed out of the driver's side window. *What* was *that movement?* He remembered the girl's flirtatious giggles, the look in her eyes as she realized she was in real trouble, the feel of her luscious golden lion's mane of shoulder length hair. The front of his jeans tightened as he remembered her screams of terror. Screams so loud they sent wildlife scattering through the brush.

"Focus, boy! Or your ass is going to end up under the jail."

Lawrence jerked straight upright. The flash of movement from the front seat of the pickup, combined with the scrambling noises in the brush, threw a different light on the situation. *That wasn't wildlife. It was a witness.* He scrambled out of the tangled covers and darted into the kitchen. He scooped the driver's license off the tabletop. "Tanya Westmoreland. Fuck, fuck, fuck! Tawny Tanya… Sam's best friend."

He slammed his fist through the sheetrock. Those two girls never went anywhere alone. The witness had to be Sam.

Chapter Forty-Two

Yellow and black crime scene tape attached to temporary wooden stakes flapped noisily in the night breeze, competing with the roar of the generators powering the mobile searchlights. The flickering lights cast eerie shadows on the rugged terrain, adding to the chaotic symphony of sights, sound, smells and feelings that made up the crime scene. Acrid smoke from warning flares hung in the air, adding a burned scent to the atmosphere.

The weight of the investigation lay heavy on Rhyden's shoulders. All around him, deputies from the sheriff's office climbed through the dense undergrowth. The beams of their powerful LED flashlights sliced through the darkness as they searched the brush for disturbed earth, drag marks or footprints. Moving slowly, they searched for scraps of fabric or discarded condoms. Many of them had cell phones in hand, videotaping their search efforts.

A slight metallic tang of spilled blood mingled with the faint scent of damp soil and decaying leaves. Each rustle of leaves and crack of twigs heightened his senses, filling him with a mix of anticipation and unease. A quick glance at the cloud-laden sky confirmed his feeling of urgency. It wouldn't be long before the heavens opened up and potential evidence washed away.

"Nothing like inviting the fox into the henhouse," he muttered to himself. He watched deputies and investigators alike clamber through the brush. *Anyone of these men could be the rapist.*

Weaving between the bright orange traffic cones blocking off the right-hand lane of the moonlit county road, Noah dodged around the deputy who waved the few remaining vehicles onward. He unfolded his lanky frame from the seat of his Challenger.

Rhyden waved him over. He held a clear evidence bag containing scraps of cream-colored cashmere. "This match the sweater our victim was wearing?"

His partner examined the scraps of cream-colored cashmere, comparing them to the image of the victim's sweater in his mind. He nodded. "Appears to."

He placed the bag into the oversized large brown paper grocery-type bag. "Hey, thanks for taking the hospital side of things tonight. I just couldn't deal with Mikki right now."

"No worries. She had her hands full with the victim's father." He surveyed the scene. "Do you think it's a good idea to have all these deputies out here?"

"No, not really." Rhyden scrubbed his face. The ache in his leg intensified. He glanced at his truck with longing. With a sharp shake of his head, he pulled his attention back to his best friend. He shrugged. "The call came into dispatch over the 911 line. How was I supposed to keep them from responding?"

Noah tilted his head to the side in acknowledgement. "Good question."

"Ranger Trammell?" A deputy called out from the brush, waving his flashlight in the air. "Can you come here, sir?"

Rhyden, followed by Noah, headed to where the deputy waited. "What do you have?"

The young man, peach fuzz sprouting on his chin, pointed to the ground. "I found a series of weird footprints."

The Rangers exchanged a weighted look.

"Weird, how?" Rhyden asked.

"The weight distribution is off."

Noah butted in, "Like the toes of the shoe are empty?"

"Yes, sir, but it looks more like a boot than a shoe. A big boot."

Rhyden patted the deputy on the shoulder. "Good catch, son. Make sure you get measurements, photographs, and casts of those prints. Let me know when the casts are ready and I'll transport them." The Rangers moved out of earshot before Rhyden spoke again. "Fuck. Well, if we weren't sure before, we know it's the same guy now."

"How's Sam handling things?"

Rhyden's face contorted into a deep frown as he replied, "What's Sam got to do with anything? She's at home with Maddie."

Noah raised an eyebrow, his expression questioning. "Do you know who the victim is? Or how she got to the hospital?"

"Just that she's a seventeen-year-old girl. I didn't wait around for more details. I needed to get out here and keep an eye on the deputies. I didn't want to take a chance that evidence might walk away." His confusion deepened as he watched his partner's face twist with a mixture of concern and determination.

Noah sighed. The lines etched on his forehead deepened. "The victim, the seventeen-year-old girl? It's Tanya. You know? Tanya, Sam's bestie," he revealed. His voice heavy with emotion, he added, "Sam took her to the hospital. She begged Mikki not to say anything but—"

"Just because Sam took her to the hospital doesn't mean she was here. Maybe Tanya called her."

He shrugged and turned away from his buddy. Dropping his eyes to the ground, he scanned the shoulder of the road. "Hey, what's this?" Tugging on a pair of latex gloves, he scooped a cell phone with a shattered screen from the ground. He pushed the home button. "Shit."

"What?"

"I thought you said Sam was at home with Maddie?" Noah asked, his voice filled with concern.

"She's grounded. Where else would she be?"

Noah tossed the phone to Rhyden. "It's Sam's."

"What the...?" Rhyden caught the phone and examined it carefully. His eyes widened in recognition. His breath caught in his throat. The realization hit him like a sudden shockwave, sending shivers down his spine. The bag holding the shreds of Tanya's sweater suddenly felt heavier. "Sam? My Sam was here?"

As they stood there, the gravity of the

situation sinking in, Rhyden felt a swirling mix of emotions rise within himself. Anguish, fear, and anger combined with a deep sense of responsibility. Everything else, every ache, every pain, every craving, faded away in reaction to the emotions.

Noah placed a comforting hand on Rhyden's shoulder, their shared determination clear in his gaze. "We will find out who did this, Rhy. And we will make sure he pays... and pays dearly."

Rhyden nodded, a steely resolve replacing his initial shock. They needed to find answers, and they needed them now.

Chapter Forty-Three

A scream ripped Sam from her uneasy sleep. Moments passed before she realized the screams came from her. Stifling the noise with a fist shoved into her mouth, she kicked her legs free from her mussed covers.

The room felt suffocating, the air heavy with the lingering scent of fear. Sam's heart pounded in her chest, its rhythmic thumping echoing in her ears. The moonlight crept in through a crack in her light-blocking curtains. It cast eerie silhouettes that danced on the walls, looking for all the world like figures fighting, struggling in the shadows. The sound of her rapid breaths filled the silence, punctuated by the distant call of a lone coyote outside. Every muscle in her body trembled, her palms slick with perspiration. She clenched her fists, trying to steady herself.

Her secret weighed her down, crushing her and devouring her ability to sleep. Each time she closed her eyes. Tanya's desperate cries for help echoed endlessly in her brain. The nightmare wouldn't release her, even when awake. *Why had she hidden?* She wasn't a coward. She didn't run from danger. *Why hadn't she gotten to her best friend sooner? Why hadn't she stopped him?*

Beads of cold sweat formed on her forehead, trickling down her face like tiny rivulets of fear. Guilt settled upon her shoulders, causing them to slump under its unbearable burden. Her trembling hands clenched into fists, nails digging into her palms, seeking an outlet for the overwhelming emotions that consumed her.

The room felt smaller; the walls closing in on her, squeezing the air out of her lungs. Every breath became a struggle, each inhale shallow and suffocating. The darkness seemed to grow thicker, wrapping around her like a shroud, strangling her, taunting her with its relentless grip. She whimpered.

In the depths of her mind, Tanya's voice echoed like a haunting refrain, a constant reminder of her own failure. The sound reverberated, amplifying the torment she felt, amplifying her regret. Her friend's pain, and her own complicity in it, bore down on her with an unforgiving force, crushing her and leaving her gasping for reprieve.

She lay in bed, her eyes staring but not seeing. The shadows of the trees outside her window danced on the ceiling, grabbing her, pulling her back into the brush on the side of the deserted road. Her room felt like a prison. The echoes of Tanya's cries grew louder, more insistent, tearing through the fabrics of her thoughts, relentless in their accusation.

Most importantly, why couldn't she remember where she had heard his voice before? Sam knew the rapist, but her mind blocked his identity.

The door to her room creaked open. The

side of her bed sagged as her dad sat on it. "Sam, sweetie, we need to talk."

The sound of her dad's voice sent a shiver down Sam's spine, causing her heart to race. Her body tensed up, and she could feel her palms becoming clammy with anxiety. His presence on her bed made her stomach churn, and a knot formed in her throat, making it hard to swallow. She squeezed her eyes closed and pretended to be asleep.

Despite her best efforts to feign sleep, Sam knew her dad knew she was awake. And she knew he knew that she knew. Her eyes drifted open.

Her dad's concerned gaze met hers, searching for answers and seeking the truth. "Where are you, Sam? What are you thinking? What's going on?"

Sam took a deep breath. *Okay. You can do this.* She shifted uncomfortably under her dad's gaze. She combed her fingers through her tangled curls, chewed on her cuticles. Avoiding eye contact, her voice just above a whisper, she responded, "Nowhere." She shrugged and pulled the quilt tighter around herself. She looked from the door to the window and back. Her gaze roamed the room, still avoiding her father's eyes. "I don't know. Everywhere. Here."

Rhyden sighed. His weight shifted on her bed causing the springs to groan. Sam chewed on her fingernails. She couldn't bring herself to look at him, fearing the disappointment she knew would be etched on his face. She could sense the mix of emotions swirling in the room—frustration, anger, worry, and a touch of sadness flavored with disappointment.

Finally, he broke the silence. "Samantha…" He paused and brushed the sweat-soaked curls from her forehead. Concern colored his voice. Without another word, he reached into his pocket and retrieved her cell phone. He handed it to her.

A sob escaped Sam's tightening throat. A surge of regret washed over her. Her knuckles whitened as she clutched the phone. She turned her face away to avoid her father's penetrating gaze.

"Oh, baby, I'm so sorry. I know about Tanya. What happened?"

Silent tears streamed down her face as she shook her head in denial.

After a shared moment of silence, Rhyden said, "Sam, we need to talk about this. You're not in trouble. I love you, but I need—Tanya needs—your help. Talk to me."

Tremors shook her body. She bit her lower lip, torn between the fear of judgment and the need to seek vengeance for her best friend. *If anyone can help you get justice, you know your dad can. Tell him. He already knows. He's your dad and he loves you. You know he does.* Guilt swamped her. "I-I can't."

"Sam." Rhyden stammered. "He didn't… I mean, you weren't… Did he…"

"Oh, Dad!" Sam sat up and clutched her father. *I never thought he would think that.* She clung to him. "No, nothing like that. I just… I couldn't save her, Dad. I hid. Like a coward. I hid and I couldn't save her. How can you stand to be near me?" Sobs tore from her aching throat.

"Shh, sweetie." He rubbed her back in soothing circles. "It's okay. You did what you could. You did everything possible. Sam, you got Tanya to help. Things could have been much worse."

She pulled away from her dad and scrubbed at her cheeks with her hands. Anger-induced heat flashed through her body. She gritted her teeth. "But, I didn't, Dad. I didn't. I couldn't stop him. And I know who he is."

Shock widened Rhyden's eyes. His nostrils flared. "You what?"

"I know who he is." Sam slammed her fists against the side of her head. "I know, but I can't remember. It's locked inside this worthless brain."

A slack expression crossed his face. He filled his cheeks with air and blew it out noisily. He took another deep breath. "Wait a minute. What are you saying, Samantha? Did you see him? Recognize him?"

"I recognized his voice." She collapsed back against the pillows. Anguish filled her voice. "I know him, but I can't remember who he is or where I know him from."

Chapter Forty-Four

With his head resting in his hands, Lawrence rocked back and forth in the worn leather chair behind his cluttered desk in the darkened shop. Working hours were long past. The rhythmic creaking of the chair echoed in the small space, mingling with the distant sound of traffic outside. The scent of gasoline and leaking coolant permeated the air, intermingled with the faint aroma of burned coffee from earlier in the day. As his father's voice grew louder in his mind, Lawrence could feel the weight of disappointment bearing down on him. His father's voice had been invading his mind more frequently. Always ranting about how disappointed he was in his son.

He jumped to his feet. "I'll show you." Forgoing his ritual preparation of dressing in his father's uniform and oversized boots, he grabbed his hidden tool kit and a set of keys from the board of patrol vehicle keys hanging by the door. He slammed out of the shop, not caring who saw him. The need was too strong.

As the fading pink-orange glow of the sun descended beneath the distant horizon, casting its final golden rays across the desolate stretch of county road, an eerie darkness engulfed the landscape, shrouding it in mysterious shadows. With bated breath, he bided his time in his vehicle, silently observing, his surroundings enveloped in a profound stillness. He waited, lights off, parked discreetly on the fringes of the shoulder.

A lone car approached, its headlights carving through the darkness like a blade. A blade similar to the one tucked into the sheath on Lawrence's belt. He sat upright in the Tahoe, his breath shallow with anticipation. He felt his adrenaline surge as the vehicle drew closer. *I'm doing things my way this time.*

The sporty convertible coupe zipped past him, its vibrant red paint glimmering under the fading rays of sunlight. In that fleeting moment, he glimpsed flowing, sun-kissed blonde hair. Reacting swiftly, he switched on his headlights and overheads simultaneously, effortlessly slipping in behind the speeding car. Engaging the sirens, the piercing, high-low, yelping wail sliced through the air, amplifying the urgency of the chase. With every nerve on edge, it felt as if the entire world spun in sync with the blaring siren.

He cranked up the volume on his radio, blasting hard rock through the speakers on the dash. Tapping on the steering wheel in time to the music, he was almost disappointed when brakes lights flashed from the vehicle in front of him. *I would have enjoyed a short chase.*

With a shrug, he shut off the sirens and the radio, leaving the red and blues flashing. He eased to a stop on the shoulder of the road behind the convertible. He turned on the spotlight mounted on the driver's side of the

Tahoe and swept it across the coupe. Not taking any chances this time. Once he knew the driver, the female driver, was alone in the vehicle, he stepped out of his and sauntered up to where she waited.

"Ma'am." He tipped his cowboy hat to her. "Do you know why I stopped you?"

The young woman, voice trembling, replied, "No, sir, I don't."

"Would you like to know?" He smirked and held out his hand. "Driver's license and proof of insurance, please."

As she dug in her handbag, her fingers trembled with a mix of anxiety and anticipation. Finally, her fingertips brushed against the smooth surface of her wallet. With a quick, shaky breath, she pulled it out.

Carefully, she opened the wallet, revealing the neatly organized cards inside. Her license, with its official seal and her photograph, stood out prominently. With a slight tremor in her voice, she uttered, "Here you go."

Her eyes darted fearfully between him and her license, waiting for his reaction. The seconds seemed to stretch into eternity as she anxiously awaited his response.

"Please remove the license and hand it to me."

She complied. "Why did you stop me?"

He stuck the driver's license in his shirt pocket and closed his fingers around the door handle. He jerked the door open. "Ma'am, step out of the vehicle. Now."

She hesitated, so he grabbed her by the upper arm and forced her from the vehicle. Abruptly, he spun her around and secured her hands behind her back with flex cuffs.

Fear radiated off the driver like a palpable force. Her breath hitched, her eyes widening in terror as she identified the sinister smirk that appeared on his face. She screamed and struggled against his grasp. Slamming her head backwards, she struck him in the face.

Growling, he rubbed his bruised cheek. "Now, that wasn't very nice, was it?" He dragged her to the patrol vehicle and shoved her into the backseat. Grabbing the duct tape from his tool kit, he silenced her screams, wrapping the tape around and around her head.

Humming beneath his breath, he climbed back into the driver's seat and put on his seatbelt. Catching her eyes in the rear-view mirror, he smirked again and asked, "Comfy?"

***

Lawrence moved with a predatory grace that usually escaped him when tripping around in his father's boots. Blending into the shadows that clung to the abandoned buildings, he stood in a room tainted with the stench of decay, blood, and feces. The flickering light from a camp lantern cast an eerie glow on his face.

His heart pounded in his chest, a wild rhythm that matched the adrenaline coursing through his veins. The young woman, bound and gagged, lay motionless on the cold, gritty floor. As he stood there, his eyes fixated on her, a twisted smile played upon his lips. The thrill of power surged through him. The struggle had been brief, but brutal.

His gaze lingered on the young woman's face. Her brilliant green eyes were now dull and lifeless. He had enjoyed watching the wide, terror-filled eyes as life fled from them. He basked in the knowledge that he had extinguished that spark, extinguished it with his own hands.

He could still feel the remnants of the struggle, the memory of her feeble attempts to break free. Reveled in the remembered chaos, the desperate muffled pleas he assumed were for mercy. It was a dance of power and control, a sick game he relished. He had never taken the game this far before, never taken another life. The young woman's lifeless form was a testament to his dominance, a trophy of his twisted desires. *See, Dad, I won.*

As he gazed upon her, a sinister hunger ignited within him, eager for the next victim to satiate his insatiable thirst for power. *Why the hell did I wait so long?*

He examined his hands in awe of the power they had held over her fragile life. *Still think I'm not man enough, Dad? Bet you never had the balls to finish it, did you? If you had, maybe you wouldn't have gone to prison. Maybe you'd still be alive.*

Chapter Forty-Five

Rhyden approached the blocked-off crime scene on foot, taking in as many details as possible. Flashing red and blue lights lit up the sky, reflecting off the ground-hugging fog. Flares closed both lanes of the road. Deputies. in bright yellow reflective vests, stood ready to wave off traffic—if any traffic ventured down the deserted thoroughfare. The air was redolent with the smell of burned rubber and gasoline.

A young, blonde woman lay sprawled, face up, across the center of the pavement. Her hair fanned out like a cloud of spun silk contrasting strongly against the pitch-black, oily pavement. A dual-wheeled pickup, its front grill adorned with roadside vegetation, rested in the ditch on the opposite side of the road The tick, tick, tick of its cooling engine showed the vehicle had not been sitting long. The flickering lights cast an eerie glow on the abandoned truck, its shattered windshield glinting in the darkness.

Rhyden's hands trembled as he crouched down beside the lifeless body. He rubbed the back of his neck before tucking his hands into his pockets. His jaw tightened as he fought the urge to return to his truck for another pain pill. Standing, he approached a nearby investigator. "What happened here? Why was I called out for a pedestrian motor vehicle 10-50?"

The investigator glanced at the Ranger, his expression one of exhaustion and discomfort, before he replied, "Not an accident. That guy" the deputy gestured toward a man slumped against the base of an ancient oak tree, "ran off the road, trying to avoid what he thought was a bundle of clothes dumped in the road. Based on the scene, I'd say she was murdered somewhere else and dumped here. Checking out the condition of her clothing, she was most likely sexually assaulted as well. Chief gave orders to contact you."

Rhyden's jaw clenched as he surveyed

the surrounding area with fresh perspective. The victim lay sprawled on the ground, limbs twisted at unnatural angles. Green eyes covered with the milky film of death stared unseeing into the night. He tugged on a pair of latex gloves and crouched beside the body. "Okay if I move her?"

"Yeah, photographer finished already."

Rhyden examined the crime scene with a methodical precision, gently rolling the girl to view markings and wounds on her back, looking for detritus beneath her body. "Someone make sure her hands are bagged before they transport her, please."

Who the hell are you? A gnawing sense of urgency settled in his gut as he contemplated the shadows that possibly concealed evidence leading to the identity of the assailant. *I will find you. I will find you soon, and you will wish you had never been born.*

His partner, Noah, squatted beside him.

"Damn. He's escalating. This is the first one he's killed, isn't it? If it's the same guy?"

"Oh, it's the same guy." An intense shot of fear slammed through Rhyden. Sam had barely avoided this monster. A shiver raced down his spine. His mind worked to piece together the puzzle of the suspect's madness. He felt the weight of the victims on his shoulders, the weight increasing with each victim, multiplying many fold with this death. Their pleas for justice reverberated inside his skull. A burning determination to stop this madman fueled a fire within Rhyden.

As the moon threw macabre shadows across the landscape, Rhyden's radio crackled to life. A voice from dispatch requesting he call the office—immediately. Stepping away from the other officers, he dialed his cellphone.

"Bennett County dispatch, how may I help you?"

"Ranger Trammell here. You needed me?"

"Sir, sorry to disturb you, but your daughter called. Said she needs you to contact her. It's an emergency. She sounded hysterical. We offered to send a deputy to her, but she wouldn't tell us where she was, and she didn't call the 911 line so we couldn't track her location beyond the nearest tower."

Rhyden thanked the dispatcher and hung up. Glancing at this cell phone, he noticed several missed calls and text messages from Sam. As he dialed Sam's number, his heart raced with a mix of curiosity and concern. His palms grew clammy. Each ring felt like an eternity, amplifying the anticipation building within him.

His mind raced with a myriad of possibilities, wondering what could have prompted such urgency from Sam. Especially after their earlier conversation. *Was she in trouble? Had something happened?* The uncertainty ate at him, creating an ever increasing tension in his chest.

With each passing moment, the suspense intensified. Rhyden's free hand involuntarily clenched into a tight fist, his knuckles turning white. He could feel the adrenaline coursing through his veins, heightening his senses and keeping him on edge.

After what felt like an eternity, the call connected. Rhyden's grip on his cellphone tightened as he held it to his ear. The physical effects of his emotions manifested in a shallow, quickened breath that escaped his lips in short bursts. His brows furrowed, creating a slight crease of worry on his forehead. *Why wasn't she answering?*

Finally, the tension broke as Sam's voice filled his ear. The sound was a mixture of relief and apprehension, further fueling the rollercoaster of emotions within him. Rhyden's shoulders relaxed slightly, releasing some of the built-up tension that had settled there.

"Dad? Daddy?" Tears choked her voice. "I need you. It's Tanya. Can you come, Daddy? Please?"

Chapter Forty-Six

Rhyden rushed up the cobblestone pathway towards the house, his footsteps echoing softly in the still night. The pale, silver light of the rising moon cast a spooky glow upon the potting soil and the shards of shattered flowerpots scattered haphazardly across the front porch. A faint scent of damp earth mingled with the muggy night air as he cautiously approached the open mahogany door, its glass panels reflecting the moon's gentle radiance.

Despite the inviting warmth emanating from within, a sense of foreboding gripped him, causing a cold tremor to race down his spine. As he stepped inside, a disheartening sight met him. A trail of destruction stretched from the entranceway towards what he presumed to be the living room. The air felt heavy with tension, and an unspoken fear hung in the atmosphere, intensifying his unease. "Sam?"

"Dad! Back here. Be careful. She's got a gun."

Rhyden's heart raced. His daughter was in a room with an unstable rape victim—who had a gun. *Fuck!*

The fluorescent light hanging in the kitchen buzzed like an angry hornet. The smoke from a scorched pan on the stovetop hung heavy in the air. He scanned the room. Empty. A single chair lay on its side beside the kitchen table. The door leading to the backyard hung ajar. The hairs on the back of his neck prickled. Crossing to the stove, he snapped off the burner and placed the burned pan in the granite sink. "Sam? Tanya? Where are you?"

A wavering voice called from outside the door. "Dad? Out here."

"Sam, baby, are you okay?"

"I'm fine, Dad. But Tanya needs help."

Hands held palms up in front of him, Rhyden nudged the back door open with his foot. Cautiously, he stepped through the opening. A street lamp cast long shadows across the yard. His eyes searched the darkness for his daughter. She kneeled in front of Tanya, her hands wrapped around the chains of the swing where her best friend perched. He gestured with his head for Sam to go inside.

Reluctantly, she stood and met her father's gaze. She searched his eyes. Apparently satisfied with what she found, she nodded. She squeezed Tanya's shoulder in support. "He'll help you. I promise." With one last glance at her dad, she headed back into the house.

Tanya sat on the swing's edge, her boots scraping against the crimson dirt below, a striking figure clad in torn jeans and a paint splattered t-shirt, outlined against the bruised sky. Her eyes, as dark as the weathered Glock she gripped, held unwavering determination. Not a hint of fear lingered in her gaze.

Rhyden dropped onto the swing next to her and waited. Trucks rumbled past on the nearby highway, filling the oppressive silence draped across the backyard. He watched moths dance around the streetlight until she spoke.

"You came." Tanya's voice was a rasp, raw from unheard screams. Bruises circled her throat from the rapist's attempt at strangulation,

"Sam called me."

"Doesn't mean you'd come. Thin blue line and all that."

"He threatened you. Used the badge." Rhyden stated, making it a statement, not a question. *Son-of-a-bitch. The arrogance...*

She huffed a laugh. "You could say that." She caressed the pistol in her lap. "But I'm not afraid of him. Not afraid of you. Not afraid of your badge-wearing buddies, either." She met his eyes, hers devoid of emotion. "Fear lets the bad guys win." She shook her head. Caressed the gun again. "He's not winning. Not this time."

"Tanya, hand me the gun."

"No." It wasn't a defiant shout, but a flat, resolute statement. Somehow, that scared him more. One wrong word or movement would send her spiraling into the abyss.

"You can't go after him, Tanya," he said, his voice laced with a deep sense of burden, like a heavy fog settling on his words. The air seemed to thicken around them, carrying the weight of responsibility. The scent of anxiety lingered in the air, a bitter reminder of the stakes at hand. "It will just make things worse for you and your family."

"Worse?" she growled at him. "How could it be any worse? My mom cries all the time. My dad can't even look at me. He wavers between anger and guilt. It's eating him alive. Sometimes he's mad at the bastard who did this to me. Other times, he's mad at my mom for the way she raised me. And then he's mad at me, asking me what I did to deserve this. What happens if I shoot him? I go to jail? I'm already a prisoner. And so is my sister. Dad won't let us leave the house. So tell me, Ranger, how could it be any worse?"

Her anger was a rigorously contained storm. The attack had turned the bubbly, up-for-anything, carefree teenager into an unflinching survivor, one willing to do whatever it took to relieve her pain—and the pain of her family.

"Tanya—"

"You don't get it, Ranger. If I don't do this, my dad will. I'm a kid, a victim. They won't go as hard on me as they would on him." She pleaded with her eyes. "I can't let anything else destroy my family. It's all my fault, anyway. I should have stayed home. I shouldn't have talked Sam into going out with me. Why do you want to help me? I dragged your daughter into this situation."

The swing creaked a forlorn lullaby as she disappeared into the shadows, a wraith consumed by the flames of her own fury.

"And she saved your life, right? She was supposed to be there."

She stood abruptly, the swing groaning in protest. The pistol dropped to the ground. Shoulders slumped, instantly looking much younger than her age, Tanya asked, "What do I do?"

"Help me."

Tanya's eyes searched Rhyden's, a flicker of doubt battling with the embers of hope. "How?"

"Tell me what happened. I know you've already told the responding officer at the hospital, but tell me. Every detail. Every sound, every sight, every scent. No detail is too small."

The wind whipped up. Clouds blew across the moon. A visible shiver traveled down her spine, causing a ripple of goosebumps to appear on her arms. Her muscles tensed and her breath hitched in her chest. Her hands, once steady, now trembled with the intensity of the shiver. A shudder ran through her, causing her to wrap her arms around herself.

Rhyden rose to his feet. He bent down and scooped up the pistol. Standing, he said, "Let's take this inside, okay? Sam can give us her input, too."

Sam hovered inside the back door, pulling it open as they approached. She looked anxiously from her dad to her best friend. Wordlessly, she stepped out of the path so they could enter the kitchen.

Rhyden pulled out a chair for each of

the girls. "Have a seat. Let's work this through." He pulled a small notebook and pen from his pocket. "Tell me what you remember. Anything, everything. Every detail, no matter how small." He nodded at his daughter. "You, too."

Silence hung heavy in the air, thick with unspoken tension. The girls exchanged a long look. Sam shifted uncomfortably in her chair.

Tanya dropped her gaze, stared at her hands, clutched so firmly together her knuckles whitened. She hesitated, then took a deep breath. "It was dark," she began, her voice dropping to a whisper. "He pulled us over. I distracted him while Sam hid in the back seat." She made eye contact with Rhyden. "We thought you'd sent him after us because Sam snuck out of the house."

A sudden feeling of heaviness expanded through Rhyden's chest. His skin tingled in shock. He jerked his head back. "What?"

Sam placed a hand on her dad's. "We didn't think that for long. Just when the lights came up behind us. I know you would never condone…" She broke off, tears welling up in the back of her throat.

Tanya refocused on her hands. Her gaze turned inward. "He was strong. And fast. He had me step out of the truck. Took my license and put it in his shirt pocket. Why did he do that? He knew all the right things to say."

Sam interrupted. "But he didn't, Dad. He asked things a real cop wouldn't ask. He sounded more like a television actor." She slammed her hand on the table. "Damn it, I recognized his voice. I just can't remember where I've heard him before." She looked up, pleading. "Why can't I remember?"

"Sam, it's not your fault." Tanya reached a hand out to her friend. "I recognized it, too, but not from where." She took a shaky breath. "He grabbed me from behind and put those plastic thingies on my wrists. He was tall, broad-shouldered.”

“You said it was dark, but he walked up to the truck. Did you see his face? What he was wearing?”

“No, he had that spotlight behind him. And he wore a cowboy hat like all the other deputies. All I saw were shadows.”

“Was he left handed or right?”

“How would I know that?”

Rhyden leaned forward. “Was his gun on the left or the right side of his belt?”

“Gun? He wasn’t wearing a gun.”

Rhyden jerked back, scratched the side of his neck. “But you said he was a deputy, right? He had to be wearing a gun.”

Tanya shook her head in denial. “He wasn’t wearing a gun. I didn’t think about it at the time, but that's weird. Isn't it?"

"Yeah, it is. Can you think of anything else? Anything at all about him?"

"He shoved his hand over my mouth. His hands were rough, callused, covered with little cuts and scars. I remember the smell. It gagged me. That sweet-sour burned sulfur odor." She turned to Sam. "Like that time we had to tow my truck to the shop. Remember?"

"Like bad differential fluid? The time we got stuck in the pasture?"

Tanya crinkled her face, squinched up her nose. "Yeah, like that."

A memory of a patrol Tahoe being towed into the shop tickled Sam's mind. The scorched odor had clung to her clothing and skin for days, despite constant scrubbing. She squeezed her eyes shut. An image of her boss up to his elbows in the burnt fluid flashed behind her eyelids. Recognition crossed her face. "Oh hell. I know who it is." Aghast, she stared at her father. "Dad, Lawrence is the rapist."

Chapter Forty-Seven

Cursing and a metallic slamming noise drew Lawrence from beneath the hood of a police cruiser in the back bay. *What the hell?* He was supposed to be alone in the shop. Sam had called with a bullshit excuse for why she couldn't come to work today. She didn't have to come to work. He would have her soon enough. Instead, he had thanked her for calling and indicated he planned on closing early today to go out of town. He walked around the corner, wiping his hands on a red rag. Citrus odors from the hand cleaner tickled his nose. His stomach growled. *Guess it is close to lunchtime, isn't it?*

The metallic slamming noise grew louder. "I know it's here. It has to be here." Sam rummaged in Lawrence's desk drawers, searching.

A fluttery sensation rushed through his chest. A grin teased the corner of his lips.

Teenage girls were so predictable. "Sam? What are you doing?"

She jumped and banged the desk drawer shut. She stumbled backwards. "Um… uh… what… why… I thought you were going out of town?" Guilt flashed across her face, chased by fear.

He nodded. "I wondered how long it would take you to figure it out." Reaching into his back pocket, he pulled out the rusty orange Groucho Marx pencil case. He shook it. The driver's licenses inside rattled. He raised his right eyebrow. "Looking for this?"

The air crackled with tension as he crossed the shop floor toward her. He smiled. "I'm glad it was you. You're so much smarter than your dad."

She backed away, trying to make herself look bigger.

Laughter rang out. Lawrence raised his hands in front of himself, palms up. "Hey, now. I'm not a wild animal. No reason to be afraid of me." Mischief glinted in his eyes. He giggled. "Bet you wish you had bear spray, don't you?"

Urgently, she looked left, right, and behind herself. The tendons on her neck stood out. Her chest heaved as she gulped air.

He continued closing in on Sam, trapping her between desk and the wall. "No place to run. But hey, you don't have to run. I like you. We have a bond. Come away with me."

With trembling hands, Sam fumbled her cell phone from her jeans.

Before she could unlock it, Lawrence slapped it from her hands. The phone clattered to the concrete shop floor, useless. He grabbed her wrists, twisting her arms behind her back, lifting her arms until her shoulders screamed in pain.

His voice rose with each word he spit at her, his previous giddiness replaced with anger. "I asked you sweetly to come with me. What more do you want? A fucking diamond ring? I don't like you that much."

Holding her in front of him with one hand, he scooped a key ring from the board of keys hanging on the wall behind his desk. "This one will do." He dragged her out the door and across the lot to a Dodge Challenger. "I've been souping this baby up. She'll get us to safety in no time, no time at all."

With an unexpected burst of strength, Sam twisted from his grip. She darted toward the back door of the law enforcement center.

A voice rang out from the law enforcement center. "Sam? I told you to stay away from here."

"Daddy! Help!" She raced toward her father.

Lawrence followed, weaving between the patrol units littering the parking lot. The scent of engine oil and gasoline filled the air, fueling his determination. With long strides, he quickly overtook the teenager. Without a word, he lunged forward, his body a blur of motion.

She tried to avoid his grasp, but he was faster. He scooped her up and threw her over his shoulder and darted to the Challenger.

She screamed for help.

Lawrence slammed his hand across her mouth. He opened the driver side door of the Challenger and shoved her inside, following quickly.

Her hands scratched at the passenger door handle, struggling to open the door and flee.

Reaching across the car, he slammed her back against the seat. He pulled a pair of handcuffs from the center console and secured her hands. He tugged the seatbelt across her torso and clicked the latch.

He sat in the driver's seat, his chest heaving with exertion. Sweat trickled down his brow, mingling with the citrus scent of hand cleaner that still clung to the red rag in his back pocket. Grabbing the rag, he shoved it into Sam's mouth as a gag, slapping a piece of duct tape over it to secure it in place. A flash of movement in the rearview mirror warned him of the Ranger closing in on the car. He started the engine and threw the gearshift into reverse.

Rhyden's footsteps echoed off the pavement like gunshots as he raced across the parking lot, trying to rescue his daughter. His fingers brushed the passenger door handle as the vehicle tore from the space.

Chapter Forty-Eight

Rhyden's fingertips brushed the cool metal of the Challenger's door handle as it was torn from his grasp. The pitch black sports car spun its tires against the pavement, burning rubber and whipping up a cloud of smoke that blinded him as the vehicle hightailed it out of the parking lot. Tiny pieces of gravel kicked up by the fleeing vehicle pelted him in the face and chest.

"Fuck!" he screamed in frustration as he spun on his boot heels and darted toward his pickup truck. Hands slick with sweat, he grabbed his phone and called dispatch with one hand while he fished his keys from his front pants pocket with the other. He cursed as the keyring snagged on the fabric and the keys slipped through his fingers.

A perky voice answered his call. "911, what is your emergency?"

Where's Elaine when I need her?
Breathless from bending to scoop up his keys
and the fear running through his veins, Rhyden
said, "Theresa, Ranger Trammell here.
Lawrence Walker just abducted my daughter.
They're eastbound on 97 from the law
enforcement center in a newer model
Challenger. Black. I didn't get the twenty-eight.
The back plates were covered with red mud."
His long strides ate up the parking lot as he
spoke. He climbed into his truck and turned the
ignition.

"Lawrence? You mean Nubbins? Our
Nubbins did what?" The dispatcher's voice rose
higher with each question. Her words came out
faster and faster. "He wouldn't… Maybe they're
going to pick up parts or on a test drive or
something. Nubbins is such a sweetheart. He
would never harm a soul."

Before Rhyden could unleash his anger
on the flighty dispatcher, a calm, professional

voice issued from his cell phone's speaker. "Ranger Trammell? This is Elaine. What's happening?"

Rhyden's heart pounded in chest, the adrenaline coursing through his veins caused his hands to shake. He gripped the steering wheel tighter. His knuckles whitened from the intense pressure as he wove through traffic. The Challenger ahead of him was a shrinking flash of shiny black metal.

Forcing the words between gritted teeth, he explained the situation to the communications supervisor. "I'm in pursuit." He skillfully maneuvered his truck between an eighteen-wheeled sand hauler and a bright blue soccer mom SUV. "We're turning north onto Old Kyote Road. Eighty-five miles per hour and speed increasing. Send backup. **Looks** like we're heading toward Redus Crossing. Any chance of getting someone ahead of us with spikes?" His heart lodged in his throat, choking off his words.

He swallowed hard. "Elaine, Lawrence is the rapist, and he has my baby girl." Tears filled his voice. "Damn it, he has Sam."

***

"Whoooee!" Lawrence jerked the leather-wrapped steering wheel hard to the left, narrowly avoiding plowing into the rear of a school bus stopped at the red light. The blare of the horn from a truck barreling toward them head-on punctuated the madness of their flight. He whipped the steering wheel to the right, forcing the Challenger back into its proper lane. The rear end fishtailed, whipping back and forth. The whine of tires on the pavement filled the cabin of the car. "Damn, this is fun."

His eyes glowed with excitement as the speedometer crept higher—95, 100, 110. The faster they went, the bigger his smile grew.

Sam trembled. She'd never been so frightened. Her pulse pounded in her ears, almost loud enough to drown out the knock-knock-knocking of the engine. It sounded like an elf beating the pistons with a ball peen hammer. *He's pushing her too hard,* she thought as she heard a harsh scream from the engine. *She's going to throw a rod.*

The hard metal cuffs restraining her dug into her wrists. The more she struggled against them, the more the pain encased her shoulders. *I can do it. I know I can. I just need to slip out of one side.* The left cuff seemed looser than the right.

She rattled the chains and begged Lawrence to release her. Her words came out as indecipherable gibberish muffled by the nasty red rag shoved in her mouth.

The fibers rough against her tongue and the back of her throat combined with the taste of the rag made her gag. The bitter acrid flavors of gasoline and hand cleaner mixed with the overwhelming chemical scent of burned differential oil and the onion-y scent of her captor's nervous sweat. Each breath she took felt suffocating. Tears welled up in her eyes, blurring her vision. With her hands trapped behind her, she couldn't wipe them away.

Waves of nausea washed over her. Bile surged up the back of her throat. Sam remembered watching a movie where the heroine vomited while gagged and choked to death on her own puke. *Don't puke. Don't you dare puke.* She squeezed her eyes shut and forced the nausea down. Tears streamed down her cheeks.

"Shut up!" Lawrence glared into the rearview mirror. "Shut up, shut up, shut up," he screamed.

She widened her eyes at him. Raised her eyebrows. *I didn't say anything.* She cast her eyes down to the red-rag-duct-tape contraption muffling her speech.

Lawrence noticed. His voice gentled. "Not you, sweetheart. I would never yell at you. Him." He gestured toward the empty back seat. "He needs to shut his fucking mouth right now." He glared over his shoulder. "Right fucking now, Dad, right fucking now." Insanity shone from his eyes.

How did I miss this? How did I not realize he was batshit crazy? All hope of having a rational conversation, of talking her way out of this abandoned her. *That's it. I'm done for. There's no way out of this.* She sagged back in her seat. A sense of total despair swamped her.

I'm sorry, Daddy. You'll never know how sorry I am I didn't listen to you. Tears continued to leak down her cheeks. Her shoulders slumped as she resigned herself to her fate. There was no escape. She turned her face away from Lawrence and rested her forehead against the window. It felt cool against her flushed skin. She retreated into her thoughts and stared unseeing at the scenery flashing past. As they topped a hill, a flash in the side-view mirror captured her attention. *What was that?*

She blinked rapidly, trying to clear the tears from her vision. Behind them, another vehicle crested the hill. Red and blue lights flashed from the grill of the truck. *Dad!* Hope surged.

***

Lawrence glared at his father. "I told you to shut up."

"Shut up, shut up, shut up. Whatcha gonna do? Cry like a little baby?" The hallucination of his father mocked him. *"Didn't I teach you anything, boy? You might outrun the Ranger, but ain't never going to outrun Motorola. Stick a fork in you 'cause you're done, boy. Done, done, done."* He cackled.

"Running? I'm not running. Why should I run?"

"I'm not running." Lawrence heard his father repeating the words in a falsetto. The voice in his head repeated, *"Not running. Not running."*

He rocked his head. *Get out of my head. You're dead and buried beneath the ground.* "Dead and rotting."

Sam's eyes widened. She struggled against her bindings.

"Not you, sweetheart. I won't let anything happen to you. Don't worry. He can't touch you. He can't touch anyone."

"Can't touch anyone? You mean like this?" A long, bony hand with scraps of leathery flesh clinging to it tapped Lawrence's shoulder.

He screamed. Sweat dotted his hairline,

rolled down his forehead into his eyes, blurring his vision. He blinked rapidly. Heart racing, he glanced over his shoulder, almost driving the Challenger off the road. No one sat in the backseat. He turned to look at Sam. "We don't need to run, do we, sweetheart? We're taking a romantic trip together, right?"

Sam nodded, agreeing with him. *Surviving capture by a madman rule number one: humor him. Seriously though, why hasn't anyone written a handbook about this shit.*

He slid his callused hand down her cheek in a gentle caress.

She flinched away from his touch, huddled against the door. Anger flared through him. He clenched his jaw. "You'll see. You're going to love me. Just like I love you." He shoved his foot harder against the accelerator pedal. The Challenger hit an incline and went airborne.

***

Sparks flashed beneath the car in front of him as it slammed down onto the road. *Hang on, Sam. I'm coming.* Rhyden buried the accelerator pedal into the floorboard, forcing every bit of speed possible from his pickup. The engine whined in protest. He ignored the noise and pushed the truck harder.

As the pursuit intensified, Rhyden's muscles tensed, his jaw clenched, and his brows furrowed with determination. The cool surface of the steering wheel felt slippery against his sweaty palms, but he refused to let go. His breath came in short, shallow gasps, his chest heaving with each beat of his chest. He glanced in the rearview mirror. *Where the hell is my backup?*

He returned his attention to the road in front of him. Through the back window of the Challenger he saw Sam struggling, saw the car door fly open. His mouth dropped open. An uncontrollable shudder swept through his body. "No, Sam, no. You're going too fast. You wouldn't survive."

The sports car swerved, almost hitting the deep bar ditch on the side of the road. He sighed in relief as Lawrence dragged her back into the car. *Never thought I'd be happy to see a kidnapper restrain a victim.*

***

The Challenger bounced back onto the road—hard. The impact jolted Sam, shaking her to her core. Seeing her dad catching up infused her with a sudden burst of energy. She wriggled her left hand free from the metal cuff clamped around it. Blood rushed back into her fingers. She swung wildly at Lawrence, catching him in the face with the dangling cuff.

He cursed and grabbed at his now bleeding nose.

Sam lunged forward, ripping the red rag from her mouth. Her face burned as the duct tape took skin with it. Gasping for air, she grabbed the door handle and shoved the door open. She leaned out. Watched the ground roll past at a terrifying pace. *Oh hell, this is going to hurt.*

She lunged toward freedom, not caring about the price her body would pay in pain. She had to get away.

Lawrence's hand reached into the waistband at the back of her blue jeans and yanked her back into the car. Her heart sank as she fought against his relentless grasp, to no avail.

The tiny town of Redus Crossing loomed ahead. Through the windshield, Sam could see the flashing yellow light in front of the school. A mile past the school sat the town's only convenience store/gas station. The rest of the town consisted of large ranches, twelve churches, and four bars. *Beer joints, really.* Sam mentally shrugged her shoulders. *What difference does it make what Redus Crossing has or doesn't have? I'm about to die. Why am I even thinking about it?*

As the Challenger approached the convenience store, a loud clattering noise came from the engine compartment, followed by a thunderous clank as a connecting rod shot through the engine block. The engine seized. The smell of burning oil and hot coolant filled the passenger compartment. Smoke billowed from beneath the hood as Lawrence coasted into the gas station.

Rhyden pulled into the gas station behind the disabled car and jumped from his truck. He pulled his gun from its holster as he raced toward his daughter and her captor.

As the car slid to a stop, Sam grabbed at the door handle, determined to escape. Lawrence wrapped his hand in her curls and jerked her across the console and out the driver's side door. Dragging her in front of him as a shield, he backed towards the gas pumps. Sam screamed. Kicked and scratched at his hands and arms, but her nails were too short to do any actual damage. *Damn it, why couldn't I be more girly? Long, sharp nails make excellent weapons.* Again she shook her head, amazed at the random thoughts echoing in her head. *A mad man is holding me hostage, and I'm thinking about manicures, really? What the hell is wrong with me?*

***

Three patrol vehicles, lights flashing, sirens wailing, roared into the parking lot. *About damn time,* Rhyden thought. The Tahoe doors popped open, and officers used them for protection as they pointed their guns at Sam and Lawrence.

At the gas pump, a lady filled her fuel tank while her young son 'helped.' She froze. Fear sucked the color from her face. She shoved her son into the SUV and quickly followed, leaving the fuel nozzle in the filler neck of the gas tank. "Get in, get down, and stay down," Rhyden heard her say before she slammed and locked the doors.

Rhyden called out to the deputies. "Hey, easy now. That's my daughter in the line of fire." He raised his hands and pushed them, palms down, toward the ground in a repetitive motion, like he was patting the air. "Put your guns away."

He placed his own weapon back in its holster and stepped closer to the couple.

Lawrence tightened his grip on Sam, wrapped an arm around her throat and ducked down behind her, making himself as small as possible. "Stop right there, Ranger. Don't make me hurt your daughter. I really don't want to. I love her."

Rhyden raised his hands slowly. Held

them palms facing forward at shoulder height. "No one has to get hurt here, Lawrence. Let Sam go. Please."

The mechanic shook his head no and stepped closer to the fuel pump, dragging Sam with him. He barked a laugh. "Little late for that, wouldn't you say? This is all your fault, anyway. You and those other badge-toting assholes. Just like my father. Always treating me like a second-class citizen. Bossing me around. Talking down to me." He sidestepped a few more paces toward the SUV at the pump. "Well, look who's in charge now. Doesn't feel so good with the shoe on the other foot, does it?"

"Come on, Lawrence—"

Lawrence snarled. "Lawrence? You're not my friend. Only my friends get to call me by my first name. That's Mr. Walker to you."

As the Ranger kept the mechanic's attention focused on him, the other three deputies tried to flank him, to slip into position behind him so someone could take him down. Lawrence saw motion from the corner of his eye. He spun around and shook his finger at the deputies. "Uh, uh, uh. I see you sneaking around back there." He jerked the fuel nozzle from the side of the vehicle. "Don't come any closer." He gestured with the nozzle. "You three, come on around front here. Let me see your smiling faces. I won't bother asking you to drop your weapons. No cop worth his salt would drop his gun. My old man taught me that. Keep your hands where I can see them."

Still trapped in his grasp, Sam whimpered.

"Stay calm, sweetie, it's going to be okay. I'm here and I'm going to get you out of this."

"Yeah, sweetheart, your dad's here. Now's a good time to tell him about our elopement." Lawrence waved the nozzle around in the air, spraying gasoline everywhere. "Go on." He jerked on her hair. Gasoline poured down her back. "Tell him."

Sam choked back a sob.

Terror, cold and sharp, pricked Rhyden's skin. His heart thundered against his ribs. He saw the raw panic in Sam's eyes, the way her breath hitched in her chest.

Lawrence raised the nozzle and sprayed a rain of gasoline over himself and Sam. Glistening drops of gasoline reflected prisms from the sinking sun. The deadly tears clung to her curls.

The mechanic jerked, a puppet pulled by invisible strings. Madness filled his eyes. "Shut up, shut up, shut up," he screamed. "Go away. Leave me alone." He sprayed more gasoline, this time toward Rhyden.

The fuel soaked through the Ranger's

clothing, turning the material cold and clammy against his skin. The fumes burned his nose, stung his eyes. He tasted it, acrid and metallic, on the back of his tongue.

"Lawr—Mr. Walker, let's talk about this. Let Sam go. You and I can work this out."

Lawrence's eyes pleaded with Rhyden. "Ranger? Make him go away. Please, for god's sake, make him go away." He dug into his pocket. Pulled out a familiar silver Zippo lighter engraved with an image of his father's badge. "If you can't make him go away, I will." His meaty hand clamped tighter around Sam, pulled her closer against his chest. "And I'll take Sam with me."

"Stop. Don't open that lighter." Rhyden's voice cracked, the words sandpaper rasping against his dry throat.

Lawrence laughed, a high brittle sound that echoed across the parking lot. "You think you can stop me? You think I'm going to let you lock me in one of your damn cages like you did my old man? Where a piece of shit can shank me like they did him?"

Rhyden took a slow step toward the man holding his daughter captive.

The metallic snap of the lighter opening froze him in his tracks. "Don't take another step." Lawrence's voice was a guttural roar.

"Lawrence, son, listen to me," he pleaded, his voice hoarse. "This isn't the way. You don't want to be like your old man. You are better than this. Better than him." He moved closer. Met Lawrence's crazed gaze with one of his own.

For a split second, sanity flickered behind the mechanic's eyes. Silence filled the air. Lawrence clutched the lighter, still unlit. He shook his head, as if clearing his thoughts.

Sam whimpered.

He looked down at her as if noticing her for the first time. His grasp around her throat lessened. He pushed her away. Stepped back from her. As he did, the lighter slipped from his grasp.

Time slowed. Everything else faded—the wind, the heat, the gas-soaked asphalt. The other officers and their vehicles with lights flashing and sirens wailing ceased to exist. The world shrank to just himself, Sam, Lawrence, and that lighter. That damned lighter, a ticking time bomb, poised to shatter his world. Rhyden watched in horror as the lighter tumbled end over end toward the pavement.

He dove for the lighter. It slipped past his fingertips and clattered to the ground. As it hit the ground, the flint wheel sparked against the pavement.

The world erupted in a deafening roar.

The gasoline fumes ignited, a wave of fire devoured Lawrence and the surrounding air. Flames danced a demonic ballet across Lawrence's body, twisting his limbs, consuming him whole. He laughed maniacally, a sound of madness followed by a primal howl of pain and fear that clawed at Rhyden's soul.

Rhyden reached for his pistol, planning to put Lawrence out of his misery. Before he could unholster the weapon, he saw Sam engulfed in a halo of fire.

She dove away from the burning remains of her captor and rolled on the scorched asphalt, her hands beating furiously at the flames that clung to her clothing. The handcuff dangling from one wrist flashed and winked in the flames. Her cry of pain, shrill and raw, tore through the inferno, a counterpoint to Lawrence's agonized bellows.

A scream clawed its way from Rhyden's throat, choked by the heat and the stench of burning flesh. Without conscious thought, Rhyden scrambled towards her, the heat a tangible wall against his face. He felt the crunch of the gravel beneath his boots. The world narrowed to a single point: Sam. With a desperate lunge, he reached her side. His hands, rough and callused, tore at the burning shirt, the fabric clinging stubbornly to her singed skin.

"Sam! Baby! Daddy's here. I'm here." He rolled with her, pushing her away from the inferno that was Lawrence. His own clothes caught fire, the heat seared his skin. Still, he rolled. His only thoughts of Sam. The world dissolved into a kaleidoscope of pain, the stench of burning flesh, and the desperate rasp of Sam's breaths against his cheek.

Mercifully, the darkness came, a cool oblivion swallowing him whole.

***

The sterile scent of disinfectant and the

rhythmic beep of a heart monitor pulled Rhyden from the darkness. He blinked, the harsh fluorescent light stabbing at his eyes. His body, a patchwork quilt of burns and bandages, throbbed with a dull ache.

Aquamarine eyes hovered above him. A messy auburn bun topped high cheekbones and a sad grin. "Ranger Trammell, we need to quit meeting like this."

Rhyden closed his eyes. *Nurse Bubbles, Mikki.* A peaceful sensation swept over him. He recognized the pull of intravenous morphine. Fighting against the medication, his eyes popped open. He tried to speak. All that came out was a hoarse croak. Clearing his throat, he tried again. "Sam?" he asked.

A hand grasped his and squeezed. "I'm here, Dad. You saved me."

With a sigh, he gave into the sedative

tug of the drugs.

542

EPILOGUE

Sam tugged at Rhyden's lapel. Straightened his tie. They stood together on the front steps of the church. Soft music drifted out the open doors. Mikki waited inside. "Dad, are you sure about this? I wish Bree were here."

Rhyden smiled at his middle daughter. "Bree had finals. But I've got you. You're coming with me, right?"

She straightened her shoulders, raised her chin. She brushed imaginary lint off of her pale green linen dress. "Of course." She threw him a tentative grin. "We're a team, right?"

Rhyden squeezed her hand. *Time to quit stalling. Let's do this.* He took a deep breath. Exhaled noisily. Nodded his head sharply. "Let's do this."

Together, they walked into the church.

Following signs on the wall, they found the room they needed. He opened the door and motioned Sam in ahead of him.

Mikki waited at the front of the room. Her eyes sparkled as she met his. She smiled encouragingly.

Leaving Sam sitting at the end of a mahogany pew, Rhyden continued on his way down the aisle to the front of the sanctuary. He stepped up beside Mikki and placed a quick kiss on her cheek. She took a seat in the front pew next to Sam.

Rhyden stepped up to the pulpit and looked out across the group of people gathered in front of him. He ran his hands through his hair, cleared his throat. "My name is Rhyden and I'm an addict."

A Word About the Author

A sixth-generation Texan with Scottish roots, Glenda Thompson can 'bless your heart' with the best of them. As a former emergency medical technician married to a South Texas lawman, she used insider information from both their careers as inspiration to build her Broken Badges universe of Texas Rangers and other first responders with hidden pasts and dark secrets.

She wanted to draw attention to subjects that often got swept under the rug and ignored. The heroes in her Broken series are all flawed. They screw up, hide secrets, and fail at solving their problems. You know, they're human.

Her first novel, Broken Toys, addresses human trafficking and a Texas Ranger who isn't the person he claims to be. She writes gritty, compelling fiction with genuine emotion.

When Broken Badges becomes too dark she also writes snarky, fantasy romance under the pen name E L Hopper.

When she's not huddled in her writing cave with Darlin', the future crazy cat lady can be found embarrassing her rather large family by dancing in the middle of a country road during a rainstorm or enthusiastically ringing a cowbell to cheer on her Grands at sporting events.

You can keep up with her at www.rattlerpress.com or

Other Books by Glenda Thompson

Broken Toys